Into the Woods

At that moment a she-wolf slunk from behind a tree. For a split second Storm looked at the wolf and the wolf looked at Storm. Storm thought *Danger* and the wolf thought *Dinner*. Then the wolf looked at Storm's sisters and thought *Pudding*.

That was the beast's fatal mistake, for it was in that instant that Storm yelled for them to climb the nearest tree, while she reached into her pocket and started pelting the wolf with rock cakes. The animal hesitated, clearly uncertain whether to give chase to dessert or stick with the entrée. Then, realizing that she was in danger of losing both courses, she gave a snarl of rage and propelled herself towards Storm's throat.

Into the Woods

by LYN GARDNER

Pictures by Mini Grey

David Fickling Books

OXFORD · NEW YORK

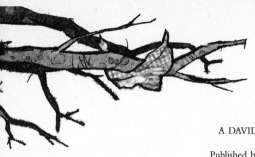

A DAVID FICKLING BOOK

Published by David Fickling Books
an imprint of Random House Children's Books
a division of Random House, Inc.
New York

Originally published in Great Britain by David Fickling Books, an imprint of
Random House Children's Books, in 2006.

DAVID FICKLING BOOKS and colophon are trademarks of David Fickling.

www.randomhouse.com/kids

Educators and librarians, for a variety of teaching tools, visit us at
www.randomhouse.com/teachers

Library of Congress Cataloging-in-Publication Data
Gardner, Lyn.
Into the woods / Lyn Gardner ; illustrated by Mini Grey. — 1st American ed.
p.   cm.
SUMMARY: Pursued by the sinister Dr. DeWilde and his ravenous wolves, three sisters,
Storm, the inheritor of a special musical pipe, the elder Aurora, and the baby Any, flee
into the woods and begin a treacherous journey filled with many dangers as they try to
find a way to defeat their pursuer and keep him from taking the pipe and control of the
entire land.
ISBN 978-0-385-75115-5 (trade) — ISBN 978-0-385-75116-2 (lib. bdg.)
1. Sisters—Fiction. 2. Characters in literature—Fiction. 3. Fantasy.] I. Grey, Mini, ill.
II. Title.
PZ7.G17931Int 2007
[Fic]—dc22
2006024350

Printed in the United States of America

June 2007

10 9 8 7 6 5 4 3 2 1

First American Edition

for Ros ASQUiTh

Contents

1
THe PiPeR RETURNS

Storm Eden was forbidden to put a foot outside the high walls that surrounded the park at Eden End. Her older sister, Aurora, had made that quite clear after Storm's last escapade, which had ended badly, with two lost shoes, one black eye and a bump the size of a robin's egg on her head. On no account was Storm to leave the park and go into the woods, except in an emergency.

'What sort of emergency?' Storm had asked.

'Only a direst emergency. Nothing less than imminent death,' Aurora had replied darkly, a dangerous glint in her eye.

So, once upon a time, here and there, now and then, Storm Eden stood disconsolately under an oak tree in the park, looking up at a cloudless sky. It was not yet noon, and the day rolled out endlessly in front of her like a piece of carpet with nothing on it. And if an empty day didn't count as an emergency, Storm wasn't sure what did. Aurora *had* mentioned death, and Storm felt quite certain that she would die of boredom if she didn't find something fun to do. Surely even her sister would understand that? Or perhaps not. But then, Aurora need never know.

Storm was sure that her sister would either be busy demonstrating her unnatural talent for house-work, by rearranging the linen cupboard for the second time that week, or perfecting her recipe for chocolate madeleines in the kitchen. And she was certain nobody else would miss her. Her mother, who hardly seemed to notice Storm's existence at the best of times, would be having a pre-lunch nap, and her father would be in his study planning an expedition in search of the legendary four-tongued, three-footed, two-headed honey dragon which was reputed to be at least one hundred metres long and have the sunniest disposition of any member of the lizard family.

Storm felt restless and hungry for something, although she didn't think it was for food. She had a round of cucumber and watercress sandwiches, a hard-boiled brown speckled egg, laid by an unreliable hen called Desdemona, and a flask filled with raspberry juice in her pockets. And she had the whole day before her.

Storm ran across the park to a place where one of the gnarled oak trees nestled close to the high walls, clambered up the trunk with the ease of a monkey, shimmied along the nearest branch that overhung the wall, took a quick glance back towards the ramshackle old house with its winking windows, lopsided chimneys and single turret to check she was unseen, and dropped to the ground on the other side.

Rooks rose from the treetops, their icy cries cutting the stillness. Storm realized she had forgotten her shoes. She shrugged and scrambled to her feet, oblivious to muddied knees and a tear in her skirt. The woods waited: mysterious, watchful and alluring. The whisper and rustle of branches in the wind sounded to Storm as if the trees were calling out to her. She took a few steps into their shadows and the thorns of a briar latched onto her arm, like sharp grasping fingers, urging her onwards into the enticing darkness of the forest.

It was then that she remembered a story Aurora was fond of telling – a story which she claimed was completely true and had happened in these very same woods. It was about a woodcutter's daughter, who many centuries ago had disobeyed her mother's orders, strayed off the path in the woods and been eaten by a wolf. Aurora always concluded the story by wagging her finger at Storm and saying, 'So heed my words, stay close to home where you are safe, and don't wander into the woods.' Storm would listen and then retort, 'Well, if I met a wolf, I'd gobble him up in a single gulp. Wolves don't scare me,' and Aurora would shake her head mournfully at her sister's boldness and reply, 'You'll come to a bad end, Storm Eden. Just like the woodcutter's daughter.'

Storm turned her back reluctantly on the forest and, skirting the very edge, set off through a copse of saplings. After a couple of miles she hit a small lane, down which a hay wagon was rumbling noisily. Hurrying after it, she hitched herself a lift on the back and made herself a nest in the spiky grass that smelled of earth and molasses, next to two dozen jars of lavender honey and three churns of milk. Lying back in contentment, she scoffed a sandwich, and soon the jolting of the moving vehicle, the heat and the drowsy hum of bees in the hedgerows sent her to sleep. She didn't know how long she dozed, but she woke with a start to the sound of surprised voices.

'Look 'ere, 'Arry, you've got a skulker in the back taking you for a free ride. You oughta demand payment from the little minx.'

Still befuddled by sleep, Storm saw rough, hairy arms coming towards her. Struggling this way and that, so she was slippery as an eel, she slithered from their grasp, and scooted across the cobbled street and through the market stalls beyond, upsetting a display of cheese, and sending a barrel of wormy apples tumbling over. She heard angry shouts and curses behind her, but she didn't stop. She bolted away from the market square, skidded past the rusty railings of a derelict church, dashed through its graveyard, thick with nettles, and crossed the waste

5

ground beyond. Soon she was lost in a maze of narrow streets with unwelcoming names such as Damnation Alley, Desolation Lane and Rat Trap Wynd. The streets were edged with identical houses with mean little windows and doors like pinched mouths.

Storm ran through Bleeding Heart Mews and into Drowned Man's Alley and found herself by a dark, oily river. Fog curled around her. Exhausted, she collapsed on a low wall behind a lidless dustbin and leaped up again in fright as two huge rats, the size of small dogs, emerged from the bin, eyed her defiantly and then streaked off. Storm's throat felt as if it was on fire and her head was muzzy. She heard a distant clock strike three. She was surprised that it was only mid-afternoon – it seemed much later. Here in the town there was no sign of the sun that shone so brightly on Eden End. Instead, the air was heavy with soot from the belching factories, and the street lamps, already lit despite the early hour, were blotches in the smog that ate up the sky.

Storm finally realized where she was: Piper's Town. She had been here once before with Aurora and her father. He had been in search of supplies for one of his expeditions and had taken them to a dark little shop in Angel Court, just off Butchery

Lane. Storm remembered studying one of the old maps displayed on its walls, her grubby finger following the winding road that straggled south-west from the mountains and Eden End until it rested over the smudge that was the town. Until then, Storm had thought her home was the centre of the universe, but the map showed it as a tiny dot compared with the town, the sea that lay further to the south, and those immense mountains.

Just thinking about the mountains made Storm tingly. Aurora had told her about them during a geography lesson that had been uncharacteristic-ally thrilling. (Aurora's geography teaching seldom extended beyond the imports and exports of dull, faraway countries of which Storm had never heard.) Apparently the mountains were mysterious and savage places – full of terrible dangers – which all sensible people avoided. Storm had decided these must be the same sensible people who would obey Aurora's exhortations not to stray outside Eden End. But, as far as she was concerned, danger equalled excitement, and Aurora's warnings only made Storm more determined to visit the mountains one day.

But that was an adventure that would have to wait. Right now, Storm was a very long way from home, and she supposed that she had better start the journey back. If only she hadn't slept for so long on the hay-cart! She decided to turn back towards the market square, hoping she'd be able to hitch another ride. If not, well, she had two legs and she would just have to walk – even if that meant arriving back at Eden End long past bedtime and getting scolded by Aurora. Her sister would probably punish her with housework and double spelling for the rest of the week. Storm pulled a face. She could already hear Aurora's reply to her apology for being so late. 'I don't like it when you're sorry, Storm Eden. You've always done more than you're sorry for.' Then, like so many times before, she would probably make Storm turn out her pockets and give up her treasures, which might include

a penknife,

a compass,

sweet
wrappers,

half-eaten sandwiches,

snails,

matches,

a file for sawing through prison bars and, on one infamous occasion, a field mouse with a damaged leg which, despite its injury, had jumped onto the kitchen floor, making Aurora scream and leap onto a chair.

Storm was still grinning at that memory when a coal-black hearse drawn by four dark horses, their heads encircled by inky plumes of feathers, careered round a corner and almost knocked her over. Scrambling out of the way, Storm stared after the sinister vehicle, wondering what a hearse was doing travelling at such speed. But as it passed through the square up ahead, none of the stall-holders appeared to be concerned. It had begun to drizzle and they were far too busy packing up their wares to gawp at hearses, or help young girls in need of lifts. Storm looked about hopefully, but all she saw was several plump rats feeding on the scraps under the stalls, and under-fed urchins throwing stones at them.

Storm wasn't interested in rats or small murderous boys, and was just about to head for the long road back to Eden End when she heard a bell and a crier calling, and spotted a tide of people walking towards an ancient wood-beamed building that she guessed was the town hall. Officials in scarlet uniforms that had long seen better days were pushing the crowd aside to make way for the aldermen. Curious to find out what was going on, Storm joined the throng as they pushed their way up narrow stairs and into a gallery that overlooked the meeting chamber. Crouching down, she squirmed her way through several pairs of legs until she had a good view of the chamber below. A thin, beautiful boy with the most extraordinary eyes – one warm emerald, the other ice-blue – patted the bench beside him and squeezed up to make room for her.

'Sit with me,' he said. 'I'll look after you.'

'I can look after myself very well, thank you,'

said Storm firmly, and she leaned over the gallery and pointedly ignored him.

The panelled meeting chamber was packed. The gallery was buzzing, but the aldermen were sunk in gloomy silence. After a few moments, Alderman Snufflebottom, a burly, self-important man with a handlebar moustache, who Storm thought bore a close resemblance to a hairy plumped-up raisin, knocked on the table with his gavel and cleared his throat.

'Gentlemen, you are all aware of the reasons for this emergency sitting of the council. The situation is grave, very grave. If we do not act quickly we will have nothing left to save. Despite our best efforts, we have been overrun. The grain store has been ravaged, food supplies are already short, and if the winter is long and hard again, many people will starve. We may wish that we had other options, but we have no choice, gentlemen, no choice at all. We are outnumbered and overwhelmed. We must bring in outside help to deal with the problem without delay.'

The members of the town council looked at each other uneasily and shifted uncomfortably in their seats. At that moment, as if on cue, several huge rats ran across the council chamber floor, leaped onto the table without any sign of fear and began chewing the pencil and order papers of the council secretary. Alderman Snufflebottom surveyed the rats, an expression on his face that Storm found hard to place. Then she realized when she had last seen that look – it was on the face of Tabitha, her favourite of the many wild cats which made Eden End their home, on the day the mother cat had succeeded in pushing over the milk churn so that she and her kittens could help themselves to its creamy contents. Yes, thought Storm, the expression on Alderman Snuffle-bottom's face was one of pure satisfaction.

'We will vote, gentleman, please, without delay. Everyone in favour please raise their hands.'

'Wait.'

All eyes turned to the public gallery. The crowd parted to reveal a tall, pale young woman. She moved to the front of the gallery and spoke calmly, her penetrating silver-grey eyes fixed on the councillors.

'Do none of you remember what happened last time we invited an exterminator into our midst? Is memory so short? Have we learned nothing from the past?'

The members of the council looked uncomfortably at each other. They remembered all too
well.

Alderman Snufflebottom peered at the young
woman. 'Netta Truelove, isn't it? I understand your
concerns, my dear, we all do,' he began patroniz-
ingly. 'But I assure you there is nothing else to be
done. Do you want to go hungry when winter
comes? Do you want babies to have their faces
gnawed by rats? There have already been stories –
mere rumours, of course, nothing confirmed – of
tragic incidents in the poorer parts of town. Rats
have also been sighted in some of the outlying
villages. And of course' – he gave a smug little
laugh – 'we have no intention of defaulting on
the payment this time around. Have no fear, my
dear, we will employ the exterminator for this one
job, we will pay him the rate for the job, and then
he will go and leave our little town in peace. I
assure you, we will make quite certain of that.'

A ripple of applause passed around the gallery,
but the boy next to Storm almost imperceptibly
shook his head.

'How can you be so sure?' began the young
woman gravely, her steely eyes sparkling with
passion. 'You all know the legends about the piper's

return as well as I do. Invite the dirty to do your dirty work for you and you risk—'

But a gesture from Alderman Snufflebottom had sent two scarlet-clad officials to Netta Truelove's side. They glared at her menacingly.

The young woman sat down shaking her head, squeezing onto the small bench next to Storm, so that Storm was squashed up against the boy with the curious mismatched eyes. Storm smiled shyly at Netta and she returned the smile.

'Now, gentlemen, all those in favour . . .' The councillors looked miserably at each other and then reluctantly they all raised their hands. Alderman Snufflebottom smiled another smug smile. 'Unanimous, I believe.' He turned to the council secretary, who was unsuccessfully attempting to rescue his last remaining papers from the ravenous rats.

'Ask Dr DeWilde, the exterminator, to step this way.'

The council secretary hurried across the chamber and pulled on the heavy oak doors. They swung slowly open, and as they did so a shaft of dazzling sunlight burst through the sooty sky, hit the high chamber window and created a pool of brightness like a spotlight in a theatre. Illuminated in it was a tall, thin, undeniably commanding man, with a livid scar running down his smooth left cheek. The man's cold, glittering eyes flicked around the room from beneath hooded lids and no one could meet his devouring gaze.

His face, thought Storm, would have been handsome but it was marred by the cruelty that lurked behind his eyes and the malice that played around his lips. Even so, he had a brooding presence and power and, like everyone else in the chamber, she couldn't take her eyes off him.

He was flanked by six slavering wolves.

There was an audible gasp from the public gallery and Storm felt a stab of fear in her stomach at the sight of the mean, muscled animals that she'd only previously seen in picture books.

There was a flash of lightning followed by an ominous roll of thunder. The man clicked his fingers and the wolves leaped forward – their jaws snapping closed around several of the rats. The council members broke into murmurs of apprehension. Someone screamed, and a woman at the back of the gallery fainted. The tall thin man cracked a mirthless smile and gave a high whistle. The wolves bounded back to his feet and lay there panting, crunching what was left of the rats between their massive jaws. The sound of teeth on bone could be heard quite clearly. A dribble of crimson blood ran down the chin of one wolf. Some of the council members shuddered and averted their gaze. A child in the crowd began to whimper.

'Ah, Dr DeWilde,' said Alderman Snufflebottom nervously, with a little fawning bow. 'Do come in.'

Dr DeWilde swept in, ignoring the alderman's outstretched hand, and strode forcefully into the centre of the chamber as if he owned it. Apart from a pied waistcoat in shades of blood, he was dressed sombrely in black, as if just returning from a funeral or shortly expecting to be summoned to one. Under his arm he carried an elegant black cane. The crowd watched, completely rapt, as if mesmerized by his presence.

There was another flash of lightning. Up in the public gallery there was a commotion as Netta Truelove stood up. Dr DeWilde looked upwards and, for a split second, his piercing glance met Storm's. She felt as if his eyes were boring into her, as if he recognized her and was trying to see right inside her soul. She gave an involuntary little shiver, and with an effort dragged her eyes from his hypnotic gaze.

Netta was walking to the door, the sea of people parting for her. At the exit she turned and looked back. 'Fools,' she said softly. 'You think you can control the wolves, but they will control you. This is madness. Everyone knows you don't invite the wolf into your house when he comes knocking. I fear for us all.' Then she was gone.

A murmur of anxiety passed around the gallery, but anxiety quickly turned to jeering led by Alderman Snufflebottom. Storm saw Dr DeWilde give a secret little smile of triumph. She scrambled to her feet, pushed her way out and followed the dignified figure of Netta Truelove, unaware that she was being followed by the boy. The crowd had begun to cheer for Dr DeWilde.

Down in the town square, Netta climbed into a small trap drawn by a handsome dun-coloured Connemara pony. She gently flicked her whip, said, 'Gee up, Pepper,' and was about to drive off, when she saw Storm watching her.

'You look like a young lady in need of a lift. Where do you want to go?'

'Eden End, please, if it's not out of your way,' said Storm.

'Hop in,' said Netta, and she turned the horse round and set off out of the town. Storm was so busy admiring Pepper the pony that she didn't notice the boy lurking in the shadows. His extraordinarily coloured eyes, one of ice-blue, the other of emerald, glittered in the darkness as he watched them depart.

'Are you hungry?' asked Netta after a short while.

'I'm always hungry.'

Netta produced two crisp red apples and some candied pumpkin.

The journey back to Eden End passed quickly as Storm and Netta munched and talked companionably. Storm wanted to ask Netta why she had been so against the appointment of the exterminator, but every time she tried to raise the subject, Netta steered the conversation back to Storm. By the time the pony and trap drew up at the end of the drive to Eden End, Storm had told Netta everything about herself: her solitary life of adventures and her scrapes and run-ins with her sister.

'Thanks for the lift,' she said. Netta gave her a hug.

'I am very pleased to have met you, Storm Eden, and I hope we'll meet again one day.' She leaned forward, and her arresting silver-grey eyes were soft. 'If ever you need my help, you'll find me in my cottage in a clearing in the woods beyond the first village after the town on the road out to the mountains. It's clearly marked.'

Storm stared at her. 'But that means you've driven me all this way and it is completely in the opposite direction from where you live.'

Netta smiled again. 'It was entirely my pleasure. If you ever pass my way, please come and visit me.'

Back in the town, the meeting chamber was clearing, and the townsfolk were hurrying towards their homes, chased by the fear that had seeped into their lives and settled like damp in a wall. Dr DeWilde stood at the window and watched the people go, his eyes cold, blank and smooth. A movement made him aware that Alderman Snufflebottom was hovering nervously nearby. Dr DeWilde felt in his pocket and casually handed over a small handful of brightly coloured precious gems as if they were mere sweets. A few scattered on the floor. Alderman Snufflebottom's eyes glittered with greed as he scrambled on his hands and knees to pick them up: emeralds, rubies, amethysts and sapphires. Dr DeWilde turned his cold gaze upon the alderman. Snufflebottom was a silly, greedy little man, but he was useful. At least for the time being.

'Come, we have work to do.' Dr DeWilde clicked his fingers and the wolves raised their heads and bayed, a long shivering cry of desolation that entered the bone marrow of all who heard it.

Out in the darkening streets, mothers quickened their step, clasping their children's hands tightly and clutching their babies to their breasts. Worry took up residence in every shadow, threat seemed to lurk behind every hedge and dustbin. People locked their doors and drew the curtains tight. All night the call of the wolves disturbed their sleep as the pack roamed the streets, catching and devouring the rats. By dawn every rodent was gone and it was raining heavily – washing away all traces of the blood that ran through the gutters and stained the streets.

2
A Beginning and an End

It was the very next day that Storm Eden first heard the wolves howl around Eden End. It was also the day that she found a sister and lost a mother.

The morning began badly. From the way Aurora arranged her mouth into a thin line, Storm knew that her sister was suspicious about her absence the previous afternoon. But thanks to Netta, she had only been a few minutes late for supper, so Aurora had no proof that she had left the grounds of Eden End. She contented herself with setting Storm hideously difficult long division straight after breakfast and sighing loudly over her torn skirt.

'As if there wasn't enough to do already with a new baby on the way,' she said grumpily as she carefully threaded a needle, holding it at a distance as if it was a highly dangerous weapon and not just an everyday piece of sewing kit.

'Baby? What baby?' demanded Storm, looking up from her sums.

'Mother's baby, you silly goose. Goodness, Storm, are you completely blind? Hadn't you noticed that's she's having a baby? It's due any day now.'

Storm processed this interesting piece of information and felt incredibly stupid. How could she not have noticed that Zella, her beautiful although seriously neglectful mother, was having a baby? She who prided herself on being told nothing and yet finding out everything that was going on at Eden End, and who had personally seen Tabitha the cat through four litters of kittens. Still, as Zella favoured long flowing clothes and held the view that exercise was so harmful to health that she seldom moved, except between her bed and her chaise longue, perhaps it was not so surprising that Storm hadn't noticed her advancing pregnancy. Particularly as in recent months Zella had been more remiss than usual in fulfilling any maternal duties. Whenever Storm had appeared in her doorway, Zella would fix her with a dazzling smile which made Storm feel as if she was being bathed in a sunbeam, and whisper exhaustedly, 'Darling, how lovely to see you. Mama's feeling a little tired. Why don't you go out in the park and leave me to rest a little.' Sustained by this flash of radiance, Storm would run off, although often with an unexplained gnawing in her stomach, even if she had just had breakfast.

But this unexpected news was thrilling. A baby would mean a companion, and a companion would mean somebody to play with. Storm wouldn't be so alone any more. She would teach the baby archery, fire-eating, synchronized swimming and how to make fireworks.

'A baby. How wonderful,' she beamed.

'Well, I'm glad somebody's happy,' Aurora said in a crotchety voice.

Storm looked at Aurora's pale face and noticed how tired her big sister looked.

'Ouch!' A tiny dot of crimson blood appeared on Aurora's finger where she had pricked it with the needle. Her pale face went ghostly white and she swayed in her chair as if about to faint.

'Are you all right, Aurora?' Storm asked, concerned by her sister's deathly pallor.

'My finger, I pricked it,' whispered Aurora, staring at the blood, her eyes wide with horror.

'It's only a tiny drop of blood,' said Storm unsympathetically. 'Nobody ever died from pricking their finger.'

'I know that,' snapped Aurora, turning from white to pink in a second. She glared at Storm, wiped her forehead with an exquisitely pressed handkerchief and gingerly picked up the needle again. Storm returned to the subject that really interested her.

'Don't you want there to be a new baby?'

Aurora put down her sewing and said, not entirely convincingly, 'Of course I'm pleased, sweetie. But a new baby is another mouth to feed and it will mean more work.'

Storm knew that Aurora meant it would mean more work for her, for much as she adored her mother, with her beautiful kitten face and smile as mysterious as the Mona Lisa, Storm also recognized that Zella was lazier than a plump, pampered tortoiseshell cat. Her mother's idea of vigorous mental and physical exercise was lying in bed eating chocolate truffles and strawberries and cream while looking at herself in the mirror. She never rose before ten and spent most days painting her nails and reading ancient copies of glossy magazines with pictures of thin, miserable women on the covers. Storm could not imagine Zella getting up in the night to look after a baby, and she very much doubted that her father would be any help either.

When Reggie Eden was not laughing and whispering with Zella, he was either away on one of his expeditions or busy planning the next one with a large DO NOT DISTURB sign pinned to his study door. Once, ignoring the sign, Storm had rushed excitedly into her father's study to show him one of Tabitha's kittens and, when he had eventually looked up from his work and peered at her over the top of his glasses, he had seemed dazed for a moment and then asked in a puzzled voice, 'Who are you?'

'Storm, of course,' she had replied indignantly, and a look of faint surprise had passed over his handsome face. He had run his fingers through his rumpled hair and said, 'My, how you have grown,' before looking down at his maps again and shooing her away.

Storm was certain that looking after the new baby would fall entirely to Aurora, who already ran Eden End with the efficiency of a sergeant major faced with a particularly unruly company of troops.

'I'll help you look after the baby, Aurora, I promise.'

'You? Help?' said Aurora, not unkindly but with a note of scepticism in her voice. 'Like when you helped with the chickens and forgot to put them away at night and a fox got them all, except Desdemona and Othello? Or when you offered to do the washing up and left both taps running full on so that the kitchen flooded?'

Storm flushed with shame and anger. She hadn't meant to forget the chickens. It had just happened. As for leaving the taps running, she had been distracted by seeing a kestrel out of the window and had pursued it into the park to see if she could find its nest. It wasn't her fault — she had been as amazed as anyone to return to the kitchen several hours later to find the tables and chairs trying to float out of the door. It was just like Aurora to bring up things she would rather forget. It was so unfair.

An unlit coal suddenly blazed in Storm's stomach. Fury swept through her body like a searing pain and hot tears throbbed behind her eyes. 'The trouble with you, Aurora Eden,' she said, 'is that you don't think that I can do anything. Well, I'll show you, bossyboots!' She picked up a heavy tray full of breakfast plates, bowls and cups and marched across the room.

'No, Storm, no!' exclaimed Aurora, rising to her feet. 'I left that tray there because the handle is crack—'

Too late. As Storm swept imperiously towards the door, the tray handle gave way and half-eaten bowls of porridge and jugs of milk and apple juice smashed to the floor.

'Oh, Storm, why do you never listen?' cried Aurora, nervously eyeing the sea of milk that was seeping across the threadbare Persian carpet

around islands of greengage and damson jam and broken crockery.

'Because as far as you're concerned I can never do anything right!' screamed Storm. 'I always know exactly where I am with you – in the wrong!'

'Oh, Storm, that's not true, sweetie, I didn't mean—' began Aurora. But she was wasting her breath. Storm had run from the room, trampling spilled milk and jam and slamming the door behind her.

Aurora sighed as she got down on her hands and knees and picked up shards of broken china. She wished that she and Storm got on better, but they always seemed to rub each other up the wrong way. They were so different, and sometimes her little sister was just downright irresponsible. Why did she never think before she acted?

Aurora stood up wearily. Through the window she caught a glimpse of Storm running through the park like a wild thing, followed by Desdemona and Tabitha. She wrinkled her nose in disapproval but, as she watched the small solitary figure leaping through the air and punching her fist at the sky, Aurora felt a smile tilt the corners of her mouth. She felt in her pocket and pulled out one of the many lists she always kept there. It read:

Things to Do

1. Rearrange linen cupboard.
2. Check Storm is having a bath every day.
3. Make madeleines.
4. Try out new recipe for broccoli and mushroom pie.
5. ~~Pay milkman.~~ CAN'T AFFORD iT THIS WEEK
6. Turn dining room curtains into new dress for Storm.

To the bottom of the list she added:

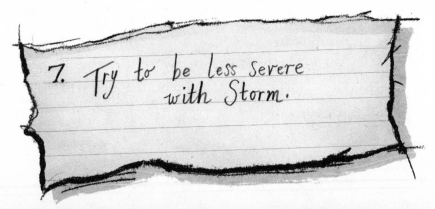

7. Try to be less severe with Storm.

She put the list back in her pocket and set off quite happily to get a dustpan and brush.

It was long after lunch before Storm dared return to the house. She was starving as usual, and hoped to snatch herself a hunk of bread and cheese without running into Aurora. But creeping inside, she was astonished to hear her mother's raised voice. Zella always spoke in a husky whisper, believing that it conserved essential energy. Storm raced up the stairs, shaking her unruly red curls as she ran, slid headlong across the polished gallery floor and skidded to a halt with an expert forty-five-degree turn outside her parents' room. She pressed her ear against the door. Her mother was agitated, gasping, 'I can't, I can't.'

Storm then heard Aurora's stern voice. 'Nonsense, Mama. Of course you can.' Aurora sounded exasperated, using exactly the same tone she employed when she was trying to explain fractions to Storm. Her voice became louder and more insistent. 'Oh, do try to make a little effort, Mummy. Push!'

Then Storm's father spoke. 'Please, Zella, my darling. Push, I beg of you.'

A few minutes later she heard a kitten-ish mewling and her father opened the bedroom door with such force that surprise and the sudden rush of air knocked Storm backwards onto her bottom. Her father thrust a small bundle into her arms.

'Look after that,' he said.

'What is it?'

'Your new sister,' he replied curtly, and shut the door abruptly.

Storm stared into the baby's dark currant eyes and the tiny screwed-up face with its mop of dark hair and, perhaps it was just a trick of the light, but for a split second it seemed as if the baby was smiling at her. Storm's heart swooped and she experienced a strange tickling sensation in her tummy. Storm had fallen in love with her little sister.

Zella had put more effort into giving birth to her third daughter than she had put into anything else in her beautiful, lazy life. The exertion proved too much. 'I knew I had it in me,' she whispered, and fainted.

After several thwarted attempts to enter the bedroom, and being shooed away by her father, Storm spent an anxious afternoon pushing the sleeping baby around the overgrown knot garden in the dilapidated pram in the company of Desdemona and Tabitha. Her throat felt sore, as if a piece of unbuttered granary toast had stubbornly lodged there. The animals clucked and purred sympathetically.

She had wrapped the child in the blanket that she herself had been given when she was a tiny baby. It was a gossamer-soft piece of midnight-blue material upon which the young Aurora had painstakingly sewed little silver stars so it looked as if the blanket was a patch of dazzling night sky cut from the starry heavens. The baby needed its warmth – the wind had got up and was lashing the trees and the sky had turned suddenly over-cast and threatening. Storm was surprised to catch a snowflake on her tongue, and even more astonished to discover that it tasted strangely sugary.

Feeling increasingly anxious about her mother, but hardly daring to discover the truth, Storm returned to the house, cradling the little bundle in her arms as if trying to protect her not just from the weather but from all the woes of the world.

In the kitchen Aurora was making up a bottle of milk for the baby. Her beautiful face was blotched with tears and she was uncharacteristically sniffly. Unlike Storm, who frequently found it necessary to resort to her sleeve in times of upset or sneezing attacks, Aurora was never without a perfectly pressed pocket handkerchief. As she was fond of telling her sister, when testing Storm on some obscure aspect of geometry or on how to correctly spell useful words such as blancmange, 'A failure to prepare is preparing to fail.'

'So, there you both are,' said Aurora as if Storm had been wilfully hiding herself and the baby away, rather than trying to make herself scarce. Seeing her sister's stricken face, Aurora softened her tone. 'You're a good, helpful girl, Storm, to look after the poor little mite,' she said kindly. 'Do you want to feed her? I'll show you how.'

She took the baby and the smudge of a child was soon sucking greedily at the milk, smacking her lips in delight. Storm watched and marvelled at the perfectly designed sucking machine but also at her older sister. Why was it, she wondered, that Aurora was so good at anything she turned her hand to, while she, Storm, was so useless and clumsy at most things? Aurora seemed to have the knack of everything, while Storm had the knack of nothing except climbing trees, lassoing, riding bareback and making fireworks. It was no surprise, she thought sadly, that her mother and father always had time for Aurora and none for her.

Indeed they seemed almost uncharacteristically protective of Aurora while ignoring Storm, happy to let her run wild all day in the park.

'Here, you try,' said Aurora, offering Storm the baby and bottle. The baby let out a roar of disapproval, but when nestled in Storm's arms, the teat of the bottle back in her mouth, she settled. Presently she burped politely, her lashes fluttered, she curled a tiny finger around Storm's thumb and fell fast asleep, snuffling like a hedgehog. Storm felt her insides turn to pink melted toffee.

'Come,' said Aurora. Storm rose and, with the baby in her arms, she followed her sister up the staircase and along the gallery into her parents' room. Zella was lying on the big canopied bed, her black tresses — so long she normally wore them coiled around her head — spread out over the embroidered lace pillow. She looked as beautiful as Sleeping Beauty waiting to be awoken by a kiss from a prince. The children's father sat by the bed, his head sunk into his hands. He looked as if he had shrunk several suit sizes in less than a day.

Storm glanced at the photograph of her parents that hung over the mantel. It showed them at their wedding, which had taken place just days after Captain Reggie Eden, the daring and handsome explorer, had rescued Zella from a tall tower atop a high mountain where, according to their mother, she had been imprisoned by a hateful old crone. Storm wasn't sure how true that was – and she was pretty dubious about her father's claim to have shinned up the tower using Zella's hair as a rope. But there was no doubt about how much her parents loved each other. In the photograph, the bride and groom glowed as if they had been kissed all over by the sun. Her mother was looking up at her new husband and Captain Reggie Eden was looking back with rapt adoration.

Storm had seen the photograph many times before, but it was as if she was seeing it for the first time. An electric shock passed down her spine as she realized with sudden clarity that Zella and Reggie still loved each other more than they loved anybody else, including their own children. They were too bound up with each other to be anything more than the most benignly negligent parents. And shocking as this new information was, Storm also found it strangely comforting. All her life she had believed that it was she, Storm Gillyflower Alice Eden, who was completely unlovable, but perhaps her parents had simply used up all their love on each other and had none

left to spare for her. She suddenly felt a terrible pity for her father, who was weeping as if his heart had cracked in two.

Storm went to lay a comforting hand on his shoulder, but he was so taken up with his own all-consuming misery that he swiped it away like a fly that was making a nuisance of itself. Storm felt her lip tremble and the granary toast feeling in her throat expanded. She would have spilled into hot tears of fury and misery if she had not felt Aurora slip a cool hand into hers and give it a little squeeze. She looked gratefully at her big sister, and found herself liking her competent, bossy sibling more than she had for years.

At that moment Zella stirred on the bed and opened her violet eyes very wide. 'Darlings, I am quite exhausted,' she whispered in her low, distinctive purr. 'But I have something to say to—'

She got no further because her husband had flung his arms around her.

'Reggie,' she murmured sleepily, 'my one true love.' Then she added testily, 'Now put me down Reggie, dear. I need to talk to Storm. This is important.'

Storm thought she must have misheard. She couldn't remember when her mother had last had anything important to say to her except 'Run along and play, darling, Mummy needs her rest.'

Aurora pushed Storm forward with such force that she almost landed on top of Zella. Her mother tugged her sleeve and pulled Storm close up against her face. Storm caught a whiff of her distinctive, delicious smell – like caramelized pineapples crossed with night-scented stocks. Zella's eyes were shut and Storm wondered if she had fallen asleep again. But when she tried to move she realized that her mother was clasping her hands with a surprisingly strong grip. Then Zella's eyes opened and looked into Storm's, as if searching for something buried there.

'Storm, my wild one, you are the strongest of us all. Only you can keep the wolf from the door. I entrust them to you. Only you can keep them safe.'

Storm was astonished. She, Storm, the strong one? It didn't make any sense. Perhaps her mother was delirious and confusing her with Aurora? But she didn't have time to ponder any further, for Zella opened the palm of Storm's hand and pressed a small musical pipe into it, closing Storm's fingers over the top.

'Our secret – use it wisely and only if you

have desperate need. Beware of its terrible power,' she whispered, and a little shudder passed through her body.

'But what am I supposed—?' began Storm.

Zella put her finger to her daughter's lips. 'It's my special gift for you. Look after it, Storm. Don't be careless with it. It's not a trinket. Whatever you do, don't let it fall into the wrong hands. If you do, you will regret it, for such an event would put you and your sisters in terrible danger. I have chosen you, Storm, because I know that you will not betray my trust.'

Then she let go of Storm, fell back on the pillow, announced, 'I am so very, very tired,' and stopped breathing.

As if they were actors who had received their cue, the baby whimpered and Captain Reggie Eden started wailing, a terrible howling desolation. Aurora burst into tears.

Knowing instinctively that there was nothing any of them could do for a grief so wild as their father's, Storm tucked the baby in the crook of her arm and tugged at Aurora's sleeve, pulling her towards the door. Her sister followed Storm meekly from the room.

As they left, Storm took a backward glance at

her dead mother and thought she saw a tear glistening like a tiny perfect diamond in the corner of Zella's left eyelid. Storm fingered the metal object that her mother had thrust into her hand and that she had discreetly slipped into the bottom of her pocket. It felt warm to the touch.

Down in the kitchen, Aurora slumped on a chair like an old teddy that had lost all its stuffing. Storm slipped into the pantry, felt in her pocket and pulled out her mother's gift. It was a little tin pipe, nothing special by the look of it. No more than nine centimetres long, and very light, as if it had been fashioned from the cheapest material. It had a dull, unattractive sheen and looked as if it was in need of a jolly good polish. It was as unremarkable as a child's toy found in a Christmas cracker. Use it wisely, her mother had said. How could you use a pipe wisely?

Laying the baby carefully on a shelf amid the jars of pickled onions, Storm put her fingers to the pipe. She blew gently, and a strange tune filled the air: tumbling fragments of melody that gave Storm a strange, shivery feeling in her stomach, as if she was going to throw up. She was puzzled. It was a trinket, but no more. Not even a particularly pretty one. And surely not of any value.

Why had her mother wanted to keep it a secret between them? And why had she warned her to beware of its power? She must have been delirious.

Anger and hot tears welled in Storm's eyes. How silly she was to think that her darling, scatty mother had chosen her in some way for some special task. Sadly, she blew the pipe again, then picked up the baby, who was watching her with big, saucer eyes. She felt eaten up with a terrible loneliness. She laid her hot forehead against the tiny child's cool one.

'Poor motherless little thing,' she murmured. 'Well, at least we have each other.' She smiled at the baby, who gazed solemnly back as if she was listening hard to every word. 'If only you could talk,' whispered Storm as the melody from the pipe faded. 'I need a friend so very badly.' The baby gave an enormous burp. Storm smiled, but felt guilty when she heard Aurora's heaving sobs.

Leaving the pipe behind a jar of pickled onions, Storm ran back to the kitchen. As she did so the back door banged open with furious force and a blizzard of snow blew into the kitchen on gusts of freezing air. Storm was so startled that she nearly dropped the child. Aurora looked terrified.

Storm ran to the door and tried to push it shut

with her shoulder, but the wind was too strong. Snow was filling the kitchen, dancing hither and thither in the air. Seeing her struggle, Aurora ran to help and together the sisters pushed with all their might. As the door finally clicked shut Storm was certain that she heard the eerie and unmistakable cry of a far-distant wolf. She looked at her sister's wan, tear-stained face. It betrayed nothing. Perhaps I imagined it, she thought. Though in her heart she knew that she had not.

3

The three Almost orphans

*I*n the days and weeks and months that
followed, Captain Reggie Eden was oblivious of
the needs of his three young daughters, and so
bound up in his own grief that he failed to
acknowledge that Storm and Aurora had lost a
mother and were in need of fatherly love, comfort

and understanding. The evening after Zella's funeral, Captain Eden locked himself in his study and refused to come out again despite the increasingly desperate pleas of his children. Aurora took to leaving trays of his favourite food and drink – shepherd's pie and best Burgundy, gooseberry fool and vin santo – outside the door. When Aurora sent Storm to collect them, they were often untouched.

The baby was growing fast. She was almost six months old and starting to crawl when Storm said, 'You know, we really can't go on calling her Baby forever.'

'Well, we could,' said Aurora, 'but it will sound very silly when she is grown up and has become a high court judge or a primary school head teacher.' So that evening when they took their father his supper, they resolved to ask what to call the child.

'Papa,' called Aurora through the door. There was a long silence. She tried again.

'Leave me alone,' came the reply.

'Papa, we want to know what we should call the baby.'

'Oh, call her *anything*,' came the emphatic reply.

'Well, it's most unusual, and not even particularly pretty, but if that's what he wants, it'll have to do,' said Aurora, shaking her head ruefully.

Storm was aghast. 'It's worse than calling her Baby.'

But Aurora was insistent, arguing – rather optimistically in Storm's view – that it was a small sign that their father was beginning to take an interest in family life.

Aurora refused to make any concession to their mother's death. She was stricter with Storm than ever, as if determined to take on the role of mother to her sister, even when Storm protested that Zella had never showed the slightest interest in whether Storm was wearing a vest or knew her nine times table or the correct usage of a comma. Much to Storm's dismay, Aurora insisted on a tight schedule of lessons and weekly spelling and mental arithmetic tests. When it came to arithmetic, Storm always felt that at some point she must have missed a crucial lesson as a result of which nothing that followed ever quite made sense. Spelling was even worse. She hated the lists of words that Aurora gave her each week to learn and tried her best to lose them, much to the annoyance of her sister. Aurora also attempted to teach Anything to talk and count, arguing that it was never too early to start an education. But these attempts were all in vain as Any, as the baby quickly became known, remained resolutely silent and promptly yawned and fell asleep as soon as she spotted Aurora with her *Teach Your Infant to Talk* manual.

While Aurora concentrated on Storm's education, Storm concentrated on perfecting more practical accomplishments such as tree climbing, diverting the river and manufacturing fireworks. The latter activity she kept secret, knowing that Aurora would explode if she discovered what Storm was up to in the greenhouse. But when, just before Any's first birthday, she finally perfected her version of fountains of fire – huge whooshing columns of red and gold sparks that rose like an unfolding ladder into the sky – she couldn't resist the opportunity to show off.

Aurora had decreed that they should celebrate Any's birthday the day after the anniversary of Zella's death so that sadness and happiness should not conflict. After an interminable morning, failing yet again to understand the intricacies of decimals, Storm spent the afternoon secretly arranging her firework display out of sight around the side of the house. For supper, to which Captain Eden was invited but failed to attend, Aurora had served all Any's favourite foods – roast potatoes, liquorice, olive pizza, Bombay aloo, broccoli, pineapple with glace cherries and grilled aubergines, followed by her extra-special madeleines and a birthday cake with lemon butter-cream icing and a single candle.

After the cake was cut, the sisters gave Any her birthday presents. Aurora had made Any seven embroidered handkerchiefs, one for every day of the week, and also gave the child her favourite recipe book – *Plain Treats for the Thrifty Cook* – which she said would prove invaluable to Any in years to come.

After much consideration, Storm gave the baby her own beloved, battered teddy, a ragged brown bear with a tartan ribbon called Ted Bear. Any hugged and kissed Ted Bear and wouldn't let go of him. After the sadness of the day before, it was the happiest of evenings, and as darkness fell Storm beckoned her sisters outside.

She lit a match. *Whoosh* went the first fountain, a splutter of green and silver sparks. With a thunderous explosion the second fizzed into life: towers of flame – red, blue and gold – shot into the sky. A third fountain erupted with torrents of orange sparks like molten lava. Any squealed and clapped her hands in excitement and delight.

Aurora's face curdled. Storm didn't notice; she was too busy assembling the *pièce de résistance* – a series of connected foaming fountains that had taken her hours of preparation and of which she was immensely proud. It was the first time she had attempted a display using a timer and she was longing to see if it would work. She lit the first fuse and stood back. With an enormous bang the first fountain sparked and sent bouquets of multi-coloured sparks high into the air; the second fountain caught alight and silver dragons erupted into the night sky; the third began to fizz, and a stream of teddy bears made out of tartan sparks illuminated the darkness. One after another the fountains burst into life.

Storm was thrilled that her simple timing mechanism had worked and Any grinned and bounced up and down on her bottom with excitement. More sparks crackled and spat. Suddenly there was the sad hiss of water on fire and the tartan teddy bears disappeared. Aurora stood next to the damp display of pulpy fireworks, an empty bucket in one hand, and two full pails of water still by her side. She was smouldering with anger. Any hid her face in her hands.

'How dare you!' Aurora screeched at Storm. 'How dare you put our lives in danger by playing with high explosives. It's reckless and irresponsible. I am doing my best to keep us safe and you're doing your best to blow us all up!'

'How dare *you*!' Storm screeched back. 'I spent hours on that. You're a killjoy, Aurora. You never want anyone to have any fun,' and she marched over to Aurora, picked up one of the pails of water and dumped it over her sister's head.

'You little horror!' yelled Aurora, spluttering and dripping, a puddle forming around her feet.

'You tinpot dictator!' retorted Storm furiously.

'Spoiled brat!' screamed Aurora.

'Little Miss Perfect!' sneered Storm.

'Don't you dare talk to me like that!' shouted Aurora, picking up the remaining bucket and pouring the contents over Storm's head.

Storm looked at the dripping Aurora for a second and then at her own soaked clothes. Her face was white with passion and fury, and then she suddenly burst out laughing. She had never in all her life seen the normally perfectly turned out Aurora look quite so bedraggled.

Aurora seemed completely nonplussed, then a tiny smile crept into the corners of her mouth and she pealed with laughter.

'Oh, I am such a mess. I need a hot bath,' she cried when she eventually stopped laughing.

'Friends?' asked Storm a little shyly, unfamiliar with this new Aurora who smiled rather than frowned.

'Friends,' said Aurora, and she crooked her little finger around Storm's and they solemnly shook fingers. Any immediately did the same with Ted Bear's paw.

It was a turning point in Storm and Aurora's relationship, and one that was strengthened the next night when, passing her father's study, Storm found the door open and the French doors leading out into the park banging in the wind. There was no sign of Captain Eden and, as she went to shut the doors, Storm thought she saw a grey shape disappearing over the distant wall of the park.

Storm's heart knocked against her ribs – she was certain that she had just seen a wolf. She looked wildly around, expecting to find her father bloody and savaged on the floor, but there was no sign of him. Instead, atop one of the tottering piles of papers and books on the desk, she saw a note addressed to herself and Aurora. It was quite difficult to decipher as it had clearly been scrawled in some haste.

I am sorry for everything and Anything.
I have to go. Forgive me,
Papa.
P.S. Aurora, don't forget to take
particular care on your 16th birthday.

Back in the kitchen, Storm showed the note to Aurora.

'Are you sure that he's gone?' her sister asked. Storm nodded.

'Aurora, what does Papa mean about you taking care on your sixteenth birthday?'

Aurora went pink as a tulip and looked embarrassed.

'Oh, it's nothing. Just a silly old prophecy made by Mama's horrible stepmother, the old hag who kept her imprisoned in the tower until Daddy rescued her. Apparently she only agreed to let Zella go with Papa if she got an invite to the christening of their first child. Well, you know Mummy and Daddy – they were so scatty. After I was born I suppose they just forgot to send her an invitation. But she turned up at the christening anyway and there was quite a scene. Mama said it made her feel so ill, she had to have a quick lie down. Anyway, the old hag was furious, and prophesied that on my sixteenth birthday I would prick my finger and fall into a deep sleep from which I would never awake. It's not true, of course – nobody believes that fortune-teller stuff. They're all charlatans.'

'But Mama and Papa believed it.'

'I suppose they did,' said Aurora with deliberate casualness. She looked at Storm from under her eyelashes. 'Maybe it was convenient for them to believe it.'

'What do you mean?'

'Just that Mummy and Daddy were useless at all the everyday stuff of life. Oh, they were beautiful, like a pair of gorgeous butterflies, and they were the greatest of fun when they made the effort. There was something golden about them. They could charm all four legs off a donkey, not just the hind ones. But when it came to the ordinary boring stuff like cooking meals, changing nappies, making sure their children could read and write and putting a note out for the milkman, they just couldn't be bothered. They were too engrossed in each other. Being protective of me was a way of ensuring that I was always around to do all those things.'

'I always thought they wanted you around because they loved you more than me,' whispered Storm.

'Don't be silly, it was because I was useful to them and they needed me. Actually I think they found me rather dull,' said Aurora sadly. She saw Storm's stricken, guilty face. 'Oh, Storm, sweetie, don't fret. It is really rather nice to feel so needed. I liked it. It made me feel special.' Aurora hugged her sister very tightly and then added forlornly, 'I suppose Papa's disappearance means we are almost orphans.'

'I believe we are,' said Storm, taking Aurora's hand. Then, with the baby held between them, the sisters spontaneously wrapped their arms around each other and pressed tight together, so that all three heads – the fair, the red and the dark – were touching.

'We may have lost our parents, but we have each other,' said Storm fiercely. 'And we'll get through this, the three of us alone, the three of us together. For ever and for always.' As she raised her head from the circle, once again she thought she heard a distant howl and her eye caught the calendar. It was only a few months until Aurora's sixteenth birthday.

4
THE BOY WITH THE EMERALD EYE

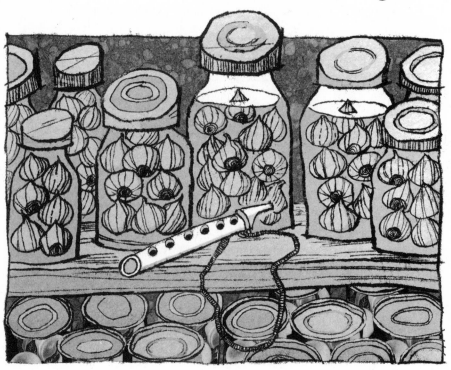

In the weeks after Captain Eden's disappearance
the sisters settled into a routine. In the early
mornings Storm tried unsuccessfully to teach
Aurora to climb trees and abseil while Any lay
watching, propped up in the pram. Mid-morning
Storm would retire to the shed in the walled rose

garden, often with Any in tow, to continue her experiments with fireworks while Aurora did housework. She deliberately didn't tell Aurora what she was doing and Aurora deliberately didn't ask. Since Captain Eden's disappearance Aurora had relaxed her educational regime considerably and had started letting Storm help her cook. On the days that Storm made fireworks and cooked, the broccoli soup would often have the smoky tang of gunpowder, which would bring a puzzled look to Aurora's face when she tasted it. In the evenings the sisters would play make-believe games together, which would often involve Storm rifling the old wardrobes for their dressing-up box, transforming herself into a valiant prince and rescuing the princesses Aurora and Anything from a fearsome dragon.

But making the fireworks was what she enjoyed most.

Bang! *Crackle!* Bang!

A huge fountain of gold and green sparks blazed, rose several metres into the air, popped and then faded to nothing in a shimmer of falling blue stars. Storm grinned at Any, who was bouncing up and down on her bottom with delight, clutching both Ted Bear and her starry blanket in her arms, and at Tabitha and Desdemona, who were watching wide-eyed too. A curl of vivid blue and green smoke rose out of the hole in the roof of the vast, dilapidated garden shed that stood amid a tangle of weeds in the old walled rose garden, hidden away from the house. Only the wall divided the overgrown garden from the woods beyond, and it was as if the latter were trying to ravage the garden and claim it back. Huge branches had crept over the wall and entangled themselves with the heavy red blooms; forest creepers were choking delicate white buds.

The final stars from the firework fell to earth. 'I can do much better than that,' boasted Storm, reaching into her pocket for another twist of gunpowder. She busied herself for a few minutes filling two roughly constructed cardboard tubes with pinches of jewel-coloured grains taken from an old wooden box with tiny secret drawers. Satisfied, she picked up one of several boxes of matches that were lying around, struck a match and lit the fuses. A blizzard of purple, orange and silver sparks erupted out of the tubes and miraculously formed themselves into little dragons that seemed to chase each other's fiery tails in whirling circles. Any's

eyes blazed with mischief and pleasure and she
gazed admiringly at Storm.

'Again?' asked Storm indulgently. Any squealed
in delight and bounced vigorously up and down
again on her bottom, which Storm took as a yes.
She bent with fierce concentration over her tubes

and containers, and so Any was unobserved as she furtively stretched out a little hand and pocketed one of the boxes of matches.

'This one,' said Storm conspiratorially, 'is going to be huge. Prepare yourself.' Any covered her ears with her hands. 'Ready, steady, go!' The match flared, the fuse caught and there was a series of increasingly loud pops and bangs. Storm and Any were laughing with such pleasure at the great crackling rafts of red and blue sparks that danced their way merrily towards the hole in the roof that they didn't notice the thin, pale boy with odd eyes – one green and one blue – creep past the shed towards the house.

Aurora was all alone indoors making the beds. Storm couldn't understand why she insisted on making the beds every day when they only got unmade as soon as you got back into them. Storm thought it was a complete waste of time, but if it made Aurora happy, she wasn't going to stop her.

In fact, making beds was doing very little for Aurora's happiness at that particular moment. Generally, housework kept Aurora's mind off all the things that worried her, and so many things worried Aurora that she kept a list in her pocket.

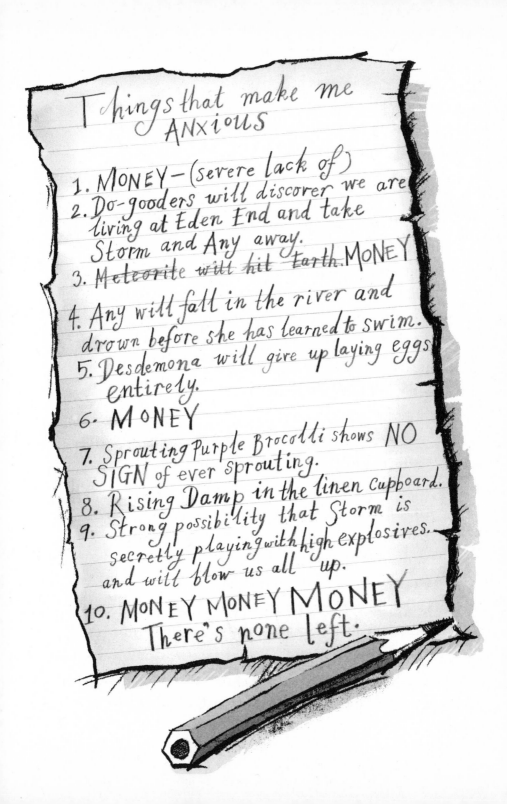

Things that make me ANXIOUS

1. MONEY — (severe lack of)
2. Do-gooders will discover we are living at Eden End and take Storm and Any away.
3. Meteorite will hit Earth. MONEY
4. Any will fall in the river and drown before she has learned to swim.
5. Desdemona will give up laying eggs entirely.
6. MONEY
7. Sprouting Purple Brocolli shows NO SIGN of ever sprouting.
8. Rising Damp in the linen cupboard.
9. Strong possibility that Storm is secretly playing with high explosives. and will blow us all up.
10. MONEY MONEY MONEY There's none left.

Not even turning out the linen cupboard, her favourite occupation, could stop Aurora worrying about numbers one, three, six and ten on her list. She was used to making do on very little. Her parents had believed they could live on love alone, and Aurora had become skilled at making meagre ends meet. She had once made Zella purr with laughter when she had declared very solemnly, 'If the wolf ever turns up at our door, he'll have to bring his own sandwiches.' Now, thought Aurora sadly, he'd have to bring an entire picnic. Supplies in the house were dwindling fast even though she had imposed strict rationing. The indigestible thought occurred to her that they might have to get through the winter on pickled onions alone.

Tears trickled down Aurora's cheek as she trailed down the stairs towards the kitchen. She was rooting through the almost empty larder when there was a knock at the door. Aurora stared uncertainly at the closed door. Eden End was as far from everywhere as it was from anywhere. Apart from a few angry suppliers demanding to be paid, nobody had called since their mother's funeral.

Cautiously, Aurora opened the door. For a moment she was blinded, not by the sun, but by the beauty of the thin boy, dressed in a grey jerkin and soft brown trousers, who stood on the step in front of her. His left eye was emerald and his right eye sapphire, and there was something about the line of his mouth – achingly soft and vulnerable – that made Aurora yearn to touch his lips with her fingertips. Aurora, although she didn't yet know it, was a great beauty, like her mother. She had skin as plush as pale pink velvet, eyelashes as long and dark as spiders' legs, and a graceful swan's neck, but this boy was so exquisite that he made her feel plain and awkward. He smiled at her and it was like catching a glimpse of daffodils on a cold, grey day. She smiled back shyly and flushed a delicate pink, like a rosebud that had opened a day too early.

'Can I help you?'

A look of surprise passed over the boy's face, the look of someone who has just caught a glimpse of astonishing beauty. He recovered himself.

'I think I can help *you*,' he said softly, in a voice that made Aurora think of brambles and autumn mists. She self-consciously raised her hand and brushed away the tear that still glistened on her cheek.

'Times are hard,' said the boy. It was a statement, not a question. Aurora nodded.

'I'm here to help,' he said, with a flash of dazzling smile. 'I am here to buy whatever you've got to sell.'

'I've nothing to sell,' said Aurora sadly.

'Oh, everybody has something to sell,' he murmured.

Aurora wasn't listening. She felt a little dizzy and light-headed. Perhaps it was lack of food. Over the last week she had eaten hardly anything, so that Storm and Any would not go without. She tried to pull herself together.

'What sort of things do you buy?' she enquired, wondering if she might be able to off-load some old furniture.

'Musical instruments,' said the boy smoothly. 'A house like this must have musical instruments. I pay a good price. You won't get better.'

Aurora's heart soared for a second as she thought of the grand piano in the ballroom, then plum-meted like a stone as she thought of the four missing ivories, one missing pedal and the family of shrews who had taken up residence inside and were happily chomping their way through the interior.

'We're not a very musical family,' said Aurora miserably, and the boy looked so disappointed that she felt a need to try and please him.

'You must have something,' he insisted.

'I'm afraid I have nothing for you, nothing at all,' sighed Aurora.

'But I am sure you do,' replied the boy. 'What about a flute or a pipe? You must have something like that? I am particularly interested in pipes. It's my special interest. I'll pay over the odds for a pipe.'

Aurora shook her head and just then a vision of the pickled onion shelf in the pantry popped into her brain. The other day when she had been counting the jars she had noticed a small tin pipe on a chain that she had never seen before, lurking behind one of the bottles. She had been about to tidy it away when Any's anguished cry had made her hurry back into the kitchen. She was sure it would still be there.

'I might just have something that would interest you,' said Aurora, and she slipped back into the pantry and found the pipe nestling amongst the jars. It felt unpleasantly hot to the touch. She stared at the pipe in her hand and wondered where it had come from. Perhaps it was a trinket that Storm had found. Her pockets were always full of rubbish. Aurora couldn't imagine such a tawdry old thing being worth anything at all, but the boy had said he was particularly interested in pipes so maybe he would pay her something for it.

'Here,' she said, smiling. She held out her hand to the boy, with the pipe nestling flat in her palm. A flash of hunger flickered in his ice-blue eye and he leaned forward eagerly. Aurora felt his fingers brush her palm and the pipe, and then just as quickly he withdrew them as if they had been scalded. He looked down into her upturned face and smiled, and fleetingly Aurora was reminded of Zella, who whenever she wanted something badly would unashamedly use the full force of her beauty and personality to make sure she got it. It was a look that made Aurora feel quite giddy. She wondered if she was coming down with flu.

'Give it to me,' said the boy winningly. He held open a small black velvet bag and Aurora made to drop the pipe in, but as she did so she hesitated. She felt torn. She longed to please the boy. If she pleased him perhaps he would accept her invitation to step into the cool kitchen and drink lemonade, and she could tell him about all her troubles. They were in desperate need of money, and the boy had promised her a good price in return for the useless old pipe. But strictly speaking, the pipe wasn't hers to sell. She should at least ask Storm before giving it to the boy. Reluctantly she withdrew the hand that hovered over the open neck of the bag. A strange look flashed across the boy's face, a conflicting mixture of anger and relief.

'It's not mine. I think it belongs to my sister. I must ask her first,' Aurora said firmly. 'Can you come back later?'

'I regret that may not be possible,' said the boy. He took Aurora's other hand in his, holding it for just a fraction of a second too long, and said, 'I am sorry I could not be of service.' He turned to leave. Aurora felt a surge of disappointment. She was just wondering whether to call him back when there was a violent explosion.

Crack! Pop! Whiz! *Bang! Bang! Bang!* A series of mighty blasts rent the air. Huge plumes of black, red and purple smoke rose from beyond the walls of the rose garden. Staccato cracks, each louder than the last, rocked the earth. The air was filled with the sound of rockets whizzing into the atmosphere. A massive bang made the ground tremble. An arc of stars rose into the sky. Aurora gasped, dropped the pipe, and ran towards the rose garden. The boy looked sadly after her, then, with a regretful shrug of his thin shoulders, bent down to where the pipe lay. His green eye was troubled. He touched the pipe, withdrew his fingers quickly as if they had been burned, and then picked up a small twig, which he used to scoop the pipe into the black velvet bag. Looking around furtively, he ran towards the driveway.

At that moment Storm, closely followed by a rueful and very sooty Desdemona and Tabitha, rounded the corner of the house holding a whimpering Any in one arm and the little wooden firework box in the other. Storm's last attempt at making a Catherine wheel display using a timing device had ended badly. The sparks had set off some firecrackers, which in turn had sent some primed rockets shooting upwards with a loud *whoosh*, making Any scream with fright and bury her head under her blanket. The garden shed had filled with dense, acrid fumes as its contents caught alight and began to explode. What was left of the shed roof had been lifted into the air with a sound like a mighty rushing wind. Storm, Any and Ted Bear were black with smoke, Any was weeping in terror and Storm's legs felt wobbly, as if they were made of half-set blancmange. She was frightened by the realization of how close she had come to blowing up herself and Any.

'What have you been doing, Storm Eden?' snapped Aurora, peering anxiously at Storm and Any's soot-covered faces and grabbing the tearful baby out of Storm's arms. Storm ignored Aurora's question; she was staring at the disappearing back of the boy.

'Who's that?' she demanded. Aurora, relieved that Storm and Any were clearly unhurt, was eager to discuss the beautiful visitor. She felt strangely intoxicated by her encounter with him and wanted nothing more than to tell the world.

'He's a musical instrument trader. He said he'd pay good money for an old tin pipe that I found in the larder on the pickled onion shelf.'

Storm's stomach did a backflip. She suddenly felt very sick. She had forgotten all about the pipe that her mother had given her. No . . . that wasn't true. She had always *meant* to go and retrieve the pipe from where she had left it, but every time she had set off for the larder she had become distracted. Guilt fuelled her anger now, and she rounded on Aurora furiously. 'How dare you!' she shouted. 'How dare you sell something that didn't belong to you. That pipe was mine. Mother gave it to *me*, not you. You had no right. It wasn't yours to sell.'

Aurora, her nerves already shredded by worry,

her encounter with the boy and the explosions, burst into tears. 'Storm, please listen, I didn't sell it. I guessed it was yours and thought I had better ask you first.'

'Where is it, then?' demanded Storm. Aurora felt in her pockets and then looked wildly around on the ground.

'I think I dropped it,' she whispered. 'When I heard the first explosion . . . the boy must have—'

Storm wasn't there to hear the end of the sentence. She had leaped on a rusty old bicycle that leaned against the wall and was pedalling like a demon down the drive. She streaked out of the gates at breakneck speed and caught a glimpse of the boy's retreating back. Redoubling her efforts, her face crimson with exertion, she set off in pursuit. The boy did not turn round, but he evidently realized he was being chased for he suddenly upped his pace.

'Stop! Stop thief!' screamed Storm.

The boy ran. But although he was quick on his feet, he was no match for the furiously pedalling girl, and Storm was so fired by anger that she had absolutely no intention of stopping until she had mown him down. Which she might well have done, had the boy not abruptly swung left and scrambled over a five-bar gate into a field of brown and white cows, and had Storm's bike not hit a large pothole at exactly the same moment. She was propelled over the handlebars with such momentum that she sailed clear over the gate and landed right on top of the boy.

The two of them collapsed into a giant cowpat, which had the consistency of curdled cream. Still Storm did not let up. She pummelled the boy's back with her fists, yelling, 'Give it back! Give me back my pipe!' Then she grabbed the hair at the back of his head and pushed him face down into the cowpat.

The boy struggled briefly, then reached into his pocket and flung the black velvet bag containing the pipe away from him. It fell in another fresh and very runny cowpat but Storm didn't care. She scrambled off the boy's back, grabbed the bag and tipped the pipe into her hand. It felt deliciously warm nestled in her palm. She slipped its chain over her head and the pipe lay against her chest like a comforting tin hot-water bottle. Then, without even a backward glance at the floundering boy, she set off for home.

Later that evening, after Aurora had finally scrubbed the last of the soot and cowpat off Storm and her clothes, Storm told Aurora all about the pipe.

'What power can a pipe have?' asked Aurora, puzzled.

'I don't know,' admitted Storm. 'But I rather suspect that that boy did. I don't think he came here by accident. He didn't want any pipe. He wanted this particular pipe. Although he gave it up surprisingly easily.'

'He was very beautiful,' said Aurora wistfully. 'He had the most extraordinary eyes.'

'His beauty is beside the point,' said Storm. 'Anyway, I didn't see his face.' She took the pipe from around her neck and fingered it.

'Have you tried blowing it?' asked Aurora.

'Of course,' said Storm.

'And what happened?'

'Nothing. But it's as if you hear in the music everything you've ever wanted – your heart's desire. It made me feel all shivery inside.'

'You mean like when you've eaten too much chocolate cake?'

'No,' said Storm. 'More like that moment when you feel totally lonely, as if you are the only person left in the whole wide world, or that moment that happens just before you know something really bad might be about to happen.'

72

'Blow it,' Aurora urged her.

Storm blew and the exquisite tune curled around the room. It hung on the air, making her feel nauseous and desolate.

The girls sat expectantly for a moment; nothing happened but for the clucking of Desdemona the hen and the purring of Tabitha the cat. Both had sneaked in and taken up residence by the fire. Aurora yawned. 'Time for bed.'

The pipe's tune was still echoing around the room. 'I won't be able to sleep,' said Storm. 'I'm too hungry. You know what I'd really like . . . ?' She looked hopefully at Desdemona. 'A boiled egg.'

'Tough,' her sister replied. 'There aren't any, and tomorrow isn't one of her laying days.'

As the melody died away, the two girls climbed the stairs to bed, arm in arm. On the way up, Storm asked casually: 'That boy, Aurora. What was so extraordinary about his eyes?'

'Oh, they are remarkable. I've never seen anything like them,' replied Aurora, delighted to get another opportunity to talk about the boy. 'One of them is icy blue and the other is green as moss.'

'Oh,' said Storm thoughtfully, casting her mind back to the council chamber and the boy in the gallery who had seemed so helpful and offered her a seat. She hadn't taken much notice of him, but she remembered that his eyes had been unusual too. Could it be the same boy? He had seemed so friendly.

'Are you hiding something from me,' asked Aurora suspiciously.

'No,' said Storm, and she hugged Aurora goodnight. If they had peered through the gallery window, they would have seen a lonely figure with mismatched eyes staring up at the house. But they were tired and they didn't.

5
Into the Woods

The following afternoon Any was asleep and Storm was sitting in the window seat in the nursery turret, reading a mildewed copy of fairytales that she had discovered in the library, and happily picking the scab off her left knee – the result of a tree climbing accident the week before.

Life didn't get much better, thought Storm as she painstakingly teased the dried blood away to reveal the soft, pink itchy scar below. There were few things more pleasurable than a cracking version of Hansel and Gretel and a good scab. Aurora was downstairs preparing a special tea because Desdemona had unexpectedly and uncharacteristically obliged with eleven eggs that morning, and Storm had managed to persuade her sister that they should celebrate.

They had eaten soft boiled eggs and soda bread soldiers for breakfast and Aurora had even let Storm have two of the eggs to make rock cakes. The rock cakes had lived up to their name as soon as they came out of the oven. After attempting to take one bite Aurora had refused to eat any more, saying that Storm's hurt feelings would soon mend but broken teeth stayed broken. They had kept the cakes for Any to use as teething rusks.

Storm looked out of the nursery turret window. A heavy mist was beginning to settle and the woods beyond Eden End looked more mysterious than ever. From her perch, Storm watched as a black coach and horses appeared over the horizon, disappeared from view, and then reappeared again, moving very slowly up the avenue of trees that led to Eden End. Squinting at the moving black blob and the horses with their black feathered plumes, Storm couldn't quite believe her eyes. Then she realized what this all too real hallucination reminded her of: a hearse, perhaps the very same hearse she had glimpsed all that time ago in Piper's Town. She felt the hairs on the back of her neck prickle with sweat.

Grabbing Any, who had been teething and grumpy all week and who immediately woke up and began to holler miserably, she raced down the 147 ½ steps of the nursery turret to the hall where Aurora had just wheeled the tea trolley laid with freshly made tea, egg and watercress sandwiches, freshly baked madeleines and rock cakes for Any. The mad dash left Storm panting for breath and a most unbecoming shade of beetroot.

'Goodness, Storm, you are a most unbecoming shade of beetroot,' said Aurora, looking up at her sister's flustered face with real disquiet. 'What's wrong?'

'We've got guests, uninvited guests,' said Storm grimly.

'Visitors?' said Aurora, looking flustered. 'Oh my goodness. It's lucky that tea is all ready. I do hope there's enough. I knew I should have made soda bread as well.' She looked worried. 'Maybe they'll want something a little more substantial. I think I'll just pop into the kitchen and heat up the rest of that nice nettle soup we had for lunch.'

'Aurora, I'm not entirely sure—' began Storm. But she was wasting her breath. Aurora was already in the kitchen wiping down the best china.

Storm dashed to the window in time to see the black coach crawl under the arch at the entrance to the courtyard like a malevolent beetle. The vehicle's driver – whom Storm recognized as Alderman Snufflebottom – halted the carriage. Its door creaked slowly open. From inside emerged a tall, thin, commanding figure, with an all-too-familiar scar. Dr DeWilde! Storm drew back behind the moth-eaten curtains to ensure she and Any could not be seen.

The doctor very carefully side-stepped a patch of nettles growing up through the paving stones in the courtyard, and looked appraisingly around, a cruel and ravenous gleam in his eyes. If the gargoyles had not been made of stone, they would have recoiled from the ruthlessness in that face, Storm thought.

Tabitha the cat and Desdemona the hen, sitting side by side in the courtyard, took one look at him and scarpered. Dr DeWilde reached into the carriage, withdrew his long, black, curved-handled cane. Then, followed at a respectful distance by Alderman Snufflebottom, he walked over to the huge wooden front door, raised the knocker and let it drop.

An ominous sound, like a clap of thunder, echoed around Eden End and died away. Any slipped her little hand into Storm's. She knew as well as her sister that this visitor was trouble – a dark shadow spreading over the quiet life that the sisters had made for themselves at Eden End.

The sound of iron on iron rent the air again, followed by a silence so empty it was as if the world had taken a sharp breath. Then a frenzy of knocking began, louder than the loudest hailstorm. Storm's hand instinctively slipped inside the neck of her dress: the pipe felt warm to the touch, like a hot potato on a blisteringly cold winter's day. Somehow its presence made her feel protected. From somewhere in the kitchen she heard Aurora call impatiently, 'Answer that door, Storm. It's rude to keep guests waiting.'

Storm sighed. She knew this visitor was not going to go away. She walked slowly across the polished floor of the great hall to the old oak front door and reluctantly pulled back the twenty-seven bolts. As the door swung open she thought she heard thunder, just a backbeat.

The man on the doorstep towered over her and Any, and he examined them like a particularly cruel cat observing a nest of defenceless mice.

'So . . . you must be Storm and Any. My name is Dr DeWilde and I believe that you have something that belongs to me.'

Storm knew instinctively that it was the pipe that he wanted. 'And I believe that you are quite mistaken,' she answered boldly, but perhaps a touch unwisely given the circumstances.

As soon as the words were out of her mouth she regretted them. There was a silence that you could have fallen into and done yourself serious damage. A small trail of spittle ran down Dr DeWilde's chin. He licked it away with a red tongue. Storm stared, both fascinated and repulsed. She felt sweaty and dizzy.

Panicked, she moved to close the heavy door, but Dr DeWilde was too quick for her. He put his elegant black leather riding boot across the threshold, hooked the handle of his elegant silver-topped cane around Storm's neck and pulled her close to his face. She could feel his hot, musky breath on her cheek. His eyes had a savage, feral

look, and close up Storm realized that they were not green as she had first imagined, but dirty yellow, like two heavily polluted stagnant ponds.

'Don't make me lose my temper, young lady, you'll only regret it,' he hissed threateningly in her ear, making every word sound as if it had both a full stop and a capital letter. 'Do as I say, or I will make life very uncomfortable for you, your sister and that brat,' he added, nodding in the direction of Any, who was giving him the benefit of her very best scowl.

'Don't stand in the way, Storm! Let our guest come in,' said Aurora, bustling in with a large steaming tureen of nettle soup and putting it down on the tea trolley. Then, completely oblivious of the exchange that had taken place on the doorstep, she walked forward and extended her hand.

'Hello,' she said cheerily. 'I'm Aurora Eden.'

Dr DeWilde bowed low and seized her hand. For a moment Storm wondered if he was going to bite it, but instead he raised it to his lips and kissed it. 'Dr DeWilde at your service. Charmed, my dear, charmed. It has long been my desire to have the pleasure. So like your poor dear mother,' he murmured.

Storm thought she might throw up, but Aurora

seemed unmoved by this revolting display of exquisite good manners and simply turned a pretty shade of fuchsia.

'You knew our mother? How wonderful! Do come in and sit down,' she said with a charming little smile. 'Make yourself at home.' She waved her arm like a grand hostess.

'Be assured that I will,' said Dr DeWilde smoothly, and stepped boldly into the hall.

'Would you like some tea?' asked Aurora sweetly, ushering him into the dining room.

'Delighted, my dear,' said Dr DeWilde, and he leaned so close to Aurora that it seemed to Storm that his teeth almost brushed her sister's pink cheek.

'Or perhaps you'd like something a little more substantial? Nettle soup?' asked Aurora, picking up the ladle and pouring hot soup into a bowl.

A look of horror passed over Dr DeWilde's face and he went very pale. 'Did you say *nettle* soup?' he said faintly, and recoiled back into a chair.

'Oh, it's quite delicious,' Aurora assured him. 'Very delicate.' And she pushed the steaming bowl towards him. Dr DeWilde leaped back to his feet as if stung.

Aurora looked nonplussed. 'It won't hurt you.

I promise.' The doctor was backing away in horror.

'Perhaps an egg and watercress sandwich instead, then?' asked a flustered Aurora, passing the plate.

'I don't mind if I do,' replied Dr DeWilde, recovering himself.

'I'm afraid we can offer very little, but what's ours is yours. You are our guest. Please help yourself to whatever you want,' said Aurora.

Storm, who had been watching this exchange open-mouthed, choked. 'Don't you see! That's exactly what he intends to do,' she shouted indignantly. 'Oh Aurora, can't you see through this sham politeness?'

Aurora turned an angry face towards her sister. 'Storm, how could you be so rude to our guest!' She smiled disarmingly at the doctor. 'Do please forgive her, Dr DeWilde. She is very impulsive.'

'That's the trouble with the young,' said Dr DeWilde indulgently. He gave a little cough. 'Actually I did come here for a reason. Your sister is right, you do have something I want. Something that belongs to me in fact. A pipe. A mere trinket. I gave it to your mother for safekeeping many years ago. I always meant to reclaim it but, well, you know how it is. Life is busy. I never got round to it. And now she is dead, I would like it back. It is purely of sentimental value. But it means a lot to me.'

Aurora started to open her mouth, but Storm interrupted. In an innocent voice as sweet and slippery as butter she enquired, 'Pipe? What pipe?'

'You know very well what pipe I mean,' growled Dr DeWilde, and he rose to his feet and loomed over Storm.

'Goodness! You're not a man to stand on ceremony, are you, Dr DeWilde,' said Aurora, looking flustered again. 'Of course, if the pipe means so much to you, I'm sure Storm will let you—'

'I don't know anything about any pipe,' said Storm fiercely. She was thinking of her mother's warning not to let the pipe fall into the wrong hands, and she was in no doubt that Dr DeWilde's hands were very wrong indeed.

'Hand over the pipe!' There was no mistaking the menace in his tone.

Storm shook her head emphatically.

'Don't play games; or you'll find that I don't play fair,' he snarled, and leaning forward, he snatched Any out of Storm's arms. Bounding lightly up the stairs, he held the terrified baby over the gallery banister railings. Any wailed piteously, holding out her arms to Storm. Aurora gasped in horror. The drop to the solid hall floor below was a heart-stopping ten metres.

'Please, no,' she screamed, then turned to her sister. 'Storm, please just give him what he wants!'

Storm glared angrily at Aurora, but Dr De Wilde looked at her appreciatively and said, 'Sensible as well as beautiful.' He descended the stairs and handed Any back to Aurora.

Aurora's shoulders sagged with relief. She looked imploringly at her sister. 'Please, Storm . . .'

'No!' said Storm fiercely.

Dr De Wilde reached for Any again and she hid her little face in Ted Bear's fur and clutched Aurora's shoulder as if her life depended on it, which it did.

Storm's eye met Dr De Wilde's and, just like in Piper's Town, she felt as if he was trying to see inside her. His glinting look was like a dagger going right through her. She averted her gaze.

'All right,' she said sulkily. 'I'll have to go and get it.' The pipe around her neck glowed hot against her skin.

'Where is it?' demanded the doctor greedily.

'Upstairs,' said Storm, and she turned as if to head up the stairs, but instead she grabbed the tea trolley and, disregarding Aurora's cry, shoved it as hard as she could at the scarred man. The trolley rattled towards Dr DeWilde with the momentum of a speeding express train, caught him off balance and hit him hard in the stomach, winding him. Hot tea and nettle soup splashed everywhere and he recoiled from the liquid as if it was poison.

'Run!' shouted Storm. 'Into the woods!'

After a moment's panicked hesitation, Aurora, holding Any tightly, made a break for the door. She pulled it open and rushed straight into the arms of Alderman Snufflebottom. He held her as if she was a butterfly that he could easily crush with a mere flexing of his hand.

Storm looked desperately around for a weapon. Her eye alighted on the pile of rock cakes. She picked up one in each hand and flung them at the alderman. The first struck him a glancing blow on the forehead, but the second was a direct hit to the nose. A third also scored a bullseye.

Snufflebottom let go of Aurora, his eyes watering, his face turning puce, and let out a holler of pain. Any, who was holding Ted Bear in one hand and her starry blanket in the other, took the opportunity to lean forward from Aurora's arms and bite him hard on the chin. Spurts of bright red blood formed around the perfect imprint of her sharp little teeth. Aurora looked quite shocked.

'Any, darling, we don't eat visitors – even if they are uninvited.'

The alderman rocked slightly on his feet, like a tree whose trunk has just been cut through, and then his burly body keeled over. Storm had to suppress the urge to yell '*Timber!*'

The children stood stunned for a second, surveying the chaos around them. Then, out of the corner of her eye, Storm saw Dr DeWilde recovering himself – a wild, dangerous gleam in his eye that did not bode well for the children.

'No, Aurora, I don't think we should stay to tidy up,' said Storm firmly, pocketing the remaining rock cakes and pushing her sister past the alderman's body and out of the house. They ran across the park, hardly daring to look back, expecting at any moment to hear the thunder of feet behind them and heavy, threatening hands on their shoulders.

'Shall I go after them, Doctor?' asked the dazed alderman fearfully, embarrassed that he had been outwitted by a gaggle of children, girls at that.

'No, Snufflebottom,' said Dr DeWilde grimly, watching the children flee. He knew that if he wanted to, he could catch them easily, but he enjoyed the idea of toying with them for a little longer. 'I have possession of the house. We must find the pipe. The girl said it was upstairs. It will be here somewhere. I can deal with the children later.' Dr DeWilde gave an unpleasant little smile. 'I very much look forward to meeting them again. They won't get away from me a second time. They are children, and children are always broken to my will.' He laughed, a creaky, cruel sound, like a door that badly needed oiling. 'I think I'll just give them a little scare.' He turned to Alderman Snuffle-bottom and licked his lips like someone savouring a particularly delicious thought. 'Release the wolves. Just two or three. Enough to let them know that I mean business.'

the better to eat you with, my Dear!"
and with a huge jump the wolf was at her

6
DanGeR!
WoLves!

Deep in the woods beyond the park, Storm, Aurora and Any huddled under a tree, shivering. It was getting dark and they were lost. After the adrenaline rush of the escape from Eden End they now felt small, frightened, and very alone. Mist was rolling in across the forest floor like a damp, white shroud and the undergrowth rustled constantly with the movement of things unseen.

Storm knew that Aurora and Any were exhausted and close to tears, and she could see from her sister's face that Aurora doubted the wisdom of actions that had left them out in the cold dark woods, and with strangers in control of Eden End.

'What are we going to do, Storm?' Aurora asked.

Storm dared not admit that she didn't have a clue. She wished she could tell her sister about what had happened in Piper's Town, then Aurora would have understood why they had had to run. But she knew that now wasn't the right time for Aurora to be reminded of Storm's previous adventures and of just how reckless she could be.

Storm felt in her pockets, wishing she had a compass, but her fingers only encountered a twist of gunpowder, a taper, a small metal file and a half-eaten peppermint toffee. She wondered whether she should have just let Dr DeWilde have the pipe. Maybe he would have left them alone after that. But she doubted it. There was something so ruthless about the doctor that she could not imagine that she or her sisters would ever be safe again. Storm shivered. She knew that he would hunt them down. Particularly when he realized that the pipe was not at Eden End, but around her neck. She had to find them help and a place of safety without delay. 'We need to get to the road that will take us to the town and shelter,' she decided.

'But which way is that?' asked Aurora with more than a hint of despair.

Storm wasn't sure. She was tired and disorientated, but she knew she couldn't betray indecision to Aurora and Any. She set off down a narrow overgrown track.

Soon the children were trudging along miserably, the low branches of the trees tugging at their arms. It had begun to snow heavily and the silence was eerie, as if a blanket had been thrown across the world. With every step the undergrowth seemed to become denser and the trees more closely packed.

It was a struggle for the sisters to put one foot in front of the other without snaring their clothes on brambles, and Storm's hands and arms were getting badly scratched from trying to clear a path.

Finally, Aurora slumped against a tree. 'It's no good, Storm. I can't go any further tonight. We're lost and we might just as well admit it.'

'We're not lost—' began Storm furiously, but her unfinished words hung in the air, cut short by a long low howl somewhere nearby. The cry was answered by a second howl, higher and more pene-trating.

'What's that?' asked a panic-stricken Aurora, grabbing onto her sister's arm.

'I don't think you really want to know,' said Storm grimly.

'Of course I want to know,' screeched Aurora so loudly that Storm clapped a hand over her sister's mouth.

'Well, if you insist,' said Storm calmly. 'Although you are really not going to like this one little bit, Aurora. It is a wolf. Certainly more than one wolf. I've heard them around here before. On the night mother died. And I saw one the day Papa disappeared.'

'But that's impossible. Everyone knows that wolves died out around here centuries ago,' Aurora said impatiently.

'Well,' Storm replied, wishing again that she'd been brave enough to admit to her trip to Piper's Town, 'somebody's reintroduced them.'

'That would be an exceptionally thoughtless and silly thing to do. It would make the countryside dangerous. Maybe they just escaped from a zoo.'

'Somehow, I don't think so,' said Storm thoughtfully. 'I think the person who has done it knows exactly what he's doing.'

'And what's that?'

'I don't know. Frightening people. Keeping them under control. Stopping them from roaming around the countryside. You'd have to have very good reasons for doing something so dangerous.'

Aurora looked at her sister suspiciously, beginning to suspect that Storm was holding something back. Then a wolf bayed again, closer than ever, and she suddenly had no desire to continue the conversation. 'Perhaps we *should* keep going,' she said with a gulp.

Storm nodded. 'Yes, I think we should.'

They stumbled on for a while, taking turns to carry Any, whose eyes somehow contrived to become rounder and wider with each howl.

'It's as if they are trying to tell us something,' said Aurora after a while.

Storm wanted to say: *They are. They are telling us that it is long past their supper time.* But she knew that wouldn't be wise given Aurora's current delicate mental state. She scanned the shadows anxiously. 'We're never going to find the road in all this snow. We'd better look for somewhere to hide.'

Like so much good advice in life it came too late, for at that moment a she-wolf slunk from behind a tree. For a split second Storm looked at the wolf and the wolf looked at Storm. Storm thought *Danger* and the wolf thought *Dinner*. Then the wolf looked at Aurora and Any and thought *Pudding*.

That was the beast's fatal mistake, for it was in

that instant that Storm yelled for Aurora to climb the nearest tree as she reached into her pocket and started pelting the wolf with the remaining rock cakes. The animal hesitated, clearly uncertain whether to give chase to dessert or stick with the entrée. Then, realizing that she was in danger of losing both courses, she gave a snarl of rage and propelled herself towards Storm's throat. Fortunately for Storm, the combination of anger and excitement at the proximity of three such tempting ready-to-eat snacks made the wolf miscalculate the angle of her jump. Not that this was any great comfort, for Storm suddenly saw two more long grey shapes appear amongst the trees.

The she-wolf growled at the newcomers, clearly irked at the prospect of having to share with so many a feast intended exclusively for one. Storm took her chance, and flung the last remaining rock cake at the she-wolf. It hit the animal squarely between the eyes. Storm saw the beast's eyes water and resisted a well-mannered compulsion to apologize, deciding instead to concentrate on staying alive long enough to celebrate her next birthday. She could see the other wolves yelping and snapping around the bottom of the tree where Aurora and Any were precariously secreted on a branch only just out of reach of the beast's open jaws. Aurora's mouth was an O-gape of complete terror.

The she-wolf had recovered both her balance and her appetite. She limped in a small circle, keeping her yellow eyes firmly fixed on Storm. Storm wanted to look away, but it was as if she was hypnotized by the animal's persistent stare.

So, she thought dully, this is how my brilliant life ends, before it has really properly begun. I am to be a superior kind of dog food.

The she-wolf crouched back on her thin haunches and then sprang forward—

There was a loud crack as the branch on which Aurora and Any were perched suddenly snapped. In a flurry of snow and foliage, bough and children were deposited directly on top of the slavering wolves below them, pinning the astonished animals to the ground.

Distracted by the breaking bough, the she-wolf who had been poised to take a chunk out of Storm's throat missed her target again and slammed into the tree behind. She yelped in pain and surprise and slithered down the trunk to lie in an unconscious heap at the bottom.

Storm turned her attention to Aurora and Any.
Here was a pressing problem. As long as her sisters
stayed sitting on the fallen branch, their combined
weight, together with the bulkiness of the bough,
was enough to keep the two wolves immobilized.
But it was clear to Storm that as soon as the children removed themselves, the wolves would be
able to escape from under the branch and give
chase.

'Stay there,' she ordered Aurora, rather unnecessarily as Aurora was in a dead faint and clearly wasn't
going anywhere. Storm cast around for inspiration
and felt in her pockets, watched by Any, who was
staring at her with big solemn eyes. Storm's fingers
found the gunpowder that she had been using to
make the Catherine wheels the day before.

'If only I had some matches,' she said out loud,
looking anxiously towards the she-wolf, who was
beginning to show signs of life.

'Here, have these,' said a small, high, clear voice.
Storm spun round, astonished. Still clasped in
Aurora's arms, Any was holding out a box of
matches for Storm to take.

Storm was so surprised she opened and closed
her mouth like a fish. Eventually some words came
out. 'Any! You can talk!'

'So it seems,' replied Any with the air of some-body very wise talking to somebody very, very stupid.

'How long?' asked Storm, still quite amazed.

'Oh, long enough. Since the day I was born. I suddenly realized that I could do it when you and I were in the pantry together.'

'Then why haven't you spoken before?' asked Storm.

'There just didn't seem to be a pressing need,' said Any. 'I don't believe in over-exertion. Life is tiring enough as it is, without lots of unnecessary talking.'

'Like mother, like daughter, then,' smiled Storm.

'I expect so,' said Any, yawning, putting her thumb in her mouth and nuzzling Ted Bear.

'These matches are just what I need,' said Storm. 'All I've got to find now is some kindling so I can make some fires.'

'Why?' asked Any.

'Because wolves are afraid of fire. They won't jump through flame.'

'You are clever, Storm,' said Any admiringly.

'So are you, Any. Most babies can't talk like you.'

There was a pause as Storm hunted around for

dry twigs and small logs to start a fire. She quickly and methodically made a number of small bonfires in a circle, enclosing all three wolves as well as Aurora and Any.

'Storm,' said Any after a short pause, 'you won't tell Aurora, will you?'

'About the talking?'

'No. She'll have to know about that, and it might as well be sooner rather than later. Although she'll probably want me to demonstrate, which will be totally exhausting. But I meant, don't tell her about the matches.'

'Why not?' asked Storm as she found larger dry logs to add to the growing piles.

'Because I don't think Aurora would approve of babies playing with matches.'

'No,' agreed Storm, laughing, 'somehow I don't think she would.'

Aurora and the she-wolf were both stirring.

'I think you are going to have to hurry up a little if we are to avoid being eaten,' said Any with the air of one who is being especially helpful.

'Perhaps you could lend a hand?' asked Storm.

'I would, but although I've completely mastered talking, I haven't entirely got the hang of walking yet.' She screwed her little face up thoughtfully and said, 'I can't entirely see the point of walking when there is always somebody around to carry you, but I expect it has its uses.'

Aurora had now revived and was staring at Any in sheer amazement, and the slavering wolves pinned beneath her with sheer horror.

'Hold on, won't be a moment,' said Storm, and she moved around the circle of unlit bonfires throwing a tiny pinch of gunpowder onto each and then tossing in a lighted match immediately after. The fires sprang into life with a pop. As the flames took hold, they merged to create a wall of fire that completely encircled the wolves, Aurora and Any, with just one small gap where there were two unlit fires.

'Now then,' said Storm to Aurora, who was looking increasingly anxious about the wall of flames, 'when I say jump, jump quickly through the gap here, and run as fast as you can in that direction. I'll light the fires and follow. One, two, three, jump!'

Aurora rose unsteadily to her feet with Any in her arms and leaped forward through the gap. The wolves scrambled up after her, but the branch was heavy and they were too slow. Just as they reached the gap Storm dropped lighted matches into the remaining two bonfires and threw in an extra pinch of gunpowder for good measure. With a roar a wall of flame rose up, leaving the furious wolves encircled by fire.

Running after Aurora and Any, Storm looked back and saw the creatures baying angrily, their eyes red in the reflected firelight.

The children ran through the woods and Aurora and Storm took it in turns to carry Any, who snuggled into their necks and hid her face from the world. After a while they could run no further. They collapsed on the ground by a small dark stream, from which they drank deeply. It had stopped snowing. The moon had peeped out; a splash of white paint in a puddle of inky sky. Both girls lay flat on their backs, gulping in the air and watching the treetops dance wildly in the wind like giddy chorus girls. Any was sleeping like a baby. After a short while Aurora raised herself up onto her elbow and spoke.

'Any can talk, then?'

'Yes,' said Storm, rolling over and looking at her sister's face.

'Good.'

'You don't seem very surprised.'

Aurora shrugged and gave a little smile.

'Why should I be surprised? I already have one exceptional sister, so it comes as no surprise to discover that I have two.'

Storm felt a warm feeling like a river of melted chocolate flood through her. This must be what real happiness feels like, she thought to herself.

After a few minutes of luxuriating in the feeling she said, 'We better move on. The fires weren't very big: when they burn down the wolves will be able to get out. They'll easily pick up our scent.'

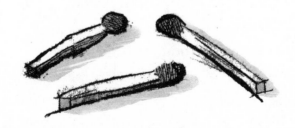

7
A house made from Sweets

After an hour of struggling through thick brambles, the vegetation suddenly thinned and the children could walk more freely under the trees. It was snowing heavily again and they were soaked through, leaving a trail of small puddles in their wake.

Whenever they stopped for a brief rest Storm listened hard. Once through the snow-furred silence she caught the sound of a far-off wolf. She shivered miserably. Could the pipe really be worth all this trouble? As if answering her unspoken thought the pipe glowed around her neck, radiating a warmth across her body. Then the trees began to thin too and Storm realized that they were following a distinct path that coiled around the tree trunks like a piece of ribbon. She broke into a run, reached a small bank, scrambled up and, to her delight, saw a narrow straight road dissecting the woods. She gestured to Aurora to hurry up.

'A road!' she said delightedly. 'It'll take us into Piper's Town.'

Aurora stood on the bank and looked first to the right and then to the left. 'Which way is Piper's Town?' she asked.

Storm hesitated. She didn't know, but she didn't want Aurora to know that she didn't know.

'Right,' she blurted. 'No, left. I'm sure it's left.'

'Storm,' asked Aurora seriously, 'are you certain, or are you bluffing? Do you have a clue where we are?'

Any raised her head from Aurora's shoulder. 'I know exactly where we are,' she said triumphantly.

'Where?' asked Storm and Aurora eagerly.

'Lost!' said Any with supreme confidence, and she put her head back on Aurora's shoulder and went to sleep again.

Aurora sighed. 'So, which way do we go?' she asked again, with a glint in her eye that Storm didn't much like. Storm opened her mouth to say right, just as a silver-grey hare shot out from behind a tree, turned left and sped up the middle of the road, its tiny footprints leaving a perfect trail in the snow.

'Left,' said Storm firmly. 'Piper's Town is definitely to the left. I'm quite certain.'

She turned out to be correct. Cold, wet, exhausted and starving hungry, they eventually saw the distant chimneys and spires of the town. Crossing an ancient stone bridge that spanned the wide river, they were soon padding down winding cobbled streets with names such as Cutpurse Way, Bleeding Heart Court and Butchery Lane, past unwelcoming houses with doors and windows shut firmly against the dark night and strangers.

It was eerily silent. Storm could hear her stomach rumbling. She thought longingly of the roaring fire at Eden End and of sitting beside it toasting crumpets and eating them with butter and drizzled honey.

'Where are we heading?' whispered Aurora.

'The town square. There's a derelict church nearby where we can spend the rest of the night,' said Storm. 'It won't be warm but at least it will be dry and then in the morning we'll get help.'

At that moment the crooked little lane down which they were walking turned a corner and in front of them was the most astonishing building. Its walls were covered in ginger parkin inlaid with sweets, and towering high above its peppermint roof was a quartet of towers constructed of spun sugar and studded with jellied fruits. But it was the smell that really attracted the children – the air around the gingerbread house was scented with the aroma of freshly baked cinnamon buns, warm chocolate muffins and hot gingerbread with sticky toffee sauce. The children stared at the building open-mouthed and Any held out her arms towards it and said one word: 'Yummy.'

Storm walked up to the white picket fence that surrounded the garden. As she got closer she realized that it was made from sweet rock and, in the garden beyond, lollipops stood to attention in the flowerbeds. Any leaned down from Storm's arms, licked the fence and said, 'Peppermint. It tastes of peppermint!' She fixed her small sharp teeth around the top of a post and took a bite right out of it.

'Any, dear,' said Aurora worriedly, 'I'm not sure

it's right to go round eating other people's property.' But Storm had already walked up the front path of the building and was nibbling at a marzipan and liquorice window ledge. Aurora followed her and broke off a piece from a chocolate window box and put it in her mouth. It was delectable. Any leaned forward and helped herself to a flower made of icing, glacé cherries and angelica. Ravenous, Storm dug her fingers into the gingerbread wall, excavated a large chunk and took a huge bite. It was the most delicious thing she had ever eaten.

The children were so intent on eating that they didn't notice the door of the gingerbread house open and they were startled when a voice suddenly said, 'Who's been eating my house? Who's been licking my fence? Who's been nibbling at my window box and gobbled it all up?'

Guiltily the children stopped stuffing bits of house into their mouths and looked up. Looming over them from the top of the stairs by the open front door was a large, plump woman with russet cheeks and eyes like apple pips. Her hair was the colour of treacle with a light dusting of icing sugar. She was wearing an old-fashioned white pinafore apron and a syrup smile, and she was holding her arms wide in a gesture of welcome. Then she descended the steps and Storm got a whiff of her crystallized-violet breath. She beamed at the children.

'My name is Bee Bumble and I am the matron here at the Ginger House Orphanage for lost, abandoned and foundling children, and you three are very welcome indeed. There's plenty more food inside. Why don't you come in, my little munchkins, where it's warm and safe, and let me look after you and feed you. Oh, my sugar plums. My little cupcakes. Come to Bee Bumble and she'll keep you safe and fat in her Ginger House. Oh, my strawberry shortcakes, my little peppermint drops, my sweet peas, stay with your Big Bee and she'll guarantee you granulated happiness.' She held out her arms to them.

Storm and Aurora looked at each other. They were half-frozen, soaking wet and completely exhausted and Bee Bumble seemed so very motherly and welcoming. From not too far away came the howl of a wolf. Aurora needed no further prompting.

'Come on, Storm,' she said. 'After all, we are almost orphans,' and she walked eagerly up the stairs and collapsed into Bee Bumble's arms. For a second Storm hesitated and then followed, holding Any.

'My poor little pumpkins. You are quite worn out. Time for beddy-byes, I think,' Bee Bumble said. She bundled them up several flights of stairs to one of the towers and put them straight to bed. Any, tucked into an alcove cot, took an experimental lick of the wallpaper and discovered, much to her delight, that it was liquorice on one side of the bed and chocolate on the other. She smiled dozily, kissed Ted Bear, clutched her starry blanket and fell fast asleep.

'What a little honey,' beamed Bee Bumble as she leaned in a motherly fashion over Any's cot. For a strange moment Storm thought the matron was going to take a bite out of the baby rather than just plant a sweet, wet kiss on her forehead. Then Mrs Bumble left, turning out the light.

'Aurora,' whispered Storm.

'I can't talk, Storm. I'm too exhausted. I could sleep for a hundred years.'

Soon Storm could hear the even breathing of both her sisters. She lay awake, fingering the pipe around her neck and looking out through the windows at the stars that shone down coldly and without pity.

* ★ ★ ★

In the morning Bee Bumble woke them by murmuring sweet nothings in their ears. She gave each of them a steaming mug of hot milk, scented with honey and nutmeg. 'Drink every last drop,' she smiled. 'It will help you grow big and strong. You all need feeding up.'

The milk was scrumptious; Aurora and Any quickly drained their cups. Storm was only sorry that she clumsily knocked her own mug over when she had only taken a mouthful. Her freshly laundered clothes were by the bed, smelling faintly of candyfloss. Storm felt relieved that she had kept the pipe around her neck. She quickly checked the pockets of her dress: a box of matches, a twist of gunpowder, a half-eaten sweet and a small metal file were still all there.

Then Bee Bumble took the sisters downstairs to the dining room for breakfast and the strangest sight met their eyes. Every surface glittered, as if the entire room had been drenched in precious gems. Brightly coloured boiled sweets, as bright as jewels, studded the gingerbread walls, while the cornices and door surrounds were made of royal icing inlaid with gum drops. The chandeliers were constructed from spun sugar and pear drops and the fireplace mantelpiece

from marzipan. A crowd of children were eagerly
pulling the sweets from the walls and eating them
– it looked as if their mouths were stuffed with
rubies, emeralds, amethysts, topaz and sapphires.
Everything in the room was covered in a light
dusting of sugar and the air was scented with ginger,
toffee and cinnamon.

In the centre of the room were four vast
trestle tables piled high with more sweet
treats. There were pecan pies, treacle tarts and
raspberry cream
sponges,
chocolate

fudge cakes the size of cartwheels, crateloads of blueberry muffins and hazelnut meringues, and slabs of candied nougat, honeycomb and peppermint fudge. Custard- and jam-filled donuts were piled high, as were sticky buns and chocolate brownies. Down the centre of each table were huge glass bowls of more boiled sweets that glistened in the light. On each side of the tables stood five-litre buckets of chocolate-chip, vanilla, and rum-and-raisin ice cream and jugs of steaming-hot chocolate fudge sauce. The centre-piece of the table was five huge swans fashioned from meringues, their necks garlanded with rainbow-coloured sweets and their backs full of trifle and jewel-like sorbets. Every dish had a little flag with a description, like the food at a children's birthday party.

Storm, Aurora and Any were open-mouthed in disbelief. Bee Bumble took the opportunity to pop an iced shortbread and a macaroon into each of the girls' mouths. Storm choked. She was so dazzled by what she saw that it made her eyes hurt. She was also appalled, not by the cornucopia of sugar – after all, she was sometimes partial to a peppermint cream herself – but by the sight of the children, who were attacking these vast sugar mountains with the eagerness of animals who had been kept without food for a month. There were dozens of them, and in complete silence they were gobbling the cakes and hunting down the brightly coloured sweets. Their eyes were glassy.

Bee Bumble pushed Storm and Aurora in the direction of the trestle tables. Any, who had the sweetest tooth, stretched out her arms longingly towards this Aladdin's cave of sparkling sugar and immediately began sifting the bowls for red sweets, like a miner searching for a rubies in the dirt. Storm held back. Peering under a table, she saw a pair of plump twins. One was fast asleep, her face and arms streaked with chocolate and sticky with hundreds and thousands. The other held her sister's head in her lap and was stroking her face gently. Storm opened her mouth to say hello just as Bee Bumble prodded her in the ribs with a surprisingly long, bony finger.

'You're much too thin, my little cupcake. You need fattening up. Eat!' It sounded more like an order than a request and Storm decided that now was probably not a good moment to ask for a plate of broccoli. Instead, she nibbled politely at a peanut-butter cookie. It was delicious, and each mouthful made her feel pleasantly sleepy, as if every aspect of her life now had rounded edges, not sharp ones. Absentmindedly she helped herself to another. Satisfied, Bee Bumble headed towards the kitchen to whip up half a dozen devil's food cakes and a death by chocolate gateau.

Sleepily, Storm looked about for Aurora and found her happily munching a chocolate éclair on the floor. She smiled up at Storm. 'Oh Storm, I feel so happy. It's safe and warm here and Mrs Bumble is so lovely. Let's stay for ever.' And before Storm could answer she had fallen into a doze and was snoring gently like a very pretty Chihuahua. Storm felt pleasantly snoozy herself. She looked around the room: all the children were either asleep or staring vacantly into space with smiles on their faces. Except for one. Storm could hear a stifled sob from beneath the table. It was one of the twins. Tears were falling down her pale face as she held her sleeping sister. Storm crouched down and crawled under the table to join them, 'Hello,' she said. 'My name's Storm. Who are you?'

The twin stopped sniffling and said, 'I am Arwen and my sister's Aisling.' She burst into tears again and sobbed, 'Aisling isn't well. She never wakes up properly. She just eats and sleeps and sleeps and eats. I want to leave here, but she won't listen to me. We always agreed on everything. Now she's changed.'

'Maybe she's just tired,' said Storm sympathetically. 'How long have you been here at the orphanage, Arwen?'

'We're not orphans,' said Arwen indignantly. 'We've got parents. But then the men with wolves came and we were brought here.' She looked utterly miserable. 'We came two days ago. I know because it was the day I had an upset tummy, so I didn't eat anything. And I've been so worried about Aisling that I haven't been able to eat since.'

Storm looked thoughtful for a moment, remembering their own encounter with the wolves. It all seemed so long ago. Then she smiled at Arwen and said in a very grown-up voice, 'Well, there you are. You're feeling low because you haven't eaten anything. You must. Those peanut-butter cookies are delicious, you know, although a little too sweet. Here, try some.'

Arwen took a cookie and nibbled at the edge. Within seconds she was gulping it down and reaching for more.

'Goodness, you were hungry,' laughed Storm, but she was talking to herself. Arwen had fallen asleep. Storm considered her for a moment with a puzzled look on her face. Then she crawled back out from under the table and wandered through the hall to the front door. She wanted to get a look at the outside of the building in daylight. She wondered how the spun sugar towers could so miraculously stay up. Why didn't they melt in the rain?

She had just begun to pull open the heavy front door when a sugary voice behind her said, 'Where do you think you're going, my little chocolate drop?' It was Bee Bumble. Storm spun round.

'I just want to get a better look at the outside of the building,' she said pleasantly.

'Of course you do, my barley sugar, and why not? You're very welcome to go outside any time you wish. But I think I heard your baby sister calling for you. The poor little muffin sounded quite distressed. I think you'd better go to her.'

Storm ran off to look for Any, and was surprised to find her fast asleep and in no distress whatsoever. Puzzled, she trailed back to the front door, but although she could see no lock, it would no longer budge. She wondered briefly if there was another exit, but then she spotted a fresh tray of peanut-butter cookies cooling on a window ledge and decided exploring could wait until later.

The rest of the day passed in a haze. Breakfast turned into lunch and lunch into supper – each meal as sugary as the last. Aurora and Any helped themselves with gusto but Storm began to feel an increasingly nagging anxiety. She had always preferred savoury foods to sweet ones, and the surfeit of sugar so early in the morning had made her feel queasy. She had barely managed to eat a thing since breakfast.

In between eating, the orphanage children dozed or sat around listlessly until, straight after supper, Bee Bumble shooed them to their rooms and into bed with an accompanying litany of sweet nothings and kisses that were like sharp little nips or bites.

Storm felt far from tired. She lay awake listening to her sisters snuffling in their sleep, and worried. She couldn't quite put her finger on it, but she knew there was something terribly wrong at the Ginger House and that she and her sisters should leave the orphanage as soon as possible. The pipe glowed warm about her neck and, brushing it with her fingers, Storm felt her mind clear. She leaped out of bed and shook Aurora and Any awake. It took several attempts before her sisters opened their eyes. They blinked at her stupidly.

'Come on! We must leave as quickly as we can,' whispered Storm. 'We've got to get out of here. Something's not right!'

'Get out? Why would we want to do that? It's nice here. I don't want to go back out into the cold, frightening woods and be chased by wolves again,' said Aurora dozily.

'Neither do I,' piped Any. 'I like it here. I'm going to stay. It's like living in a sweet shop,' and she put her thumb in her mouth and closed her eyes.

'Aurora, Any, what on earth is wrong with you?' Storm said angrily. 'We've got to leave. This place is no better than a prison!'

Aurora smiled sleepily. 'Don't be silly, Storm,

we can walk out any time we want. There are
no locks on the door. Mrs Bumble and I sat
together on the front steps earlier when she was
giving me her recipe for orange almond cake.
You wouldn't believe it, Storm. It hasn't got any
flour in it at all. She is a quite astonishing cook.
I could learn such a lot from her.' And with that
she turned over, curled up in a ball and fell back
to sleep.

Storm slumped back onto her own bed. She
suddenly felt very tired and weak. The pipe
burned around her neck. What had happened to
her sisters? They were not themselves. For a
moment she wondered whether she should just
walk down the stairs and out of the Ginger
House, but she knew that she could never bring
herself to leave them behind. *The three of them
together. For ever and for always.* If she could not
persuade them to leave, then she had no choice
but to stay too.

It was then that Storm heard a slight scuffling
noise. It was coming from the opening to a large
liquorice pipe up near the ceiling. Storm had
seen similar holes high up in every room of the
orphanage and realized they were designed to
waft a constant sweet aroma of baking into the

air. She had even considered climbing into one to see if it might lead outside, but Bee Bumble always seemed to appear just as she was considering how to scale the wall. Apparently someone else had managed it though, because a single green eye was now shining luminously out of the darkness.

Storm sat bolt upright, scared and curious. She didn't know if the eye belonged to a human or an animal. But then a soft, sad voice said wistfully, 'Your sister. She's the gentlest, most beautiful girl in the world.'

Storm threw back the covers and went eagerly to the wall beneath the pipe. The voice sounded vaguely familiar. 'Don't I know you from somewhere?' asked Storm. She thought she heard distant movement from somewhere in the house. She stood on tiptoe and called: 'Can you help us? Can you help us get out . . . ?' Outside the room there was the sound of footsteps, and the eye vanished back into darkness.

'Please . . .' whispered Storm urgently.

Heavy footfalls sounded from behind the door, the eye glittered briefly back into view and the disembodied voice said hurriedly, 'Whatever you do, don't eat the food!'

Storm leaped back into bed and pulled the cover over her head just as the door swung open. Bee Bumble stood on the threshold. She eyed the children intently for a few moments and then, convinced they were fast asleep, she left.

8
THE EXTREMELY BIG OVEN

In the morning, Storm tried again to persuade her sisters to leave the Ginger House. When they refused she told them about the warning voice in the night – although she left out the bit about Aurora being the most beautiful girl in the world because she didn't want her to become vain.

'So,' she concluded, 'I think it's for the best if we all stop eating the food that Bee Bumble serves up.'

At that moment Bee walked into the dining room with trays of chocolate-chip cookies and orange and vanilla cupcakes, and, much to Storm's disgust, Aurora stood up eagerly to take them from her.

'Such a sweet girl,' said Bee Bumble. 'Quite delicious.' She looked at her appraisingly. 'Although you still need fattening up. Then you'll be truly scrumptious.' She licked her lips as if savouring the thought.

Aurora blushed. 'So tell me, Mrs Bumble, how do you get your sponge cakes to rise like pillows? Do you favour the creaming or the whisking method? And might I hazard a guess that your devil's food cake is an entirely fatless creation?'

'Oh, my little cupcake! What a delight it is to find someone who shares my passion for the great culinary arts, who is willing to sacrifice herself upon the hot and steamy altar of gastronomy. How

I will coddle you. Step this way into my kitchen.'
And she steered Aurora away, leaving her sister to
clench her fists in frustration. Storm turned to
protest to Any, but the baby had already crawled
away to feast on more treats.

And so it continued over the following days.
Aurora refused point-blank to listen to any criti-
cisms of Bee, and Storm had absolutely no luck
persuading Any to forgo the groaning tables. In
fact, when she refused to carry Any to her favourite
puddings and sweets, the child soon discovered
that her legs worked perfectly well after all. She
hunted out the gem-like sweets and toddled
between the cherry pies and profiteroles on
chubby little legs that were getting chubbier by
the day. The more she ate, the more she wanted.
And when Storm remonstrated with her, she fixed
her sister with a melancholic look and said, 'In my
short, unhappy life I have already been deprived
of my mother, my father and my home, and now
you want to deprive me of the only food avail-
able. You are being quite unreasonable, Storm.
Every child knows that sweets are an important,
indeed essential, part of a balanced diet.' Then she
clambered onto Storm's lap and kissed her face,
so it was like being licked by a small dog with

very sugary breath, and all but melted Storm's exasperation away.

By the sixth day, though, Storm thought she would go mad, not just from frustration with her sisters, but with boredom. The occasional howl of a distant wolf had made her think twice about trying to explore the grounds again and, with the other children interested in nothing but eating, she found herself spending hours lying on her bed, staring up at the opening to the liquorice pipe, and fretting over the strange warning she'd been given. Part of her wondered if she'd dreamed the whole thing. Could there really be anything wrong with the food? Her sisters were looking a little plumper, but otherwise they seemed happy. And Storm couldn't deny that they were safer here than in the woods, or back at Eden End in the clutches of Dr DeWilde. Even so, she'd tried to eat as little as she could, which was a real struggle when all the treats were so terribly tempting.

Now she stared glumly out of an upstairs window, trying to ignore the rumbling in her tummy and wondering if she'd ever see home again and if the pipe was really worth all this bother. If she had just handed it over to Dr DeWilde, maybe she and her sisters would still be safe at Eden End. It was all her fault, she thought miserably.

The day had turned unruly: the wind gleefully toppled chimney pots and swirled tatters of leaves past the sugar-spun panes. Sudden rain hit the window like gunfire, startling her. The sky above the orphanage had turned inky, and somewhere far off Storm heard the first rumbles of thunder. She decided to check on Any, who had been nervous of loud bangs ever since their misadventure with the fireworks.

Storm needn't have worried. She found her sister huddled under one of the tables in the dining room, fast asleep, her arms wrapped around Ted Bear and her starry blanket, and her face smeared with chocolate. She looked so peaceful that Storm felt like chiding herself for worrying that the orphanage was unsafe. She crept quietly away so as not to disturb her. But at the door Storm suddenly spun round. The sticky, snoozing Any had reminded her of the twins, Arwen and Aisling. Storm realized that she hadn't seen them for several days. She felt a dreadful coldness inside and, crawling back under the table, shook her sister gently awake.

'Any, Any, wake up. I need to talk to you,' she

whispered urgently. Any opened her eyes, looking dazed. 'Any, you know the twins, the dark-haired ones with plaits? Where are they?'

'Gone,' replied Any, and promptly shut her eyes again.

Storm shook her sister, more roughly this time. 'Gone? Gone where, Any?'

'Just gone. I don't know. With the others, I expect,' said Any, and she fell straight back to sleep.

Storm shook Any much harder. 'Wake up! This is important, Any.'

Any sat up grumpily and yawned.

'What others, Any?'

'The other children. All gone. That big hand-some blond boy with freckles. Little Henna, and that horrible Rudi, who would never share the pistachio ice cream with the rest of us. I am glad he's gone. We all are. The pistachio ice cream is particularly scrumptious.'

'But *where* have they gone, Any?'

'I don't know, but I know when they went. The day before yesterday. They were here at lunch but not at supper. I know because I got the pist-achio ice cream all to myself.'

'Didn't you wonder where they went?'

Any shrugged. 'I heard two girls talking. One

of them said children leave and new ones come all the time. Now, Storm, I really am quite exhausted. I must get another nap in before lunch.'

Storm sighed; she could tell she wasn't going to get any more sense from her baby sister. She was about to go looking for Aurora when Any opened one eye and said in a small voice, 'I love you, Storm. I'm already missing you, even before you've gone.'

Storm smiled and took her little sister in her arms. Any curled up her arms and legs like a tiny newborn baby, put her thumb in her mouth and snuggled up sleepily. 'You make me feel safe, Storm,' she snuffled happily.

Storm held her tight and whispered, 'I'll always look after you, Any. I'll always protect you, whatever happens.'

Any was already snoring.

Storm laid the baby back on her starry blanket and crawled out from under the table. There was a flash of lightning and it was as if a light bulb had lit up in her brain.

Storm's heart knocked in her chest. She suddenly realized that the children who had disappeared were the plumpest in the orphanage, and she was positive that they had been deliberately fattened up for some terrible purpose.

Storm was distraught. Any's non-stop diet of strawberry cream shortcake, peanut-butter cookies and iced fruitcake meant that she was popping out of her clothes alarmingly. If anyone was an ideal candidate for going missing from the orphanage it was her own little sister.

She ran to tell Aurora of her fears, and found her sister in a room near the kitchen, piling one huge tray with choco-late and pear charlottes and pecan pies, and another with blancmanges,

fairy cakes and lemon cheesecakes.

Aurora listened while Storm explained her fears and then said airily, 'Goodness, Storm, don't fret so. There's sure to be a perfectly reasonable explanation as to why those children aren't here. They've probably been fostered or something.' She peered into Storm's worried face. 'You know your problem, Storm Eden? You've got an overactive imagination. You don't seriously think anyone is going to go round eating children in this day and age, do you? It's preposterous. People don't do that kind of thing. It is too ridiculously wicked even to contemplate. And I think you're wicked to go round implicating Mrs Bumble in such a thing. When I think of everything that lovely woman has done for us. She's even given me her secret recipe for shoo-fly pie. She's been like a mother to me.' She paused. 'In fact, I'm hoping she might adopt me.'

Storm stared at Aurora open-mouthed, but her

sister simply reached into her apron pocket and pulled out some of the little flags used to label the food. 'Here, do something useful: help me label these,' she said, handing Storm a pen. 'You do the pecan pie, fairy cakes, lemon cheesecake and blancmange.' Storm scowled, and started scribbling impatiently.

Aurora leaned over and glanced at her labels. 'You've spelled blancmange wrong. It doesn't have an H in the middle,' she said.

'Oh, what does spelling matter?' said Storm irritably. 'It's not important. What's important is—' She stopped. Aurora had put her head down on the table and fallen asleep, a contented smile on her face.

Storm groaned. She was sure now that they were all in terrible danger – Any most of all – but she also knew that she would find it impossible to coax Aurora out of the Ginger House. It was as if she was under some terrible spell that had to be broken.

Maybe if I can just get her outside, Storm thought. She glanced at the wind-swept window, wondering if it would open wide enough for them to squeeze through. It was then that she saw, with a jolt, that an all-too-familiar black carriage was standing in the yard, its horses impatiently stamping the ground.

Her heart in her mouth, Storm crept over to the kitchen door and tried the handle. It was shut firm. She put her ear against the keyhole.

'I'll have half a dozen of the little darlings very soon,' came Bee Bumble's sugary voice. 'Six succulent little piggies, as plump and sweet as meadow grass. Just the way you like them, Dr DeWilde.'

Storm stifled a gasp. Dr DeWilde and Bee Bumble were in league with each other! She and her sisters were in even greater danger than she'd thought.

The voices beyond the door dropped lower and Storm could only pick out the words 'pipe' and 'consignment of children' and something that might have been 'mountains'. Then the sounds abruptly ceased and she just had time to duck behind a huge churn of buttermilk before the door opened and Bee Bumble and the doctor walked swiftly through the room.

'The cub's more trouble than he's worth,' Dr DeWilde was saying.

'His heart's not properly frozen, my dear doctor. You can see it in his right eye. It's still green.'

'I told that old ice hag she hadn't kissed him hard enough,' grumbled the doctor, 'but she said that any more and she would kiss him to death. She assured me the ice splinter in his heart would bind him to me, but he's unreliable.'

'That's the trouble with those mountain witches,' said Bee Bumble. 'They're double-dealers. I should know, my sister's one. If they can cheat you with a half enchantment when you've paid for a full one, they always will.'

The two headed for the front door, engrossed in their conversation. Storm tiptoed out from behind the churn and through the open door to the kitchen. She wanted to have a good look around while Bee Bumble was out of the way.

The room was huge, dominated by a vast range over which hung dariole moulds, copper jelly-rings, fluted pie dishes and pastry cutters. Next to the range was the biggest oven Storm had ever seen. It was big enough and hot enough to roast a person. And, like in the dining room, the floor of the kitchen was covered in a thin layer of sugar.

Storm's eye was drawn to several huge sacks of flour in the corner. The coating of sugar on the floor around them was disturbed, as if the heavy bags were frequently moved. She hurried over to the bags and, with a grunt of effort, managed to shift one. Underneath was a trapdoor. Storm grasped its metal handle and opened the lid. Peering in, she could see rough-hewn steps descending into darkness. An oil-lamp sat on the top step.

Casting about, Storm spotted a box of cook's matches and quickly fired up the lamp. Then she ran down the stairs and found herself in a narrow passage. The passage looked like it passed right under the entrance to the Ginger House and, sure enough, as Storm crept along it, she heard Bee Bumble and Dr DeWilde's muffled voices over-head. She ran lightly onwards.

The passage continued for several hundred metres in a straight line that ended at another small flight of stairs. At the top of the stairs was another trapdoor, sealed with a strong bolt.

Storm was worried that she had already been quite long enough and that Mrs Bumble might return to the kitchen and catch her, but she was also excited to have discovered a possible way out of the Ginger House. She drew the bolt, lifted the trapdoor and found herself in a rectangular brick-lined room with a staircase spiralling around the walls, upwards into darkness.

Storm realized immediately where she was: the crier's tower in the market square. It must be how they smuggled orphans out of the Ginger House without arousing suspicion, she decided. For a second Storm was tempted to walk to freedom. But now, more than ever, she couldn't leave Aurora and Any in the clutches of Bee Bumble. She turned and raced back down the passageway and had just heaved the flour-sacks back into place, and was attempting to smudge the sugar trail around them, when the kitchen door was flung open and Bee Bumble strode in, followed by Dr DeWilde.

Storm's heart hammered with fear, but she tried to look nonchalant. 'Water. I needed a glass of water,' she spluttered.

Bee Bumble eyed Storm suspiciously. Storm looked directly back. The matron's face was as smooth as glacé icing. For a tiny, fleeting moment Mrs Bumble's eyebrows knitted together and a frown cut her forehead. It was as if a land slip had suddenly occurred on her face. Her eyes narrowed to slits and the pupils flashed red. Then Dr DeWilde pushed past her, a malicious little smile playing around the corners of his mouth.

'So, Storm Eden, we meet again. Nothing, I can assure you, could give me greater pleasure.'

'I know what you two are up to: you're in league with each other,' shouted Storm recklessly.

'And I am going to tell. You're wicked and evil. You're fattening up children to eat them!'

Dr DeWilde's smile broadened. 'My, what an imagination you do have, Storm Eden. I think you've been reading too many fairytales,' he drawled pleasantly. He turned to Mrs Bumble. 'Do you think that we have a spy in the Ginger House, Mrs Bumble?'

'Indeed, I think we might, Dr DeWilde.'

'And what do we do with spies, my dear Mrs Bumble?'

'Why, my dear Dr DeWilde,' squawked Bee Bumble excitedly, 'we put them in the Hansel, of course.'

9
A meeting with Hansel

Aurora stood in front of the Hansel, a huge chocolate truffle in one hand and a large slice of Madeira cake in the other. A bolt of lightning hit the spun-sugar tower and for a moment the room was engulfed in a dazzling brightness.

'Oh, come on, Storm. Eat! It's for your own good. If you don't eat you're going to fade away to nothing.'

'You're just trying to fatten me up,' said Storm, shivering in her underwear atop a crude bed of dirty sheets in one corner of the wooden cage. She'd draped one of the sheets around her shoulders, and tried to wrap another around her legs.

'Of course we are,' said Aurora, smiling at Mrs Bumble, who sat beside her on a chair which, apart from the cage, was the only piece of furniture in the otherwise bare room. 'We're worried about you. You're all skin and bone. Poor Mrs Bumble has been beside herself. She's put you in here to try and help you. But you've got to help yourself. She's made these especially for you. If you eat everything you're given for a week, she's going to let you out of the Hansel.'

Storm looked at Aurora despairingly.

'Aurora, that woman has bewitched you. She's in league with Dr DeWilde. She's a witch and the Ginger House is under some kind of enchantment. Think about it! The way it's made entirely from cake and sweets, the way the sugar towers don't melt whatever the weather, the way the children eat the food and grow fat and content.

The way they mysteriously disappear. Something truly dreadful is happening to them. Please believe me!'

'A liar, as well as a troublemaker who listens at keyholes,' sighed Bee Bumble, shaking her head sorrowfully, the malicious gleam in her eyes hidden from Aurora.

Aurora nodded sadly.

'Sometimes, Storm, I think there's something terribly wrong with you, the way you go around making things up. You're a fibber.'

'She is, my delicious Aurora. She is a dreadful fibber. She lied to dear Dr DeWilde about the pipe, too. She told him terrible porky pies. Such a pity.' She leaned forward confidentially towards Aurora. 'I don't like to see dear Dr DeWilde in a temper. You never know what he might do. He is so very volatile.' She paused and looked Aurora sympathetically in the eye. 'I don't suppose you have any idea where the pipe might be, my little cupcake? You'd be doing me such a service if you did. Dr DeWilde is growing impatient. I'd show you my secret recipe for baked Alaska . . .'

Another flash of lightning lit up the room, but Storm's face was already bleached white. She felt the pipe glow hot around her neck.

For a tiny second Aurora hesitated and then she said, 'Of course, dear Mrs Bumble, it's around her neck. That's where she keeps it.'

'Aurora, how could you!' cried Storm as Mrs Bumble advanced towards the cage.

Storm's struggles were to no avail. She fought like a tiger, but it was hopeless. Within seconds a triumphant Mrs Bumble held the pipe, jiggling it from hand to hand as if it was a hot potato just taken from the fire.

'Come,' she said to Aurora. 'We will leave your sister to reflect on what happens to nasty little liars.'

Aurora looked at the food in her hands. 'Come on, Storm, please have something to eat.' Storm made a noise like a wild animal. Aurora sighed. 'Well, if you won't eat it, I know someone who will.'

'Any?' asked Storm sharply.

'Yes, it's lovely the way she'll eat anything. She's turning into the most delicious little piglet, all plump and juicy.' Something in Aurora's words struck a chord with Storm. She remembered how Mrs Bumble had used almost exactly the same words about the orphans when talking to Dr DeWilde. Horrified, she pleaded with her sister.

'Aurora, please don't give any more food to Any. She is getting so plump and it is putting her in terrible danger.' But her words fell on deaf ears. Aurora simply picked up Storm's dress and cardigan from the floor and followed Mrs Bumble out of the room, a sweet smile upon her face. Storm fell back against the rumpled sheets, racked by a feeling of utter misery.

Mrs Bumble was waiting in the corridor for Aurora, struggling to hide the cunning look that was creeping over her features.

'Here,' she said, giving Aurora the pipe. 'Put this in your pocket. Keep it safe for me. Neither your sister nor any other parties with an interest in the pipe will guess that you have it. I know that I can trust you completely, my little sugar plum.'

'Yes,' said Aurora earnestly. 'You can trust me, Mrs Bumble. I would do anything for you.'

The following night, just past midnight, Aurora was busy in the kitchen. She'd just put a Dundee cake into the huge oven and was about to give her sister's dress a good wash. Storm had no need of it in the Hansel, so it was the perfect opportunity to give it a scrub and darn one of the shoulders which had a large tear. Aurora emptied out the pockets carefully, putting the contents – a box of matches, a twist of gunpowder, a half-eaten sweet and a small metal file – in one of the kitchen drawers. Then she washed the dress thoroughly. It didn't take long, but it was enough to make her feel dozy and, after she'd laid the dress out to dry, Aurora sank wearily into a chair. She felt tired all the time lately, even when she first woke up in the mornings. Tired, but content. Her mind drifted, her eyelids fluttered and within seconds she was asleep.

A few minutes later the door of the kitchen opened and a thin figure made a cautious entrance. Looking anxiously around to check they were alone, he walked across to Aurora and gently shook her by the shoulder. Aurora's eyes slowly focused.

Standing in front of her was the boy with odd eyes. He was paler and thinner than when she had last seen him at Eden End, blue veins clearly visible beneath his white skin. He looked ethereally beautiful. He looked ill and frightened. Aurora's heart skipped a beat; she felt sleepy and confused.

'You!' she breathed.

'My name's Kit,' whispered the boy. 'I'm here to help you. You and your sisters are in serious danger.'

Aurora stood up unsteadily and tossed her mane

of golden hair. 'Help? I don't need any help. I'm perfectly well. We're all fine. Mrs Bumble is very kind to us.'

The boy eyed her pale cheeks, her dull, vacant eyes. 'Have you been eating the food?' he asked urgently. 'You have, haven't you?' He sighed sadly and his face crumpled. 'Oh, Aurora.'

Aurora stood stiffly beside him, her eyes glassy. For a second the boy hesitated, then he tilted her face upwards towards his, cupped his hands around her cheeks and kissed her very tenderly on the mouth. Gently, he let her go. For a second Aurora stood very still, swaying slightly, and then a look of shock and surprise animated her features and, like a stone statue that has been magicked into life, the colour crept back into her skin and the sparkle reappeared in her eyes. She yawned, blinked and stretched like a cat.

'I feel so strange,' she laughed. 'I feel as if I've been in a long deep sleep.'

'You were enchanted by Bee Bumble's magic potion,' said the boy, reaching into a huge spun-sugar flowerpot and showing her a small bottle of murky liquid. 'She's a witch. She puts a drop into every batch of cakes and puddings. It makes people sleepy and content.'

Aurora stared wonderingly at the boy. 'You woke me up, didn't you? How did you break the spell?'

The boy blushed. 'No time for that now, Aurora. Your sisters are in dire danger. Dr DeWilde is on his way here to tell Bee Bumble he wants another consignment of orphans. We must hurry. Where's Storm?'

'Locked in the Hansel.'

'Then you must help her escape at once,' Kit said, with a worried frown and his green eye troubled.

Aurora gave him a suspicious look. 'How can I be sure that you're trustworthy? You tricked me before at Eden End when you stole the pipe.' Her eyes widened as she realized something. 'You were trying to take it to Dr DeWilde!'

'I didn't want to . . . he made me,' said the boy, so miserably that Aurora had to resist the urge to fling her arms around him and comfort him.

'Why should I believe you?' she demanded.

'Because you need a friend and I need one too. Very badly.' He smiled his melting smile, like the first ray of spring sunshine after a hard winter. He put his hand on Aurora's and said softly, 'You can trust me. I promise.'

Aurora was flustered. She wanted desperately to believe him, but he had tricked her once and he might do so again. 'Prove it, Kit,' she whispered.

There was a tiny cough from the doorway.

'A pretty scene!' sneered Dr DeWilde. He was leaning insolently against the door-surround, watching them. Fear flashed through the boy's emerald eye and he dropped Aurora's hand as if it was a red-hot coal. Dr DeWilde took a step, leaned forward, locked the curved handle of his cane around the boy's fragile neck and pulled him close.

'Plotting, cub? After everything I've done for you?' He pulled the boy right up to his face and hissed, 'You're my creature, cub. Mine entirely.' Then he pushed the whimpering boy to the ground and looked hard at Aurora. 'You would do well to remember that, too, my dear.' He reached into his pocket and brought out a handful of coloured sweets that looked like bright gems. Kit's icy-blue eye had a ravenous, greedy look. Eagerly he reached for the sparkling gems. Dr DeWilde laughed and aimed a vicious kick at the boy.

'See!' he said lazily. 'He will do anything for a handful of my precious sweeties. Anything that I ask. Anything at all. The greedy little pup would even betray you.' He picked the crumpled figure off the floor by the scruff of the neck and said, 'Come, cub, I have work for you.'

The boy's beautiful face flushed red and Aurora averted her eyes as he meekly followed Dr DeWilde out of the room.

Aurora stood for a moment looking thoughtful, then she went to the drawer where she had put the contents of Storm's pockets and took them out. She reached for a mixing bowl and two of the small flowerpot-shaped dariole moulds and began to make chocolate madeleines. When she had put them in the oven, she got down another bowl and started to make a pie.

10
ACROSS
tHe
FROZeN
RiveR

She's getting thinner, not fatter,' screeched Bee Bumble furiously, poking Storm with a bony finger through the bars of the Hansel. 'She must be forced to eat.'

Aurora stood next to Mrs

Bumble, holding the plate of madeleines, her eyes downcast.

'Look, Storm, I've made your favourites,' she said. 'Do try one, please.'

Storm scowled back at her with eyes like burning coals. 'I wouldn't touch anything you cooked,' she hissed. 'I wouldn't trust you not to poison me.'

'Now, now. Temper, temper,' said Mrs Bumble. 'Your sweet sister is only trying to do her best for you. Such a delectable girl and such a talented cook.'

'I do my best to please, Mrs Bumble,' said Aurora meekly, still keeping her eyes on the ground. 'You have taught me everything. I'm very grateful.'

Storm gave a snort of disgust. 'Do please take this mutual admiration society elsewhere,' she yelled angrily.

Bee Bumble's eyes flashed threateningly. 'Come, my little sweet pea, we will leave her. Clearly she's still not hungry enough. But she will be. In a few days she'll be begging us for food, and then we can stuff her full.' Mrs Bumble waddled towards the door.

'I'll just leave her these madeleines,' called Aurora, 'in case the silly child changes her mind.'

'Don't bother,' spat Storm. 'I wouldn't eat them if they were the last edible thing left on Earth.'

'But I made them especially for you, Storm,' hissed Aurora. 'As a surprise.'

'I don't want your surprises, Aurora,' Storm hissed back. Mrs Bumble stood tapping her foot impatiently by the door.

'I made them because I thought they might remind you of Eden End. Of our home,' said Aurora, pushing the madeleines through the wooden bars of the Hansel.

'Come on, Aurora, don't dally,' snapped Mrs Bumble. 'I need you in the kitchen. We need to prepare extra cakes for breakfast. Dr DeWilde will be here before noon.'

'Of course, Mrs Bumble, I am entirely at your service,' replied Aurora.

Storm watched them go. Angrily, she picked up one of the madeleines and threw it across the cage. It fell to the floor in tiny pieces. In a rage she picked up another. It flew across the cage, hit a bar and broke open. Storm jumped up, hardly daring to believe her eyes. Glinting on the cage floor, amid the crumbs of broken cake, was a small metal file.

She picked it up and set to sawing through the

bars. But then she stopped, a thoughtful look on her face. Tucking the file behind her ear, Storm turned to the sheets and began tying them together.

It took Aurora two hours to escape Bee Bumble's attentions in the kitchen. She snuck back to the tower room just as Storm was sawing through the last of the struts and helped her sister squeeze free of the Hansel.

'Here, you'll need these,' she said, handing Storm her dress and cardigan. The temperature had plummeted that morning and outside it was snowing; flakes as big as teacups were falling from the sky. 'I put everything back in your pockets,' she added.

'Thanks,' said Storm, and as Aurora passed her the dress she took her sister's hand and squeezed it. 'I'm glad you're yourself again.'

'So am I,' said Aurora, and she reached into her pocket and pulled out the little phial of murky liquid.

'What is it?' asked Storm.

'Bee Bumble's magic potion. She's got half a dozen little bottles of the stuff hidden in the kitchen and a drop goes into every batch of cooking. Here, have a sniff.' She held out the phial to Storm, who was enveloped in a fragrance of tangy vanilla overlaid with the scent of oranges and lemon rind.

'Oh, it's so delicious,' said Storm, yawning languidly. She reached eagerly for the tiny bottle. 'Let me have another whiff.'

Aurora laughed and held the bottle away from Storm. 'That's what it does to you. It enchants you. It's as if it makes you happy and sleepy at the same time, so you don't care about anything.'

'Not even being eaten,' said Storm darkly, taking the phial from Aurora and pocketing it. 'By the way, how did you escape the enchantment?'

'You remember that boy with the mismatched eyes? Well, his name's Kit and . . .' Aurora trailed off suddenly, blushing furiously. 'Um . . . Never mind – I'll tell you later. Come on, let's find Any and get out of here.'

The girls crept down the twisting stairs, along the landing and up towards their room. Storm pushed open the door and rushed in to gather Any in her arms and smother her in kisses.

But the cot was empty. Any was gone. The only sign that she had ever been there was the tartan ribbon that had been tied around Ted Bear's neck. It lay on the sheet like a reproach.

As Aurora reached for the ribbon, Storm put

her hand in the cot. The sheets were still warm. The sisters stared at each other with white, frightened faces and raced for the stairs. Stealthily they crept down the final flight. Then Storm ran towards the dining room. A crack of light shone through the door, which was slightly ajar. Through it she could hear Mrs Bumble and Dr DeWilde's voices. Storm peered through the crack. Laid out on the table were a dozen small children, trussed and gagged. The smallest and nearest child was Any!

Storm twisted her head to whisper to Aurora, but her sister wasn't there. Then Storm heard a noise from the kitchen and, cold with fear, she crept down the corridor. Bursting through the open door, ready for anything, she found Aurora busy wrapping up a golden-crusted pie in a clean tea towel.

'Aurora, what on earth are you doing?' she hissed angrily. 'How can you possibly be thinking of food, when your baby sister is lying trussed up on the dining-room table and is about to be made into a sausage.'

Aurora pocketed the parcel and followed her sister back into the hall. 'Do you have a plan, then?' she whispered. 'How are we going to rescue Any?'

Storm didn't have time to answer because at

that moment the dining-room door swung open. The sisters caught a glimpse of Any's helpless, beseeching eyes, and then Dr DeWilde was striding towards them.

'My dear Mrs Bumble,' he growled. 'I fear there has been a serious lapse in your security arrangements.' He reached for the girls.

Storm kicked him hard on the shin and he doubled up with a yelp. Then she dragged Aurora towards the front door. Half-expecting it to be locked, she pulled as hard as she could. It swung open. And she quickly slammed it shut again in horror. A wolf stood sentry under the porch, its teeth bared. There was no escape that way.

'Lock all the doors,' yelled Dr DeWilde. Storm grabbed Aurora's hand and headed for the stairs.

'Any!' cried Aurora.

'Later,' said Storm. 'Let's save ourselves first,' and she took the stairs two at a time, pulling Aurora behind her. They ran upwards, aware of the thump of feet behind and Mrs Bumble's wheezy breath. On the first landing Storm turned and pushed a huge box of freshly-folded chocolate blankets back down the stairs behind them. Dr DeWilde and Bee Bumble had to squeeze themselves against the wall as it crashed past, breaking into great chunks as it went. Meanwhile the girls galloped up the next flight, heading for the tower room where Storm had been imprisoned in the Hansel.

'There's no escape this way,' gasped Aurora, but Storm took no notice and continued up the twisting stairs. Their pursuers were only a couple of bends below them and they could hear Dr DeWilde's furious shouts.

As they staggered into the Hansel room, Storm slammed the door behind them and wedged the chair against its handle. 'That should keep them out for a few minutes,' she gasped. Then she pulled a sheet from the cage, tied one end to a bar she hadn't had to break, and hurried to the window, a fat snake of knotted linen trailing behind her.

'Over here, Aurora. This is our way out. I tied the sheets earlier in case I had to make a quick exit. We can climb down.' And she smashed the sugar-pane with her fist.

Aurora blanched.

'You'll have to do it, Aurora. There isn't any other way. And if we don't get down, we can't save Any!'

Aurora peered out of the narrow window. The frozen ground looked very far away. Storm saw the panic in her sister's eyes. 'Be brave, Aurora.'

'I can't,' her sister whispered.

'You'll have to. You haven't got a choice, unless you've just sprouted wings. Come on – I know you can do it.'

'I wish *I* did,' said Aurora in a small voice.

Storm busied herself with the linen rope. 'Ready?'

'As ready as I'll ever be.' Aurora was shaking as Storm helped her onto the window sill. The handle on the door began rattling furiously.

'You'll be fine,' her sister assured her. 'Just lean out, don't look down and don't let go. When you get to the bottom, run for that old stone bridge we came across on the way here. Remember? And make sure you're not seen! I'll meet you underneath it. Right, off you go.'

Aurora stood on the window ledge, clasping the twisted sheet so tightly that her knuckles turned white. She didn't move.

'I said go,' said Storm impatiently. 'Do you want your sister to be made into a pork pie? Do you want to end up as pâté yourself?'

Aurora was frozen to the spot. 'I can't, Storm, I just can't—'

Before she could finish Storm heard the heavy thud of a door being rammed. She looked wildly around, and with one swift gesture and a whispered 'sorry' she pushed her sister off the ledge. Aurora gave a gasp of terror and her mouth formed a perfect O of surprise. But she clung to the twisted sheet and, with trembling legs, her brain in neutral, she somehow made it down the side of the building – buffeted by the icy wind.

She was almost at the bottom when she felt a tug and an added pressure on the twisted sheets. Storm was zipping speedily down the rope and catching up fast.

Just as Aurora's feet touched the wonderfully solid ground and sank into fresh snow, she heard an angry shout and, looking to her left, saw the door of the Ginger House burst open and Dr DeWilde emerge. From the other side of the house came a heavily perspiring Bee Bumble.

For a moment Aurora was frozen with indecision, then Storm landed beside her and was pulling her away from the orphanage and through the garden of lollipop flowers.

Their pursuers were converging upon them from different directions and although Storm was confident that she and Aurora could outrun either of them, she knew that together the adults would have a good chance of cutting off their escape route. Storm's brain went into overdrive. 'Do exactly as I say, Aurora,' she panted as Dr DeWilde and Bee Bumble bore down upon them. As the two adults came closer, to Aurora's surprise Storm jolted to a halt and stood completely still. Dr DeWilde and Bee Bumble were now so close that the children could hear the latter's wheezing.

'Right, Aurora, on the count of three we duck . . . One . . . Two . . . *Three!*' The children ducked down just as Dr DeWilde and Bee Bumble reached out to grab them. There was an almighty thwack and the crunch of bone on bone as the heads of the doctor and the matron collided. Then they slid to the ground and lay in the deep snow, quite still.

Storm and her sister headed off at a gallop, through the gate in the picket fence and along the too-quiet cobbled lanes of the town. Not daring to look back, they pounded through the outskirts, then took a zigzagged short cut across a field and through a small coppice, not slowing until they reached the road leading to the old arched stone bridge that straddled the frozen river.

Storm took a good look around to check that nobody was watching and then slid down the steep, nettle-covered bank to the cobwebby darkness beneath the bridge. Aurora followed wearily and they both lay down, gasping for breath.

After a few minutes Storm managed to croak, 'We'll stay here until dark and then go back for Any.'

'It was hard enough getting out,' Aurora protested weakly. 'How will we get back in?'

'I think I can get in through the liquorice pipes,' Storm replied, just as the air was cut by the long mournful howl of a wolf and an answering melancholic cry.

Storm sat bolt upright. 'Why is it that I am living my life like a girl who has got *lunch* written all over her?'

Another howl split the air, much nearer this time.

'I think we'd better cross the river, and try to find a very tall tree,' Storm decided.

The children got up wearily, ready to scramble back up the bank, when they heard the warning rumble of an approaching wagon. They waited as it trundled overhead, then they scrambled up the bank and onto the bridge.

A sixth sense made Storm race after the wagon. With a superhuman effort, she gained on the vehicle. Reaching out, she managed to loosen one of its canvas doors. Suspended on hooks around the sides of the vehicle were a dozen little orphans trussed and bound like sides of bacon. The smallest

and nearest was Any, who stared out at Storm with desperate, terrified eyes.

The wagon began to move faster. Her muscles aching, her throat on fire, Storm put on another spurt of speed. 'Where . . . ? Where are they taking you?' she gasped.

From Any's gagged mouth came an indistinct noise that sounded like 'Pie Man's Squeak'. Then the wagon accelerated and Storm was left behind.

She stumbled back across the bridge and fell blindly into Aurora's arms, tears thick in her eyes. She feared they had lost Any for ever.

Then Aurora broke away, pointing back down the road towards Piper's Town. Five wolves were racing towards them.

Storm knew at once that there would be no time to flee for the trees. But she thought she could perhaps distract the beasts long enough for Aurora to escape. She looked nervously at the river with its thin layer of ice. The snow had ceased and a weak sun was trying to break through the clouds. Storm didn't think it was strong enough to melt the ice, but it was impossible to tell exactly how thick the ice was under its dusting of snow. She looked back at the wolves. They were gaining fast. She had no choice.

'We've got
to split up to get across
the river,' she told Aurora. 'It's
our only chance. See that twisted old oak tree
down the bank on the far side?' Her sister took
her eye off the wolves long enough to nod. 'Cross
the bridge and then head into the forest and hide,
preferably high up, somewhere on a line with that
tree. Keep an eye out for me and I'll join you
there when I can.'

Aurora was shaking. 'What about you? How
are you getting across the river?'

'Oh, I thought I'd do a little walking on
water,' said Storm with deliberate casualness.

Then she added lightly, 'I'm going over the ice.'

Aurora gripped her arm. 'Don't be a fool, Storm. The ice isn't thick enough!'

'I'll take my chances,' she insisted. 'The wolves will hunt as a pack and they can't go two ways. If we split up there's a chance that one of us will make it and be able to save Any.'

Aurora opened her mouth to protest, and Storm laid a silencing finger tenderly across her sister's lips. 'Hop it, and quick.' She pushed her sister towards the bridge and, after a final worried backward glance, Aurora set off at a steady run.

Storm turned to face the approaching wolves. Her stomach cramped with fear and she had to resist the urge to run. She had to be sure that the wolves followed her, not her sister. They were so close now that she could see their white teeth: rows of savage pearls, beautiful and lethal. Storm yelled at them to be sure they were focused on her and not Aurora, then she spun and slid down the bank, and stepped gingerly onto the ice. It creaked but held firm.

Picking her way across the surface, more skating than running, Storm headed upstream and away from her sister. The icy surface groaned under her weight, but she was quick and light, and her beady eyes picked out the more solid patches of ice as she hopped from one to another.

The wolves raced down the bank and out onto the ice in pursuit. The animals were lean and lithe and sniffed out the more solid patches by instinct. They quickly gained on her. She could hear their thick panting breath.

There was a snap of a jaw, and a gaping hole appeared in the back of her skirt. Storm cried out and took a desperate leap. Her feet hit the fragile ice and crashed straight through. She was plunged into the icy water – so cold it was like a lethal hug, squeezing all the breath out of her. For one terrifying moment, as the current tugged her down, Storm thought she would be trapped under the ice, but her fall had caused the surface to crack and splinter, and she was whirled downstream amongst the jagged chunks.

The wolves plummeted too, and were soon drifting as helplessly as Storm. They snarled and gnashed their teeth at her, but the current pulled them away from where she floundered and carried them downstream at speed. Every time a wolf was hit by a loose piece of ice it would growl in surprise and anger.

Aurora, meanwhile, had reached the twisted oak. She was about to clamber up when she saw the wolf-pack drift past in the increasingly swift current. Horrified, she looked for her sister and spotted Storm struggling in vain to reach the bank. She was in slower-flowing water than the wolves but Aurora knew she couldn't survive long in such freezing conditions.

Aurora cast desperately about and spotted a long branch on the ground. Storm was bobbing ever nearer. Unless she hurried she would be too late. Aurora heaved the branch towards the bank and, as fast as she could, pushed it out over the water.

As Storm drew level with it, Aurora gave one last mighty push. But her lack of physical prowess made her misjudge her thrust and she accidentally bopped Storm on the head. Her sister went under, rose again spluttering and coughing, and just managed to grasp the branch before she was swept away. Awkwardly, Aurora started heaving the branch back towards the riverbank.

At last she got the exhausted Storm lodged between two tree roots and, more hindering than helping, aided her sister onto the bank.

For a few moments Storm lay panting and shivering in a puddle of water. Then she looked up at Aurora and said a little testily, 'What were you trying to do, hitting me on the head like that? Help me drown?'

'I was trying to save you, Storm!' said Aurora, biting her lip.

'I know, silly,' said Storm, grinning. 'But it was a close-run thing.'

Aurora studied her sodden, bedraggled sister.

'Storm, you are disgustingly filthy. You need a good scrub and a change of clothes.'

'Aurora,' said Storm wearily. 'Just at this moment, cleanliness is the least of our worries.' She shivered and rose shakily to her feet, leaving a trail of puddles behind her. 'Come on. We have to find Any.'

11
The Strangely Silent Village

The sun was lower in the sky as Storm and Aurora followed the ragged road that wound away from town, into the woods and towards the distant smoky peaks of the mountains far beyond. They were exhausted and hungry and they knew that there was no help in the town, only danger. Their only option was to follow the road taken by the covered wagon that had spirited Any and the other orphans away from the Ginger House.

'At least it will feel as if we're trying to stay in touch with her,' said Storm. 'And maybe we'll find someone who knows how to get to Pie Man's Squeak.'

They walked in silence for what seemed like hours and Storm felt more despondent with every step. Her clothes were soggy, and she couldn't help feeling that both she and Aurora shared some of the blame for their little sister's absence. If only she had planned their escape from the Ginger House better, and if only Aurora had resisted falling under Bee Bumble's spell. But it was too late now. Any was gone and they might never see her again. Tears began to pour down her face.

'Storm?' said Aurora hesitantly. Angrily, Storm brushed her sister's hand away.

'Storm, let's sit down for a minute. You're completely exhausted,' Aurora said gently.

'Sitting down's not going to help!' yelled Storm angrily. 'I've lost everything. My mother. My father. My home. My little sister *and* the pipe!' She fell to her knees in the middle of the track and started sobbing. Aurora sat down beside her, put her arm around Storm and waited patiently until the sobs subsided. When Storm stopped hiccupping she said softly, 'You haven't eaten properly for weeks, Storm. You must be starving.' She reached into her pocket and pulled out the tea cloth and opened it up to reveal the glorious pie, all yellow and buttery.

'Have some. It's just what you need.'

'Need?! Don't you ever think of anything other than cooking and cleaning, Aurora?' Storm shouted angrily, and she brought her fist down violently upon the pie's perfect crust, smashing it to smithereens. It disintegrated, and thick gravy poured over the edges and spurted across Storm's already filthy dress. She stared into the centre of the devastated pie. Glistening amidst the gravy, broccoli spears and mushrooms was the pipe. Her fingers shaking, Storm reached in and took it. It felt wonderfully warm and comforting to hold. She licked off the gravy and slipped the pipe's chain over her neck. Then, a little sheepishly, she turned to Aurora. 'How?' she asked.

Aurora looked a little abashed and then said lightly, 'Oh, you know me, I always enjoy cooking with new ingredients.' She looked ruefully at the sodden tea cloth. 'A pity we didn't get to eat it.

It was your favourite, Storm.'

They sat in silence for a few minutes and then Storm crooked her little finger and offered it to Aurora.

'Friends?'

'Friends,' replied Aurora firmly. 'Friends and sisters.'

'Aurora,' said Storm hesitantly, 'I need to tell you something.'

Aurora looked seriously at Storm. 'Is this some kind of confession?'

'Yes,' said Storm, and she told Aurora all about her first adventure in Piper's Town, the appointment of Dr DeWilde as the exterminator and her journey home with Netta Truelove.

Aurora listened wide-eyed and then she said: 'I knew you had been up to something you shouldn't have been, Storm Eden. I can always tell.' She took Storm's hand in hers. 'And from what you've said, I think you were right not to give the pipe to Dr DeWilde.'

Storm chewed her cheek inside her mouth. 'I'm not so sure,' she said miserably. She pulled the pipe over her head. 'I don't think this useless old thing is worth losing Any for.' Angrily she made to throw the pipe away, but Aurora stopped her.

'It was Mother's special gift to you. She wouldn't have given it to you if it wasn't very important. You know Zella, she wouldn't have wasted her breath.' Storm smiled wanly and put the pipe back around her neck, where it tingled as if in greeting.

'Come on,' said Aurora brightly, rising to her feet. 'We've got a sister to rescue.'

The track through the forest was rutted and over-grown. A grass pathway had sprung up along the middle of the road, and mallow and buttercups, queen's lace and shepherd's purse waved cheerily in the breeze, their heads nodding up and down as if encouraging the girls onwards. After a while a distinctive silver-grey hare lolloped across the road and sat on the green ribbon of grass watching them intently, its ears pricked and its curious silvery eyes alert. As the girls neared, it bobbed elegantly ahead, then sat in a patch of speedwell, seemingly waiting for them to catch up. This happened several times. Storm watched the animal. It seemed strangely familiar. She had seen those bright silver eyes somewhere before.

'Have you noticed anything strange about that hare?' asked Storm.

'It does seem unusually sociable.'

'It's behaving very oddly. Hares are shy creatures. Hare today and gone tomorrow. They don't
like human company, but it is almost as if this one
is human. Are you thinking what I'm thinking?'

'All I'm thinking is that it's a pity we don't
have a cooking pot, a fire and a few bay leaves. I
know an excellent recipe for jugged hare.'

'Aurora!' said Storm, shocked.

'All right, all right, I wouldn't dream of
eating it,' said Aurora crossly. 'I was only
joking. Although I am so ravenous I'd even
consider eating a woolly mammoth right
now – if one turned up with apricot
stuffing on the side.'

The hare stopped licking its
fur and cocked its head on one
side as if listening to this
conversation. It stood
up on its hind legs,

raised its nose to the air and sniffed. Then it turned and headed towards the side of the road, constantly looking back at the children as if encouraging them to follow. Storm ran after it.

The hare plunged into the thicket and Storm pushed her way through the brambles in pursuit.

'Storm, come back! I can't see you!' Aurora cried fearfully from the track.

Storm took no notice. She was convinced that the hare knew where it was taking her and she followed with mounting excitement. She was disappointed when she reached a small clearing, only to find the hare sitting on a large hollow log washing its fur.

Storm waited, hoping that the hare would move off, but it sat contentedly licking its silver-grey coat all over.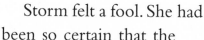

Storm felt a fool. She had been so certain that the

hare was more than it seemed; that it had magical powers like the animals in her storybooks. But just as she resolved to go back to Aurora, her eye caught something red in one of the bushes on the far side of the clearing. She ran to investigate. It was a wild raspberry bush, thick with juicy berries. Storm crammed a handful into her mouth, the juice spurting down her chin. They were the most scrumptious thing she had ever tasted.

'Aurora!' she roared. 'Come here!'

Her sister came struggling through the undergrowth and Storm pulled her joyously across the clearing.

'Shut your eyes, Aurora,' she ordered as they drew close to the bush. 'Now stand still and open your mouth.' She plucked a handful of heavy berries and popped them in her sister's mouth. Aurora chewed for a second and then beamed a huge red beam.

'Oh, Storm, this is so much better than woolly mammoth. I should never have doubted you or the hare. Where is it, by the way?'

Storm looked around but the hare was gone.

'It's just a great pity that it didn't arrange some cream to go with the raspberries before hopping it,' said Aurora, laughing, her hands and clothes sticky with fruit and her face alight with a fragile, fleeting happiness.

The laughter was short-lived. The sunlight hardened. Night bore down fast, and a dampness filled the clearing and clung to the girls like a ghostly companion.

Suddenly they heard the rattle of wheels and hooves back on the path. Ignoring Aurora's frantic looks, Storm crept nimbly to the edge of the clearing, lay on her stomach and peered through the bushes just in time to glimpse a horse and carriage. The horse's mouth had a sherbet foam ring, and its soft dark flanks were striped with blood where it had been driven too hard.

The carriage came to an abrupt halt. Storm froze. Dr DeWilde climbed down the steps to the ground, carefully avoiding a patch of nettles. He stood just metres from her. She dared not move or even breathe. His dead eyes flicked lazily around, then he raised his head and sniffed the air.

'They came this way,' he growled to himself. 'But they won't get far. I have the baby sister, and I will have the girls and the pipe too.' He grinned wolfishly up at an exhausted-looking Snuffle-bottom. 'Pipes have the odd habit of turning up in the most unexpected places, and I have every confidence that this one will make its way to me. And when it does I will destroy that little family. I will make those girls wish they had never been born!'

He leaped back into the carriage, which surged away to the heavy crack of the alderman's whip and the terrified neigh of the horse.

Storm felt sick, as if something repulsive had just crawled up her spine. She fingered the pipe. It was as warm as fresh buttered toast.

She decided to spare Aurora the details of what she had heard, saying only that they were on the right road to find Any. Reluctant to venture any further that night while the doctor was on the prowl, Storm suggested they try to sleep in the hollow log. Shivering, they crawled in − after Storm had done a quick recce to assure Aurora that there were no earwigs, spiders or other beasties lurking there. Once settled inside, she wrapped her arms around her sister. 'We'll get through this, the three of us alone, the three of us together. For ever and for always,' she said.

'But there are only two of us now, Storm,' said Aurora in a small, exhausted voice. 'We've lost Any.'

'We'll find her again,' Storm insisted. 'I feel it, just as I can feel my heart beat or my breath on my hand. The three of us are like bits in a jigsaw puzzle. We belong together. It makes us complete.'

At the first grey light the children awoke, stiff with cold. In the mean dawn, the dew-drenched raspberries were less inviting, and Storm thought longingly of the Eden End kitchen on frosty winter mornings, with Aurora standing at the range stirring honey and cream into bowls of steaming porridge. But it was raspberries or nothing and both girls ate until they could eat no more.

Back on the track with the sun warming their backs, the children felt their spirits revive. The trees began to thin and gave way to open countryside, across which they could see the track winding up a distant hill. Huffing and puffing, they climbed to the top of the escarpment, sat down and gazed around. It was as if the whole world was spread out like a quilt below them. There were handkerchief fields of brown, green, yellow and gold intercut with hillocks, small copses and streams that glinted in the sun like silver thread. The track meandered lazily across this idyllic picture-book landscape towards a distant village, complete with a church with a needle-thin spire. Its weather vane winked merrily in the sunlight.

'It's gorgeous. It looks like a dinky little toy

village, a giant's plaything,' said Storm, turning delightedly to Aurora, who was staring intently across the landscape with a puzzled look on her face, as if searching very hard for something she had lost.

'Come on,' said Storm, all tiredness forgotten. 'Let's go down to the village and get help.'

Aurora didn't move.

'Aurora, what are you waiting for?' asked Storm impatiently.

Still her sister didn't move.

'Aurora, have you turned to stone?' yelled Storm angrily.

Aurora looked calmly up into her sister's frowning face. 'Wait, Storm. Sit down and take a really good look.' Something authoritative in her tone made Storm sit grumpily by her sister's side. She glared across the valley.

'What do you see?' asked Aurora.

'Exactly what you can,' glowered Storm. 'I see fields, streams, a river, houses and a church . . .'

'And what *don't* you see?' asked Aurora.

'What do you mean, what *don't* I see? You can't see something that's not there!'

'Precisely,' said Aurora. 'There is an absence.'

Storm looked at Aurora as if her sister had gone mad. 'Aurora,' she said in a dangerously sweet tone that her sister recognized from the arithmetic lessons of old as heralding an explosion, 'could you please tell me exactly what you mean before I dash your brains out and bury you in a shallow unmarked grave.'

'Well, think about it another way, sweetie,' said Aurora patiently. 'Can you *hear* anything?'

Storm listened intently for a second. 'Nothing,' she said.

'That's right. Nothing, and then more nothing.'

Storm rose to her feet angrily. 'So?' she screeched with a hard edge of sarcasm in her voice. 'Is nothing plus nothing, more nothing or less nothing?'

'It's nothing. Nothing at all. Not even the song of a bird. Not the buzz of a bee. Now, what can't you see? What's missing from the landscape?'

Storm looked again across the serene scene, and as she did so her heart somersaulted down into her big toe. Her legs folded as snappily as a deckchair and she sank down beside Aurora.

'No smoke from the houses,' she whispered. 'No animals in the fields. No people, no carts on the road. No birds, no butterflies . . .' Her eyes scanned the view desperately. 'It's empty. Completely empty.'

'Lifeless,' said Aurora with a hard finality.

179

'Why? What does it mean?' asked Storm quietly.

'I don't know,' replied Aurora. 'All I know is that I don't like it. It's unnatural. Spooky.' She shivered as if something cold and clammy had brushed her skin. 'Come on, let's go and investigate. But slowly, and very cautiously.'

The village was much further away than it appeared, but long before they reached it they knew that something was terribly wrong. The lack of noise was oppressive. Storm had never realized that silence could be so loud. She wished she could turn it down. She spoke in a whisper, as if afraid of disturbing the still air and unleashing some terrible force.

Eventually, the road stopped snaking back on itself and they found themselves within sight of the first houses. Without speaking, they both stopped and sat down by the hedgerow. Aurora rubbed a blister on her toe and Storm absent-mindedly picked some daisies and twisted them into a chain.

'So, are we going on?' she whispered.

'I don't see that we've got much choice,' replied Aurora.

'We could always skirt around the village.'

'We could, but it will add on miles, and why

bother? We know the village is deserted. We haven't seen any sign of life.'

'All right, then,' said Storm, rising to her feet and putting the daisy chain around her neck. 'Let's go on.'

As they started down the road lined with the first buildings, a soft breeze rippled around them. They crept past the little pink and white houses, their doors closed and their windows shuttered and blind. They heard nothing except their own soft footfalls which the silence seemed to magnify, so that once or twice Storm cast a fearful look back, thinking that perhaps she had heard a third set of footsteps.

There was never anyone there.

Storm had to concentrate hard on putting one foot in front of the other. Perhaps it was sheer exhaustion, but it felt more as if so much vanished presence made walking through the streets like wading through glue. She sensed all around her the absence of those who had lived, worked and played in these small houses. It was as if the air was full of hidden laughter and vanished voices, just as her head was full of Any's vanished smile and voice. There was nobody to see her, but Storm felt incredibly self-conscious, as though she was an actor on a giant stage or the guest of honour at a surprise party and sooner or later the villagers would all pop up from behind a wall and chorus, 'Surprise! Surprise!'

Slightly apart from the other houses, and atop a small rise, was a tiny whitewashed cottage, its windows unshuttered. Ignoring Aurora's whispered protests, Storm ran to the window and, standing on tiptoe, pressed her nose against the diamond panes. She could see an unfinished game of checkers laid out on a side table next to two half-drunk glasses of juice. On the floor a sad-eyed doll flopped sightless across an open book of fairytales. Someone had been in the middle of reading *Rapunzel*. It looked as if the inhabitants of the room had been called away by a sudden emergency and would shortly return to pick up their games and book and carry on where they had left off.

Storm's gaze took in more of the room. A child's rocking horse stood in the corner, and with a little gasp Storm realized that it was still gently moving, as if its rider had only just dismounted. In the grate a fire burned merrily. On the table a meal was laid out on a checked tablecloth: corn-on-the-cob glistening with butter, steaming mashed potatoes, roasted carrots, parsnips and onions. Storm pressed her nose harder against the pane. Her tummy rumbled. She was so hungry: she felt as if she could smell the food. She wanted to devour it. She put her hand on the door handle and the door swung open. The room seemed to be whispering to her to step inside. She moved over the threshold and reached out a hand towards one of the buttery corn-on-the-cobs and raised it to her mouth.

Suddenly the corn was knocked out of her hand by a furious Aurora.

'Storm!' she shouted. 'Don't be a fool. Don't eat the food! Have you learned nothing from the Ginger House?' She pulled a reluctant Storm back out onto the front step.

'Just a little taste,' pleaded Storm. 'I'm so hungry.'

'No,' whispered Aurora sternly, and she pulled the door firmly shut. 'It's dangerous here. This place is enchanted. I can feel it.' She shivered. 'We mustn't linger here. We certainly shouldn't eat the food.' She pushed Storm down the street.

The silence was oppressive. Passing another house, Storm stumbled over an empty milk bottle that nestled close to the front step. It fell onto its side with the clank of glass on stone and rolled noisily across the street, creating a terrifying cacophony in the silence. The children clutched each other and held their breath. Nothing stirred. But against Storm's breast, the pipe glowed and throbbed as if it recognized where it was and was trying to sing out.

Walking almost on tiptoe now, they reached the end of the street, which opened out onto a small pretty square. A sudden creaking noise made Storm's heart thump. Across the square, the sign for the Hanged Man inn swung back and forth in a gust of wind. Somewhere an unlatched door was banging. Storm crept over to the pub and peered through the window. All was silent. She walked to the door and tried the handle. It opened easily. Holding her breath, she pushed it gently open. The hinges squeaked painfully through lack of use.

'Storm,' whispered Aurora urgently, 'what are you doing? Don't you ever listen to a word I say?' But Storm had already slipped inside. Very reluctantly Aurora followed her sister. They were in a room with a low-beamed roof.

Half-drunk mugs of beer stood on the bar. A game of cribbage had obviously been in full swing. Everything was covered in dust. It was quieter than the grave. Aurora shuddered.

'Come on,' she urged, nervously. 'Let's go.'

But as she stepped back into the square again, the sky turned black and cracked open. Huge hailstones fell, hitting the ground like bullets and tearing painfully into her skin. It was like being peppered with shot. Hastily, she retreated back inside.

'Let's stay until it clears,' said Storm, and she felt the pipe tingle as if in excitement.

Aurora looked aghast. 'If you think that I am going to stay here among all this . . . all this . . . all this . . . *dust* . . .' she spluttered.

'What else do you suggest? At least it's sheltered and warm,' said Storm irritably, pointing to the hail falling from the furious sky.

'All right, we'll stay. But only for as long as absolutely necessary. I'll tidy up a bit and get rid of the worst of the dirt.' She took out her handkerchief and polished the nearest table. Storm smiled to herself. Aurora looked the happiest she had seen her for days.

The Hanged Man

12
A GAME
of
BONES

Storm wandered beyond the bar, the pipe pulsating and burning under her dress. In a narrow corridor beyond she found a small door with a key in its lock. She tried the handle. It didn't budge. She turned the key, and with a teeth-wincing squeak it clicked open.

A Game of Bones

Pushing back the door, Storm found herself at the top of a small flight of steps leading down into a large, dark cellar that ran under the entire ground floor of the inn. Feeling in her pocket for the box of matches that Any had given her, her heart stuttering at a sudden, intense memory of her lost baby sister, she struck a match and cautiously started down the steps. The cellar smelled musty. A cobweb feathered her face and she squinted and brushed it aside, peering into the dark shadows. Squat barrels, once full, Storm guessed, of beer and cider, lined the edges of the room. A stub of candle in a holder sat on top of one of the barrels and Storm used another match to light it. Candle in hand, she crept over to the far corner of the cellar. Her eye was caught by something half hidden by one of the barrels. She peered behind the barrel and gave a little cry: curled in a corner was a small skeleton, a child's skeleton. She gave a tiny gasp, but there was something so fragile and tender about this little pile of bones that she was not in the least frightened. Her heart racing, Storm knelt beside it. Around the child's white wrist bone was a small silver bracelet. Tenderly and very carefully, Storm twisted the bracelet. The underside was engraved with a name: HOPE GOODCHILD. Storm stood up and, taking a tattered sheet that was draped over one of the barrels, she laid it gently down to cover the little skeleton. 'Rest in peace, Hope Goodchild,' she whispered softly. 'Rest in peace.'

As she turned to leave, her eye was drawn to an open barrel. It was filled to the brim with pome-granates, and the golden-orange fruits on the top had been cut open, revealing the seedy red pulp glistening like drops of precious blood within. They were bewitchingly beautiful, like priceless rubies. Storm hesitated. She just couldn't resist. She leaned over to touch one, her mouth already watering as she imagined sucking up the sweet, juicy flesh. She raised the fruit to her lips to eat, and at that moment the candle guttered and went out.

Still holding the fruit, longing to sink her teeth into its crimson flesh, Storm struck another match. It sizzled, burst into a tiny swell of light and then died. She fumbled to light another but her fingers were cold and awkward and the tip broke off. Never mind, the fruit would taste just as delicious in the half-darkness. She raised it to her mouth.

As the flesh brushed her lips, the door at the top of stairs slammed suddenly shut – plunging the cellar into a thick oily slick of darkness.

Storm gasped: never before had she been in

such total blackness. It was darker than the darkest
starless night. It was so dark it was as if someone
had thrown a thick blanket over her head.

She held her breath, and in the screaming
silence all she could hear was the pounding of her
own heart. Something slimy touched her face and
mouth and she shivered and gagged. She needed
something to take away the horrible taste in her
mouth. She raised the pomegranate to her lips
again, and as she did so she felt rather than heard
a horrifying sound and something leaped by her
face, screeching and wailing like a banshee and
knocking the pomegranate from her hand. Storm
opened her mouth and nothing came out. She
sucked at the darkness and screamed, the noise
filling the void in her head and the terrible cold
clammy darkness, joining in unison with the
shrieking of whatever terrible thing she had
unleashed in the cellar.

Blind, still screaming, feeling as though her
bones were turning to dust, Storm fell to the
ground and curled into a small quivering ball of
fear. Her entire body was filled with pain, as if
the screaming was stabbing at her head and guts.
She was oblivious to the door flying open at the
top of the cellar stairs, to Aurora's frightened gasp

as something streaked past her and into the hallway, the clatter on the steps and then her sister's firm, gentle arms wrapped around her sweat-soaked body. She lay sobbing like a baby against Aurora, who held her tight and rocked her. 'It's all right, Storm,' she crooned. 'It's all right, sweetie.'

Eventually Storm dared to open her eyes, blinking in the light thrown by the small lantern at Aurora's side. She sat up slowly and looked around. The lamplight had chased away the demons and wraiths. All she could see were the ropes and twine and tools hanging on hooks from the low ceiling, cobwebs and boxes and barrels around the edges. Storm blinked.

'There was something horrible here . . .' She shuddered at the memory of the squalling, shrieking spectre. Then she looked into Aurora's face. A tender smile was playing around her sister's lips.

'It was a cat, Storm, only a cat,' she said gently.

'But the door! It slammed shut on its own as if the room was haunted.'

'The wind, Storm, nothing but the wind. I opened the front and back doors of the pub to get a good blow through and it created a draught, that's all.'

Storm burst into tears afresh. 'I was so frightened,' she sobbed. 'I thought I was going to die.'

'I'm not surprised. It must have been pitch black down here,' said Aurora soothingly. 'Come on, let's go up.' She helped Storm to her feet.

'The pomegranates,' whispered Storm suddenly. She looked inside the barrel. Instead of the luscious ripe fruit that had so attracted her, the barrel was full of small wizened balls like little lumpy grey skulls. Tentatively, Storm put out her hand to touch one and it crumbled to dust.

Aurora was watching her carefully. 'You weren't thinking of eating one of those, were you, Storm?' she asked, horrified.

'They looked so tempting. As if they had just been picked.'

'Well,' Aurora said tartly, 'it's lucky you didn't eat them or who knows what might have happened to you. Most unhygienic. You have that cat to thank for a lucky escape.'

Storm looked thoughtful. 'Maybe it *was* trying to warn me; maybe it knew.'

Back in the front parlour of the inn, a small tabby cat with hazel eyes was sitting on the bar, washing itself with a complete lack of concern. It stretched languidly, jumped onto the floor and rubbed itself against Storm's legs as if trying to push her towards the door.

'This cat is definitely telling us it's time to leave,' said Storm. 'And I think we should take its advice.'

'So do I,' Aurora said briskly, and she opened the door and the two of them walked out, arm in arm, into the hail and thunder.

They hurried through the silent village past more shuttered houses towards the church and graveyard. As they drew nearer the churchyard, with its gravestones like upturned bookends, they heard a noise. Storm clutched at Aurora's sleeve and put a finger to her mouth. There it was again: a child's voice — pure and unearthly — carried on the breeze. The air she was singing was beautiful, a tune to make you both shudder and exclaim in delight. But when the girl got to a certain point in the tune, she broke off and began over again. This happened several times: the child never sang all the way through to the end.

She wasn't quite sure how, but Storm recognized the ghostly melody instantly, and knew exactly how it finished. And so, it seemed, did the pipe. She'd almost forgotten she was wearing it, but now the instrument glowed and tingled around her neck as if over-excited. She peered over the wall and, on a distant tumbledown grave, saw a small solitary figure sitting with her back to them. It was a little girl, aged about six or seven.

Clambering over the dry stone wall, Storm picked her way through the lichen-covered grave-stones. Aurora followed.

The child was engaged in a game, her dark head bent low and her brow knitted in fierce concentration. All the time she sang, always halting at that very same point. The girl was playing dabs, and as Storm drew nearer she realized with a prickle of horror that she wasn't using stones, but small bones – human bones. The little figure looked up. Aurora bent and took the child's hand in hers. It was icy.

'Goodness,' she said, 'you're frozen through. You need a long, hot bath. My name's Aurora, and this is Storm. What's your name?'

The child screwed up her face as if trying to remember something. 'I've forgotten. I did have a name but I lost it. I look for it every night on the gravestones.' Her expression was earnest. 'I look hard, reading all the names, even the difficult ones, but I never find it. It's not here.'

'Where are your parents?' asked Aurora.

'I've lost them.'

'Well, we'll find them for you; they can't be far. Maybe they've just wandered behind one of the mausoleums.' She whispered to Storm: 'It's very negligent of them, to leave her all alone in this weather.'

'Where do you live?' asked Storm.

The girl looked puzzled. 'Here, of course. I live here.'

'In a graveyard?' asked Aurora, looking shocked.

'On your own?' chipped in Storm.

'Of course not, silly. I live with my baby twin sisters. We're together here.' The child gazed at Storm and Aurora. 'Have you come to live here too?'

'Certainly not,' said Aurora. 'We live in a house.'

The child looked thoughtful. 'A house. I think I lived in a house once.' She frowned. 'It was like a house. It was an inn. But now I live here. I wouldn't want to live anywhere else. I like to be near my family.' She stood up and skipped off the grave singing her song again, and Storm could see the faded writing carved in the stone.

VICTORIA AND SARAH GOODCHILD
AGED THREE DAYS.
TOGETHER IN LIFE
AND
TOGETHER FOREVER IN DEATH.

The date was several centuries previously.

Storm's spine felt as if someone was running a finger down it.

'Where are the rest of your family?' asked Storm gently. The girl looked stricken. 'I don't know. I've been waiting for them for so long now. I'm so tired, but I can't sleep until they come, until we're all together again. If I knew how the song ended, I think they might come.'

'How do you know that song?'

'I heard it. In the inn. My brother and I were playing hide and seek and I'd gone into the cellar to hide. There was laughter in the bar overhead. Suddenly it went quiet; it always went quiet when a stranger walked in. Then I heard the music. Pipe music.' The girl's eyes shone. 'It was so beautiful. I heard such wonderful things in that music. But I'd only caught a snatch when it began to fade, as if the player was moving further away. I heard the feet of the people in the bar following after the tune and I wanted to follow it too. I ran up the cellar steps, but I couldn't get the door open. I think my brother must have guessed I was hiding there and locked me in for a joke.' Tears rolled down the little girl's cheeks. 'I banged and shouted and I waited and waited. But nobody ever came. Something must have stopped them. I know they would never have abandoned me willingly. They loved me.' The girl broke into song again, stopping in exactly the same place. Against Storm's chest the pipe was buzzing and humming. But Storm was oblivious. She was staring at the child, her mouth dry and her hands clammy. She realized that she knew this little girl's name.

The girl didn't notice Storm's consternation. She said brightly, 'Will you play a game with me?'

'Of course we will,' said Aurora, feeling terribly sorry for the lonely little girl, and wondering why Storm was looking so pale. 'We'll play with you until your parents return.'

'We'll have prizes,' said the child excitedly. 'I try to make my baby sisters' home nice, but it's hard: there are no pretty flowers in the church-yard, only weeds. If I win, you give me that daisy chain round your neck as a garland for the grave, and if you win I'll give you . . .' She thought hard. 'I'll give you a surprise.'

So for the next hour the three children sat on the grave in the drizzle playing dabs with bones until they were wet through and frozen.

'Enough,' said Aurora after they had played ten

games and the little girl had won six.

'I win! I win!' cried the girl.

'Yes, you win,' smiled Storm, and she carefully lifted the daisy chain over her neck and gave it to the child, who draped it with enormous care over the twins' grave. She stood back to admire her work.

'You played well. So you'll get a prize too.' She skipped happily behind one of the gravestones and emerged smiling with something held behind her back.

'Shut your eyes. Now open them.'

The sisters did so, and there in the girl's outstretched arms was Ted Bear. Aurora gave a little miaow of surprise. The child noticed their startled expressions and a look of hurt stole over her face.

'Don't you like it?'

Aurora recovered herself. 'I love it. It's the best prize I've ever won. Thank you so much. Where did you get a marvellous prize like that?'

'From the wagon. It passes this way every few days, always at night, always on the blackest nights. They stop at the pump by the gate for water. I heard them talking once. They said the children were plump enough to survive the journey without food, but they must have water. I hide so they don't see me. Nasty men.' She surveyed the sky. 'They won't come tonight, the moon is too bright.'

'Who gave you this teddy?' asked Storm urgently.

'Nobody. I found it. On the road by the gate, after the wagon had gone.'

'Do you know where the wagon goes?'

The child shook her head. 'No.' She paused. 'But I know who does.'

'Who?' cried Storm and Aurora together.

'Netta Truelove. She knows everything.'

Storm's heart leaped with excitement. Netta Truelove! The young woman whom she had met at the town hall in Piper's Town that day that now seemed so long ago, and who had helped her get back to Eden End. Netta Truelove, who had said to her that if she ever needed a friend, she was there and would help. Storm felt like kissing the girl.

'Where? Where do we find her?'

'Oh, up there,' said the child, waving an arm up the hillside with its rows of tumbledown gravestones and ravaged angels with sad disfigured faces. 'She's up there.'

Storm's mouth went dry again. 'You mean she's

in one of those graves?' she whispered, hardly daring to hear the answer.

'No, silly,' laughed the child. 'She doesn't live in the graveyard. She lives in the clearing in the woods, up beyond the village.'

Aurora bent down to the child. 'We would like it very much if you came with us.'

The little girl smiled a dazzling, sweet smile. 'But I can't leave. This is where I belong. I've got to wait for my family. I know that this is where they will come, because this is where my baby sisters are.' She pointed at the words on the gravestone, 'Look! For ever together.' The child sang again.

Aurora pulled at Storm's sleeve. 'We can't just leave her here. She'll catch her death of cold in this weather.'

'Aurora,' whispered Storm gently, 'I think she's already dead. Many centuries dead. I know who she is. I found her skeleton in the cellar of the Hanged Man. Her name is Hope. Hope Good-child. And she's a ghost.'

Aurora turned almost as pale as Hope. 'Surely not?' she whispered, watching the child as she resumed her solitary game of dabs.

'I'll prove it to you,' said Storm, and she called

out to the girl: 'Hope. Hope Goodchild.'

The child spun around, her face a beam of joy and delight. 'That's my name,' she said wonderingly, and she ran forward and clasped Storm's warm hands in her icy ones and said: 'You gave me back my name. Thank you.' Hope pulled hard at Aurora's arm, stood on tiptoe and planted a frozen kiss on Aurora's cheek. Aurora looked as if she was going to faint.

'Come on, Aurora. Let's go and find Netta,' said Storm, and she started pulling Aurora back towards the gate. The girl had skipped away and resumed her plaintive snatch of song again, her ghostly voice echoing through the silent, milky graveyard. She was reaching the point in the song where she always broke off, unable to carry the air any further because she didn't know the notes. Storm felt the pipe burn and tingle around her neck. Quickly, as she walked towards the road, she pulled out the instrument, took a deep breath, and blew.

As the child's voice faltered, the pipe took up the tune. The sound of the instrument swelled over the graveyard in a great mushroom of music, and entwined within it was the joyous laughter of Hope Goodchild. The pipe burning in her hands, Storm blew harder still and the sound magnified as if it was trying to fill the whole world up with its sweet music. The tune lingered.

At the gate the sisters looked back through the swirling mist. Hope was sitting quite alone on the gravestone with its daisy garland. As Storm and Aurora walked away they heard her begin her plaintive song once again, her tune mingling with the dying sounds of the pipe in a ghostly round. And this time Hope didn't break off her song, but continued singing it right through to the very end.

A Game of Bones

Storm and Aurora smiled at each other as they plodded wearily up the hill in search of Netta. If they had glanced back again they would have been very surprised to see that Hope was no longer alone. Standing on the stone grave were six people: a beaming man who held two tiny sleepy babies in his arms and a laughing woman and a young boy, who joyously hugged Hope as if they would never, ever let her go.

13
Dinner At True Love Cottage

Storm and Aurora stood in the clearing in the woods in front of a crooked little cottage with a thatched roof and wisteria-clad white-washed walls. A curl of smoke rose from the chimney. There could be no doubt that this was Netta's cottage because at the edge of the clearing was a small signpost. The signpost had two arms. The arm pointing towards the house said, TRUELOVE COTTAGE; the other, pointing away, declared THE REST OF THE WORLD.

The sisters knocked long and hard at the door of the cottage, but there was no answer.

'She must be out,' said Storm disappointedly. 'But she can't have gone far because the fire is lit.'

Aurora, who was quite exhausted, sank to the ground and buried her head in her knees. A little tabby cat, looking remarkably like the one from the inn, rubbed its ears against her legs. Storm peered through the letterbox. She saw a table laid for three people. A bowl of soup steamed at each setting and there was a fresh-baked cottage loaf sitting next to a large pat of pale, creamy butter and a bowl of ripe tomatoes.

'She must be around,' said Storm excitedly, her mouth watering. 'She's expecting somebody. The table's laid and there's food set out. It looks yummy.'

Aurora lifted her head and said sharply, 'Storm Eden, you should know it's very rude to look through other people's letterboxes, and you should also know by now that anything that looks like a free lunch almost certainly comes at a price.'

'I'm going in anyway,' said Storm, turning the handle on the door.

'Oh no, you're not,' said Aurora, leaping to her feet and barring Storm's way. 'I once heard a terrible story about a girl walking in the forest who came across an empty cottage and made herself at home there. It turned out the owners were really violent, ferocious types. Part of the notorious Bruin family. Apparently she had a very narrow escape. I know for a fact that it's true because Betty in the post office in the village knows somebody who knows somebody who was the girl's third cousin twice removed.'

Storm sat down grumpily on the step. She was so tired, hungry and wet that she longed to rush into the warm cottage and help herself to the food, but she also knew that Aurora was right to be suspicious. She sighed very loudly and had just started biting her fingernails, ignoring Aurora's disapproving look, when a silver hare darted across the clearing and ran around the back of the cottage. It had just disappeared from sight when the front door was flung open and they heard Netta Truelove's laughing, silvery voice: 'Storm Eden, how lovely to see you. And this must be Aurora.' The little tabby cat rubbed against Netta's legs.

'Is that your cat?' asked Storm.

'Yes,' said Netta. 'Cobweb is my eyes and ears.' She grinned. 'Sometimes I think that she is a witch's cat, she's so clever. But come in, girls, out of the weather. You're both soaked through. You need baths and a change of clothes.'

Aurora gave a heartfelt sigh. 'That would be pure bliss.'

Some time later Storm and Aurora were huddled in front of a fire, bathed and wrapped in warm towels, and full of spiced pumpkin soup, doorstep slices of fresh-baked bread thickly spread with butter, and apple cobbler and custard. The girls told Netta everything that had happened to them and Any.

'So,' concluded Storm in a rush, 'we've got to find this place called Pie Man's Squeak before Dr DeWilde eats Any up.'

Netta smiled and fixed them with her serious silver-grey eyes. 'The place you are looking for is called *Piper's Peak*, and it is indeed imperative that you get there very soon if you want to see Any again. You have no need to fear that she is going to be eaten: that is not Dr DeWilde's way. But a terrible fate awaits those who are taken to Piper's

Peak.' Her grey eyes were serious. 'They are doomed to become slaves in the Piper's kingdom.'

Storm and Aurora gasped in horror.

Netta continued quickly, 'But you've made an excellent start by getting through the village unscathed. It's enchanted, you know. Stay there for the night or allow any of the food to pass your lips and you would be doomed to stay there for ever.'

Aurora shivered. 'Why do you live in such an awful place?'

'I've always lived here,' said Netta, 'and somebody has to give passing travellers a helping hand.' Then she added lightly, 'Besides, I've been waiting for someone. I've been waiting a very long time. But I think that maybe my wait is over.'

'What happened in the village?' asked Storm.

Netta shivered. The little tabby cat jumped on her lap and purred. 'Well, I know you will be familiar with the ancient story of Piper's Town and how the Pied Piper, enraged that the town refused to pay him for ridding them of a plague of rats, led all the children of the town away. He bewitched them with the tune he played on his pipe, and they danced after him across the mountains and into the highest peak of all. That's how

Piper's Peak got its name. The children's desperate parents searched all over the mountain for them, but no trace was ever found. There has always been talk of a great gemstone mine hidden in the mountains, where the descendants of the children lured away by the Pied Piper worked as slaves digging for precious stones. But few believed it. They put it down to old wives' tales.

'What fewer people know is that, around the same time as the events in Piper's Town, something similar happened in other smaller, more isolated villages too. But in these places it wasn't just the children who disappeared, but entire populations. That's what happened in the village you passed through. One day it was a thriving community; the next it was entirely deserted: every man, woman and child had disappeared overnight. Even the animals were gone. There wasn't even a cockroach left.'

'But there was somebody left,' said Storm excitedly, and she told Netta about Hope Goodchild and finding the skeleton in the cellar and using the pipe to show the little girl how to finish the song.

'Ah, little Hope and the Goodchilds,' said Netta with a soft smile. 'You did the right thing, Storm.

209

I tried to help her but it wasn't in my power. You have released that poor little girl from centuries of loneliness and allowed her to rest in peace.' She sighed. 'Such a lovely family: always so kind, and they never served anything other than a full measure of brandy at the inn, not like some cheating landlords.'

A puzzled look passed over Storm's face. 'But I thought you said this all happened centuries ago, so how could you possibly have known them . . . ?'

Netta ignored Storm's interjection and continued with her story. 'In more recent years I heard rumours that something was going on again in the mountains. The forests and the mountains beyond the villages have always been wild places: nobody travels there if they can possibly avoid it. Those who venture into the wilderness seldom return. People say they are haunted places, best left to ghosts, wolves and the ice witches. People have short memories; they easily forget what they do not want to remember, and although they kept alive the story of the Pied Piper, they forgot the warning that the Piper had given as he led the children out of the town.'

'What warning?' asked Storm.

'As he stood on the low hill that overlooks the

town, he took the pipe from his mouth for just a few seconds and shouted, "I will return!" and the words echoed around the hill and down every street and byway and alley.

'Centuries passed. Then a couple of winters ago bad things started to happen. In the villages nearer to the mountains there were stories of howling wolves and children who disappeared. Occasionally a ragged, starving traveller would turn up on this side of the mountains, claiming that villages on the other side were entirely deserted – no sign of life, entire populations completely vanished. They talked of somebody called the Exterminator. The travellers' ravings were put down to mountain madness. Maybe people didn't want to believe them; maybe they thought that history wouldn't and couldn't repeat itself. That's why I was in the town that day that I met you, Storm. I had heard that there had been another invasion of rats, as there had been centuries before, and I heard gossip that the Exterminator had been invited. It all seemed too convenient. I wanted to see if what I feared was true.'

'And what did you fear?' asked Storm, wide-eyed.

'That the legend had real truth in it. That if

we didn't learn from history, it could happen again. That the Piper had indeed returned, but in a new form – as Dr DeWilde, the Exterminator – and that this time the people of Piper's Town, led by Alderman Snufflebottom, would be all too eager to dance to his tune. What I saw convinced me that the old legend was true. But I knew that I couldn't do anything alone. I also knew that Dr DeWilde was not yet all-powerful, that he didn't have the thing he needed to make him invincible. So I came back here and waited. I knew something or somebody would turn up sooner or later.' She smiled and added, 'And now you have.'

'Us?' shrieked Aurora. 'What can *we* do?'

'Rescuing your little sister would be a good start,' said Netta firmly.

'All on our own? Why can't you come with us?' asked Storm.

'I have other business that I must attend to. You are not the only ones who need my help. I have every confidence that you two can succeed without me.'

'But what do we have to do?' asked Storm.

'You'll have to find a way to get inside Piper's Peak. They say the mountain is impregnable: nobody has ever been able to find a way in or a way out, so you'll need some help. There is talk of a secret disused mine shaft that leads right into the mountain, but nobody has discovered the entrance – or if they have, they have never returned to tell the tale. But I have made studies and I believe that there is one person who knows its exact location and has the map upon which it is marked and the key you'll need to get inside. Her name is Mother Collops, and you two are going to have to pay her a visit,' said Netta seriously.

'Mother Collops? Who is she?' asked Storm.

'An ogress, if you're inclined to believe that sort of village tittle-tattle,' said Netta lightly.

'An ogress!' whispered Aurora faintly. 'Don't ogres eat children?'

'It's probably just gossip that she's an ogress,' said Netta soothingly. 'She knows more about the legend of the Pied Piper than anyone alive. And about Dr DeWilde and Piper's Peak. Mother Collops' map and key will lead you into the very heart of the mountain.'

'How do we get them off her?' asked Storm.

Netta spoke gravely. 'You'll have to ask her for them. Very politely.' she said.

Storm looked nonplussed and said with a sarcastic edge to her voice: 'You mean you want us to walk up to a well-known ogress and say, "Excuse me Mother Collops, but would you be so kind as to hand over the map and key to Piper's Peak," and she'll give it to us and wave us on our way with her blessing? Somehow I don't think so.'

'It's your only chance of saving Any and the others who have been snatched away. You have to accept all Mother Collops' hospitality and refuse nothing, thank her profusely and then ask for what you want. You mustn't just try to take it,' said Netta patiently. 'If you try to sneak in and steal the key she'll lose her temper, and I can assure you that is not a pretty sight.'

Netta pointed away to the moorland beyond, across which were scattered several massive boulders. 'That happened last time she got in a temper. Something to do with some lad and a beanstalk, according to gossip.'

'It must have been some tantrum,' said Aurora brightly. 'Maybe you've met your match, Storm?' Storm grinned sheepishly.

'No,' continued Netta. 'You need to ask her for the map and key very politely and offer to play her for them. Apparently she loves games, particularly if the stakes are high.'

'What kind of games?' asked Storm.

'Any kind of game. Backgammon, ludo, tiddly-winks. Poker. But her favourite is hide and seek.'

'Sounds like fun,' said Storm chirpily.

'No it doesn't. It sounds perfectly horrid, like a cat toying with a mouse before eating it,' said Aurora.

'Something like that,' replied Netta grimly. 'But I have every faith that you two can outwit her. It really is the only chance you have of saving Any.'

'Then we'll take our chance,' said Storm firmly, and she took Aurora's hand in her own and held it tightly; it fluttered like a trapped butterfly.

'I'm frightened, Storm. I am frightened of Dr DeWilde, of Mother Collops, of the mountains, of everything.'

'Well, I'm sorry, Aurora,' snapped Storm, 'but you're just going to have to get used to being frightened. We're going to save Any, even if it kills us.'

Later, as dusk fell, Storm went out into the garden. The moon had come out early and hung in the sky like a great wobbly tear. A silver-grey hare streaked across the grass towards the pumpkin patch. Storm had thought she was quite alone, but to her surprise she suddenly spied Netta by the

duck pond adjoining the pumpkin patch. She was
casting a small paper boat onto the water. As Netta
let it go she threw a match into the fragile little
boat. It bobbed across the glass surface of the water,
a little blaze of fire that left a trail of sparks behind
it, before it crumpled and sank, leaving no trace.
Netta looked up, her strange silver-grey eyes
serious, and held out her hand. Storm walked along
the water's edge and Netta put an arm round her
as the two crouched on the damp grass.

'What are you doing?' asked Storm.

'Casting away my demons, before they grow
fat with gnawing at me. Do you want a go?'

'Do I have demons?'

'Everyone has demons. Only some people don't admit it.' Netta looked at Storm. 'Maybe I am speaking out of turn, but I think you're angry, Storm Eden. Angry with your mother for leaving you, with your father for being useless, with Aurora for not being brave and with me for not having all the answers. Above all, I think that you are angry with yourself. You are punishing yourself because you think you are to blame for Any being taken.'

Storm began to cry quietly, and Netta hugged her and, just for a second, Storm thought she caught a faint whiff of a smell that was something like her own dead mother's distinctive scent.

'Why can't you come with us to visit Mother Collops?' asked Storm wistfully.

Netta clasped Storm's hand tightly. 'Believe me, Storm, I would if I could. But these are dangerous times. I have other pressing work to do. There is a boy who needs my help. He has nobody else; at least you and Aurora have each other. But I will be closer than you think.

'Come,' she said, after Storm's tears had subsided. 'Let's go in. You'll need to make an early start for Hell Lane. It's a long climb to Hell Heights, where Mother Collops lives.'

14
A Stroll up
Hell Lane

Hell Lane did not immediately live up to its name. Netta drove the children to the start of the lane in a trap pulled by Pepper. The pony was delighted to see Storm and pranced along shaking his head to remind her what a handsome, clever fellow he was.

Unless you knew that Hell Lane was there it would have been impossible to detect, as its entrance lurked behind a tangle of briars and overhanging trees. When the main road took an unexpected twist, Netta stopped the trap in the middle of the road, stepped down and started to walk straight into a dense blackberry thicket.

Storm and Aurora looked at each other and then followed her into the bushes.

About five metres in, almost hidden by the brambles, they saw an old wooden signpost pointing forward, upon which was carved the legend HELL LANE.

Storm felt a quiver of anticipation pass through her body like a tiny electric shock: their journey to rescue Any was really underway.

Netta disappeared further into the thicket and Aurora followed, but Storm hung back. She ran her hands over the carved signpost, feeling the rough indentation of the writing beneath her fingers, and as she did so she whispered, 'I *will* find you, Any. I will save you and the others. I promise.'

At that moment, her fingers located another line of much smaller carved writing. Storm brushed away the dried-on mud and peered at the letters. In the gloom she could just make out the words: GO FORWARD AND BE EATEN; GO BACK AND REGRET IT FOR THE REST OF YOUR LIFE.

Storm raised an eyebrow, murmured 'some choice' to herself, hoisted her knapsack onto her shoulders and set off after the others, deciding it was best not to mention the warning to Aurora.

She found Netta and her sister sitting on a small bank by the side of a wide, picture-postcard lane edged with wild flowers. As she pushed clear of the brambles she thought she saw a glint of light as Aurora quickly pocketed something. Looking flustered, her sister said, 'Netta has to leave us here.' She nodded towards the path. 'But it doesn't look too bad, does it?'

Storm said nothing, but she caught Netta's eye, and in that second a look passed between them that said they both understood that, however dangerous the past had been, the future that lay ahead was more perilous still.

'No, not bad at all,' said Storm, forcing herself to sound cheerful. 'Let's get going.'

She hugged Netta fiercely and felt her throat constrict. Netta returned the hug and whispered, 'I wouldn't send you off on your own if I could come myself. And I wouldn't do it if I didn't have complete faith in you. Take care, Storm. And think before you leap.' Then she embraced Aurora tightly. 'I wish I could do more for you, but I can't. You must do it for yourselves. Good luck, my dears, you will need it.' And she threaded her way back into the thicket.

The girls set off up the path. After a few minutes, Storm glanced back and saw a watchful silver-grey hare sitting in the very spot where Netta had disappeared.

At first the path was strenuous but not difficult and Storm set a cracking pace. But after just a mile or so the terrain became more treacherous. The tiny beck that had run down the side of the lane soon widened into a stream that spilled across the track, making the going slippery. Storm and Aurora slid all over the place on glistening chocolate mud and the stream quickly became an icy torrent. Both girls fell over frequently and they were soon wet through and splattered with dirt. The banks on either side of the path gave way to high rocky walls that rose sharply upwards. This narrow gorge was gloomy and dank, with strange twisted ferns and toadstools nestling in the dark, secret places that had never seen full sunlight.

They were not the first to come this way. On the rocky walls of the gorge many had left evidence that they had passed by carving their initials and names into the rock and adding a date.

J & R were Here

CELiA 4 OLiVER

Squirrel loves Bear

Winnie and Willie

Some of this graffiti was centuries old. Storm felt cheered to think of so many walking this way before her, and the fact that Hell Lane had clearly not always been such a creepy place, for many of the entwined names were those of lovers.

223

Waiting for Aurora to catch her up, she gazed around at the carved names and one inscription caught her eye.

Storm's heart skipped a beat and, when Aurora eventually arrived panting by her side, she silently pointed at the engraving, hardly able to speak, such was the mix of emotions in her heart.

When Storm finally tore her eyes away from the inscription and looked at Aurora, she saw tears glistening in her sister's eyes.

'Do you really think . . . ?' Storm's unfinished question hung in the air.

'I do,' said Aurora, sniffing. 'It must be.'

The sisters might have lingered longer beside their mother and father's names but for the unmistakable sound of a wolf howling somewhere far, far away.

Struggling ever upwards and ever wetter, grabbing each other for support as their legs slid from beneath them, Storm and Aurora were surprised when, after a violent twist, the path opened out flat at a crossroads where another ancient wooden signpost offered four choices.

Aurora looked longingly back in the direction they had come from, but Storm barely paused, merely glancing at the signpost before grabbing her sister by the arm and striding purposefully onwards.

'Storm! Wait! It says danger,' said Aurora, pulling back.

'I know – I can read,' Storm said impatiently, shaking her arm free and marching on.

'Well, shouldn't we heed what it says?' her sister called, hesitant.

'Not if we want to find Any alive. You really shouldn't believe everything you read, Aurora. It's a terrible habit. It will get you into big trouble one day.'

Aurora smiled wanly and hurried to catch up. 'It's just that I feel so scared not knowing what is going to happen, what dangers we are up against. If I only knew exactly what it was I had to be anxious about, I know I wouldn't be so anxious,' she confessed in a small voice.

Storm took her hand. 'I do understand, Aurora. I feel the same. It's like when you set me one of your horrible tests and the worst moment is just that second before you allow me to turn the paper over and see what the questions are. Once I know what I'm up against, it's never as bad as I'd pictured it in my head. It's the waiting and the not knowing that is so terrible. But whatever dangers are in store will come soon enough and then we'll wish that—'

Storm never finished the sentence, for at that moment there was snarl. She just had time to hear Aurora's scream of horror and catch a glimpse of flashing amber eyes and rows of razor teeth before she was pinned to the ground, her mouth pressed against matted fur and her nostrils filled with the earthy, ripe smell of wet wolf. She felt a shudder of hurt coil throughout her body as her head hit the ground and a hot white pain in her shoulder radiated across her chest as needle teeth sank into soft flesh.

I am going to die, she thought, with surprising clarity and even more unexpected calmness. The pipe around her neck burned red-hot. The wolf raised its head and opened its jaws for the kill. As it did so, two loud cracks cut the air. The wolf yelped in fear, leaped to its feet and bounded away.

Storm lay dazed on the ground. A stain of crimson was spreading slowly from her upper arm across her shoulder, but she didn't care. She felt as still and peaceful as a reclining stone effigy in a country church. Apart from the tightening pain across her chest, everything was pleasantly fuzzy. The face of her dead mother floated in front of her. She saw little Any's sad, beseeching eyes. She felt the pipe warm against her cold skin. Then she heard someone yelling in her ear.

'Storm! Storm! Breathe! You've got to breathe.' Shock had made Storm hold her breath. She opened her mouth and sucked greedily at the air like a newborn baby. Her lungs expanded painfully, her mother's smiling face drifted away, her head cleared and she struggled to sit up. Aurora was kneeling beside her, quivering like a baby deer and transfixed by the tiny, smoking mother-of-pearl pistol that she still held in her quaking hand.

Shakily, Storm sat up and took the pistol from her sister's trembling fingers. Aurora stared at her empty hand as if in shock and whispered, 'I actually pulled the trigger. I shot a wolf.'

'Strictly speaking, you missed,' grinned Storm, 'but it did the job. I'm impressed, Aurora, although given how much your hands are shaking it's lucky you didn't hit me.' Aurora turned a whiter shade of pale. 'Are you all right, Aurora? You look as if you're going to faint.'

'It's the shock,' said Aurora, feeling inside her knapsack and pulling out a small thermos. 'We both need some of this.' And she poured two cups of strong, sweet tea.

Storm looked at her sister in amazement.

'You brought tea with you?'

'What's wrong with that?' said Aurora defensively. 'It's come in useful, hasn't it?'

Storm raised an eyebrow. 'I suppose so, but we're not exactly going on a picnic, are we? You'll be telling me next that you brought salmon and cucumber sandwiches.'

Aurora blushed. 'Egg mayonnaise and cress, actually.'

'Oh well, if you've gone to the bother of making them, I suppose I'd better eat one,' said Storm, still grinning. They sat for a few minutes in silence munching sandwiches, then Storm said lightly, 'Where did you get that pistol?'

There was a tiny chafing silence, then Aurora replied, 'Netta gave it to me.'

Storm looked a bit cross. 'Why you and not me?'

Aurora squirmed. 'I don't know.'

'You do,' said Storm hotly, egg spilling down her chin.

'Well, if you must know, she said she thought it would be safer with me. She was worried that you'd be too reckless with it.'

'Me? Reckless?' spluttered Storm indignantly. Then she added grudgingly, 'I suppose she might have a point, given past history. Only a very small point, mind you. Anyway, it was rather lucky you had it, otherwise I'd be dead by now.' She handed the pistol back to Aurora and said in a gruff voice, 'Thanks.'

Aurora tied a neat bandage around the gash in her sister's shoulder and they sat companionably for a few more minutes before heading on up the track, keeping a wary eye on the rocks above in case they were attacked again. Shock and the wound to her shoulder had taken their toll on Storm and she suddenly felt exhausted. So for once it was Aurora who led the way, helping her sister when the going got rougher.

Late in the afternoon, when the girls were about ready to drop, they came to a flat rocky outcrop by a waterfall and stopped to drink the cool clear water with relish. The temperature had dropped, and it had begun to snow again, great white flakes falling from a sullen sky. Storm glared up into the gloom. She was sure the weather had never been so volatile in the past.

She looked about for shelter and caught sight of a large crack in the rocks, half hidden by tall ferns. She picked her way to the opening and peered into a short tunnel. As her eyes grew accustomed to the gloom, she could see that the tunnel opened out into a bigger chamber.

Ignoring Aurora's protests, Storm clambered in. It was warm and dry, with a smooth rocky floor and, at the far end, a small slit that let in the fading light from above. She called out to her sister. 'Come on. It's a cave. And it's warm and dry. We can rest for a couple of hours and go on when the moon comes out.'

Aurora scrambled after Storm, watched from the bushes by a pair of small silver-grey eyes.

Storm smiled at her sister. 'It's not exactly a palace, but it's warm and out of danger.'

'Danger!' said a voice very clearly.

Aurora clutched at Storm, who spun wildly round trying to locate the voice. It sounded strangely familiar but she couldn't quite place it. She yelled back, 'We're armed. Beware!'

'Beware!' said the voice, and something detonated in Storm's brain as she realized that the voice reminded her of her dead mother's.

'I am going to die of fear,' moaned Aurora, who was holding onto Storm's good arm so tightly that it hurt almost as much as her injured one.

'Die of fear!' came the voice.

'We must go back,' wailed Aurora, retreating towards the cave entrance.

'Go back!' said the voice.

'It's a terrible warning,' whimpered Aurora. She fumbled for the mother-of-pearl pistol.

'A terrible warning!' retorted the voice.

'Run for your life,' cried Aurora, and took a few steps forwards before her knees buckled beneath her. She sprawled to the ground and the pistol fell from her shaking fingers.

'Run for your life!' the voice urged.

'No thanks,' Storm shouted back, a sudden sparkle stealing into her green eyes. 'I think I'll just stay here. But you'd better shut up.'

'Shut up! Shut up! Shut up!' replied the voice.

Aurora raised her head from the ground and pleaded with Storm, 'Please be quiet! You're scaring me to death!'

'Death! Death! Death!' replied the voice.

Storm grinned. 'It's nothing to be afraid of, Aurora, it's just a silly old echo.'

'Echo! Echo! Echo!'

Aurora looked at Storm in amazement tinged with admiration. 'How stupid of me. Of course. An echo. There's no reason to be afraid.'

'Be afraid!' replied the echo.

'Be quiet, echo. I am staying whether you like it or not, and I am not going to talk to you. You are a dead thing,' said Storm firmly.

'You are a dead thing!' came the echo.

A flicker of uncertainty passed across Storm's face. 'Echo, be gone!' she cried.

'Be gone!' returned the echo.

'Generally,' said Storm, 'I refuse to act on un-solicited advice. But there is something very creepy here. I think we had better go.'

'Go! Go! Go!' wailed the echo. The sisters didn't wait to hear any more. They ran for the tunnel and scrambled through it as fast as they could.

They set off through the snow without pausing or speaking, following the path ever upwards. It was only later that Aurora realized that she had left the pistol on the floor of the cave.

15
JeLLy BaBies
of DooM

It was close to midnight when Storm and Aurora caught their first glimpse of Hell Heights. The path lurched to the right and, as they turned the corner, the snow abruptly ceased. Rising up in front of them was a castle, stern and unwelcoming. Bats flew around the tallest tower, which stretched upwards, like a forbidding finger reproaching the sky. The place looked deserted.

The sisters climbed the icy stone stairs and stood in front of an oak door. The huge iron doorknocker, in the shape of a grinning, open-mouthed ogre – the legs of his victim still protruding between his teeth – was covered with frozen cobwebs. Weather-beaten signs proclaimed:

NO HAWKERS

NO PEDDLARS

especially with SHiNy ReD apples

RUN NOW if you KNOW what's GooD for you

RiNG the BeLL entireLy At Your OWN RiSK

You CAN'T SAY You HAVEN'T BEEN WARNED

'Well,' said Storm, 'at least Mother Collops has a sense of humour.'

'It's no joke being eaten,' said Aurora exhaustedly. 'And that's what's going to happen to us if we ring that bell.'

'So what do you propose?' said Storm furiously. 'You know we need Mother Collops to help us find Any. Netta says she's our only hope, and if that means risking being eaten, it's a risk worth taking.'

'Oh, let's just get on with being eaten, then,' Aurora sighed. 'I'm so tired it can't come quickly enough.' And she pulled hard on the bell.

It took a long time for the ugly jangling to die away. But nothing stirred.

Storm pressed her hand against the door. It creaked open to reveal a vast hall, smothered in cobwebs. The girls walked slowly in, gazing at the dusty chandelier, the threadbare Afghan rug and a woodworm-riddled rosewood table. A tiny 'tut, tut' involuntarily escaped Aurora's lips as she ran her finger over the dusty windowsill. She looked up guiltily and caught her sister's eye. Storm grinned.

'Hello?' called Storm hesitantly. There was no answer. 'Hello, is there anybody there?' Silence. At the far end of the huge hallway was a gallery, from which two wide sweeping staircases descended on either side in a horseshoe formation. Below the gallery stood a huge saggy red velvet chaise longue.

There was no sign of a living soul but somehow Storm still felt that they were being watched. Pushing open a door set in the wall beneath the gallery, the children found themselves in another chamber. Although still extremely dusty by Aurora's exacting standards, this room was warmly lit and a log fire blazed in the grate. In front of the fire was a small table laid for two. In the middle of the table were three covered silver platters. Storm lifted one of the lids and underneath was a salver of broccoli and succulent carrots like tiny fingers. The second revealed two aromatic potato-topped pies. The third dish was of ripe fruit: bunches of grapes tumbling over blushing peaches and wild strawberries.

Storm's eye was attracted by a large mirror on one wall. Written in the dust on its surface were the words:

Welcome. Help yourselves. Have seconds if you like. Thirds if you can manage them. This is a house of plenty.

'Well,' said Storm, pulling back one of the mahogany chairs, 'let's tuck in.'

'Maybe it's another trick or enchantment,' Aurora said, frowning.

'Come on, remember what Netta told us. We must accept Mother Collops' hospitality and refuse nothing. Anyway, it's scrumptious,' Storm said through a mouthful of pie.

Aurora looked suspiciously at the carrots. 'They might be poisoned.'

'Who's being over-imaginative now?' said Storm, although it sounded more like 'Whoa ben ova imgeentiv nia?' as her mouth was full of potato.

'Don't talk with your mouth full. It's rude,' said Aurora sternly.

'It's rude not to accept hospitality when it's offered. We mustn't do anything to anger Mother Collops,' retorted Storm. But Aurora was too nervous to eat and she suddenly cocked her head anxiously.

'What's that noise?'

'What noise?'

'A tapping sound.'

'I didn't hear anything,' said Storm, helping herself to more broccoli. As she did so she looked at the mirror. A new message was superimposed in the dust:

Your beds await you.

Aurora looked at her sister in horror. 'We're not spending the night here. We'll be slaughtered in our beds and turned into sausages! We need to find Mother Collops, persuade her to give us the key and the map and get out quick.'

'And how exactly do you propose to do that?' said Storm angrily.

Aurora's eyes filled with tears. 'I know I'm being cowardly. I'm not brave like you. I'm just me. And at the moment I feel like a very small, very frightened version of me.'

Storm took Aurora's hand and squeezed it. 'You can leave and go back to Netta's, if you like. I know this is hard for you, and I know how brave you're being. I wouldn't think less of you, Aurora, if you decided to go.'

'Leave?' said Aurora, staring wildly at Storm. 'Leave, and let you face Mother Collops alone? What kind of a sister do you think I am? I will never, *ever* abandon you. Whatever the circumstances. I'd die first!'

'Well, I am pleased that's settled.' Her sister smiled, and then turned on her heel and marched up the narrow staircase. It led to a bedroom, a vast gloomy room with an ornate double bed and ragged purple hangings, tartan wallpaper and a painted ceiling depicting a giant coiled sea-serpent devouring seven whales in a blood-red sea. Two crisp white nightdresses were laid out on the feather eiderdown.

Later, lying in bed, their frozen feet thawing on four huge hot-water bottles, Storm said quietly, 'I'd never, ever abandon you either, Aurora. Whatever the circumstances. I'd die first too.' In the dark Aurora smiled, and then fell into an uneasy sleep.

In the morning they found a delicious breakfast of sausages, crispy bacon, scrambled eggs, soft white rolls, curls of butter and marmalade laid out for them. Even Aurora tucked in, although her appetite was still dampened by anxiety. After eating, Storm explored the house further, her sister trailing nervously in her wake, jumping at every unexpected noise.

'Listen,' she said, suddenly stopping. There was

a quiet tapping noise. 'There's that noise again. What is it?'

Storm shrugged. 'Ignore it.' She felt increasingly wound up and frustrated by the waiting. It was now three nights since the terrible events at the Ginger House and she felt that Any was slipping away from her. She knew that unless they caught up soon, Any could be lost to them for ever. With increasing desperation she led them through the maze of cobwebby rooms full of wardrobes stuffed with mouldering ball gowns. Eventually they found themselves back at the top of the staircase that led down to the entrance hall. Looking down, Storm's heart skipped a beat. There on the circular rosewood table was an ornate key lying across a large map. Beyond, the front door stood open, beckoning freedom. Storm felt light-headed. All the waiting had raised the tension in her stomach to the point where she was like an over-stretched elastic band ready to snap. In her excitement she forgot Netta's warning. The key and map were within her grasp, and she was intoxicated by the sight. She didn't hear Aurora's desperate cry of 'Stop! It's a trick!' She bounded down the stairs.

Aurora yelled frantically, 'Don't touch the key, Storm. It is there to test us. Don't touch it!'

But all Storm saw was the means to save her
baby sister. She grabbed the map and key
triumphantly and ran for the open door. Beyond,
Storm could see the snow-covered lawn stretching
away to Hell Lane. Her heart pounding, she raced
towards it, unheeding of everything except this
tantalizing vision of freedom. She was a metre from
the open door when it slammed shut, the sound
reverberating with a dreadful finality around the
hall. Still she didn't halt. She reached the door and
tugged furiously at the handle. It didn't move. She
turned to the windows. None budged. Distraught,
Storm ran back to the closed door and threw her
body against it like a caged animal.

'Open! Open up, you stupid, stupid thing!' she
raged.

After a few seconds of fruitless pounding she
fell to the ground, sobbing uncontrollably. Aurora
came slowly down the staircase and bent over her
sister. Storm shook her off in a fury, and as she
did so the sisters heard the tapping noise again. It
was much nearer this time.

The girls turned their heads fearfully to look
up to the top of the stairs. The tap, tap, tap grew
louder, and then something strange moved into
sight: a huge decrepit old woman, dressed in a

tattered, layered white dress so that she looked like a walking wedding cake that had been left out in the rain. The woman stared down at them through filmy eyes. The tapping that they had heard was the sound of the stick she used to find her way around the labyrinthine house.

The old lady's face was cracked with anger.

'How dare you!' she said, pointing her stick at the girls. 'How dare you come into my house and abuse my hospitality! I offered you everything that I had, but you are just like the rest. You try to take advantage of me and steal my mementoes from me. My most precious things. Is this the way to repay my kindness?' She glared at them. 'You will be punished!' She felt in her pocket, pulled out a jelly baby and bit off the head as if to underline her threat.

Storm was so despairing that she couldn't speak. Aurora took control of the situation. She squared her shoulders and headed up the stairs towards Mother Collops. Peering into the old lady's rheumy eyes, she politely proffered her hand and said, 'Hello. So pleased to meet you. My name is Aurora, and this is my sister Storm.'

The old hag's face crinkled with suspicion, then split into a gummy smile. 'I think I'll find it more convenient to call you Lunch and Dinner,' she said, popping another jelly baby into her mouth.

Storm followed her sister up the stairs and, smiling her best smile at the ogress, asked, 'Do you live here all alone?'

'Yes,' said Mother Collops mournfully. 'Quite alone.'

'It must be very lonely for you,' said Aurora sympathetically.

'It is, something bitter. My family all abandoned me long ago. I never get any post, except bills,' said the ogress, sadness further clouding her milky eyes.

'I wouldn't like that at all,' said Aurora in commiserating tones. Storm glanced down at the vast and saggy chaise longue positioned underneath the balcony, then stole a quick glance at Aurora, who shook her head imperceptibly and frowned.

Storm took no notice: she leaped forward and shoved Mother Collops hard. The old lady tipped forward and plunged over the top of the balustrade. She landed in the middle of the chaise longue and bounced up and down as if on a trampoline. Storm grabbed Aurora and pulled her towards the stairs.

'There must be a back way out of here,' she hissed. 'We must get out before she recovers herself.'

'What if she's really hurt?' whispered Aurora.

Storm pointed to Mother Collops, who was still bouncing helplessly on the chaise longue, legs akimbo and clothes flapping around, a sound suspiciously like a giggle rising from her lips.

'Look, she's perfectly fine,' said Storm impatiently. Mother Collops immediately stopped bouncing and lay very still.

'I'm going to check,' said Aurora. 'She seems like a sad lost old lady to me, not a blood-drinking ogress.'

'Oh come on, Aurora. She's trying to trick you. Save your sympathy for somebody who deserves it. Like your defenceless baby sister,' said Storm angrily.

'No, you've gone too far this time. I'll just make sure she's not hurt,' said Aurora.

Storm's face twisted with disbelief. 'Really, Aurora, can't you see it's a trick?'

'I'll catch you up,' said Aurora firmly.

'Don't bother. I never want to see you again as long as I live,' screamed Storm, and she raced down the stairs and through the door beneath the gallery.

Aurora headed slowly down towards the chaise longue where Mother Collops had fallen. The old lady lay quite still, with her head bent at an awkward angle and her eyes closed. Aurora reached out to feel her pulse, and at the moment the ogress sat up suddenly, grabbed her by the wrist, and burst into peals of laughter. Aurora screamed.

'Only pretending, ducks! Oh, it's such fun. Look at your face. I keep the chaise longue there for just such eventualities. It's not the first time I've been tipped over the balustrade by naughty children. Is your sister always so impulsive?'

'Yes,' said Aurora in a shaky voice.

'Oh, I like a girl with attitude. Your sister is a girl after my own heart.'

'Then why do you want to eat her?' demanded Aurora.

'It's what ogres do, my chick,' said Mother Collops sadly. 'It's expected of us.'

'Well, I am glad she's got away,' said Aurora indignantly.

'Oh, she won't have got far,' said Mother Collops confidently.

She was right.

Holding Aurora in a surprisingly strong grip, Mother Collops set off through the rambling castle, arriving at last in a vast stone-flagged kitchen with a huge range in one corner and a door in the other. Suspended above the door in a net was a squirming, snarling, snapping creature. It was Storm.

Mother Collops was delighted. 'One of my booby-traps. The castle is covered with them. It gives me something to do on the long, dark winter evenings. Playing tiddlywinks against yourself gets very dull,' she added miserably.

Up in the net Storm twisted this way and that like an exceptionally angry wild tiger.

'I'll let you down,' said Mother Collops, 'if you hand me the key and the map.' She slowly lowered the net.

Released, Storm sullenly handed them over.

'Now, my little chickadees,' said Mother Collops settling into a chair and helping herself to another jelly baby, 'why do you want the map and key so badly?'

Storm was beyond speech, so Aurora explained about Dr DeWilde, the orphanage and Any's disappearance, only leaving out the bit about the pipe. When she had finished, Aurora said imploringly, 'So will you help us? Please, Mother Collops, please.'

The ogress sat quietly for a while, as if fighting her own emotions, and then she said, 'I don't like being taken advantage of; give an inch and people take a mile. I'll tell you what: we'll play a game. Hide and seek. You'll hide, and I'll seek. If I don't find you in sixty minutes I'll give you the map and key and let you go. But, if I do discover you, then –' once again it looked as if Mother Collops was undergoing a terrible internal struggle – 'then, I'll have you both for my dinner.'

Aurora's face betrayed her fear for just a second, but then she collected herself. 'It's a deal,' she agreed, offering to shake the ogress's hand. 'No double-crossing, mind you.'

'Wouldn't dream of it, ducks,' said Mother Collops, cutting through the net that enclosed Storm. 'I'll count to a hundred. If I haven't found you when the clock has finished chiming midday, you'll be the winners. If I have, I win.' She began counting.

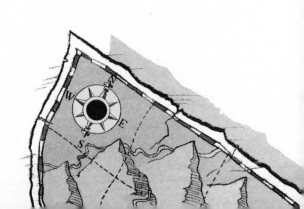

Aurora held out her hand to her sister but Storm brushed her away with a glare. She opened her mouth to say something barbed just as Mother Collops said 'Ten' in a very loud voice. The girls fled, racing along the corridor up the curved staircase and through more rooms.

'Where are we going to hide, Storm?' asked Aurora breathlessly.

'In the tall tower,' her sister replied. 'You can only access it via the stairs on the other side of the castle. It will take her ages to get there.' From far away they heard the ogre's excited yell, 'I'm coming to get you, ready or not!' The girls sped through the castle and up the narrow spiral staircase that led to the tower room. Once inside they clambered into one of the wardrobes, pulled the door closed and slumped on the floor behind the ball gowns and feather boas. It smelled of moth balls, and the feather boas tickled Storm's nose, making her sneeze. 'Sssh!' warned Aurora. Storm held her nose and shuffled closer to her sister.

After what seemed like hours they heard the sound of Mother Collops' stick on the stone floor. The tap, tap, tap came closer and the door to the room creaked open.

'Come out, my little chicks. I know you're there,' said the ogress.

The sisters held their breath.

'Where are you, duckies? Are you under the –' there was a pause as Mother Collops tapped her way across the room – 'bed?' There was the sound of her cane scraping under the bed.

'No little chicks under the bed,' the ogress sighed disappointedly. 'But I know my little ducks are in here somewhere. I can smell them.' The tap, tap, tap came closer still. The sisters could hear Mother Collops' raspy, excited breath. 'Now I've got you, my little ones!'

The door of the wardrobe was pulled open and Mother Collops peered sightlessly into the dark interior. Her stick jabbed wildly through the clothes. 'I know you're in here, my little chick-adees,' she called. Again her stick poked through the clothes, coming dangerously close to stabbing Storm in the eye. It plunged about viciously again and again, but only encountered thin air and fur coats.

The ogress sighed dejectedly. 'No chicks for Mother Collops here,' she said, pushing the wardrobe shut.

The old crone turned to leave and the girls

heard the castle clock begin to chime midday. *Bong.*
Mother Collops reached the door. *Bong.* The girls
held their breaths. *Bong.*

The ogress's stick had dislodged one of the
feather boas and it had fallen across Storm's face,
making her nose itch. A sneeze began to build.
Bong. Mother Collops pulled the door of the tower
room closed as Storm, unable to stop herself, let
out an explosive sneeze. *Bong.* The tapping of
Mother Collops' stick ceased. The ogress turned
back. *Bong.* Tap, tap came her stick across the floor.
Bong. The door swung open again. *Bong.* Storm
and Aurora could hear Mother Collops wheezing
over the sound of their own blood thumping in
their heads. *Bong.*

'Come on, my pretties. I have you now!'

Mother Collops raised her cane and rifled
through the wardrobe with it again. *Bong.* The hard
tip connected with soft flesh, prodding Storm and
Aurora in the ribs and causing them to cry out.
Bong.

'Found you! I win. I win!' cried Mother Collops
triumphantly. The clock chimed the last stroke of
the hour with a dreadful finality: *BONG!*

Storm and Aurora scrambled dejectedly out of
the wardrobe, close to tears. Quick as a flash,

Mother Collops yoked them together, pulled them down to the kitchen, tied their hands and suspended each from a hook on the wall.

Storm immediately began covertly playing with the knots as Mother Collops tapped her way over to a huge pot bubbling in the centre of the range.

'The perfect temperature, duckies,' she announced.

Storm struggled to free her hands. If she could just get loose, there was a meat clever on the edge of the table within easy reach. The last knot came free just as Mother Collops turned back towards her, smiling brightly as if she was offering Storm a wonderful treat.

'You first, little chick,' she grinned.

Storm dropped from the hook and lunged for the cleaver. But as her fingers brushed the handle, she felt something dig into her collar at the back of her neck. Her feet left the ground and she was swung dizzyingly through the air and left suspended high above the cooking pot.

Mother Collops burst into excited laughter. 'It works! Another one of my little booby-traps. Look! Now I only have to pull this lever and you'll drop straight into the pot.'

Storm hung limp in defeat. She could see

Aurora struggling, but she knew that even if her sister succeeded in freeing herself, it would be too late. Storm closed her eyes and thought of Any. The pipe around her neck began to burn so hot it singed her skin. Suddenly she hated the little instrument. Almost nothing had gone right since her mother had given her the pipe. Raising a hand, she ripped it from her neck, breaking the chain, and flung it across the kitchen. It bounced on the floor and landed at Mother Collops' feet. The old lady bent to the floor and groped for it. She ran her fingers over the surface and a look of amazement passed across her face. She pulled out a huge magnifying glass and peered at the pipe. The look on her face turned to joy and she sank into her rocking chair with tears falling.

Suspended above the pot, Storm was becoming uncomfortably warm as steam rose from the bubbling liquid below. The ogress looked up from the pipe and seemed horrified. 'Oh, my chickadee, I better get you down,' she said anxiously. 'I never intended to hurt you. I only wanted to give you a bad fright.' She quickly swung Storm away from the pot and helped her down.

Bewildered, Storm quickly cut the ties on her

sister's wrists, then both girls looked curiously at the weeping ogress.

Mother Collops suddenly clasped Storm's hands and whispered, 'Zella's girl. I should have known.' Then with a solemn look, she returned the pipe to Storm.

'You knew our mother?' Storm asked, astonished. Mother Collops nodded.

'She died,' said Aurora quietly.

'You poor mites,' sighed Mother Collops. 'You've got quite enough to deal with, without thinking I was going to make you into child roly-poly.'

'Exactly how many children have you cooked and eaten?' asked Aurora fearfully.

Mother Collops looked flustered. 'None. To tell the truth, I've never eaten a single child. Not even a small one.'

'Then you're not really an ogress?' asked Storm.

'Certainly not. I am a life-long vegetarian,' replied Mother Collops testily.

'So you were only pretending that you were going to cook us and eat us?'

'Yes, ducks,' said Mother Collops sheepishly. 'I know it's wrong, but it's lonely and isolated out here and if I didn't make people fear me, they would come in the night and throw stones. Or worse. I had to find a way to protect myself. People are afraid of what they don't understand – of anything different. And I've always been different, even when I was a girl,' she sighed. 'It's partly my fault: I have a truly terrible temper.'

'So do I,' confessed Storm sympathetically.

'It runs in the family,' nodded Mother Collops sorrowfully.

'What do you mean? Runs in the family?' whispered Storm.

'Because you are my great-granddaughters, of course. Both of you. Rapunzel – Zella as she preferred to be called – was my granddaughter.'

'Zella was your granddaughter?' asked Storm, unable to believe her ears.

'Yes,' sniffed Mother Collops. 'Her mother, my daughter, came to a sad end, running off like that. That's the trouble with children, they always abandon you,' she said weepily. 'You give them everything and then they grow up and leave you with only your memories of the past and your fears for the future. You never realize you are living happiness until it's squandered and you are quite alone. Now I rattle around this old house with only loneliness and fear for companions. It makes me suspicious and nasty.'

'I don't think you're nasty,' said Aurora kindly. 'But you must stop pretending that you eat children. It doesn't give a good impression.'

Mother Collops nodded tearfully and offered her bag of jelly babies to Aurora and Storm. She leaned forward confidentially. 'Make sure you eat the legs first, my dears, so that they can't run away.'

Storm smiled and took one. 'How did you know we wanted the map and the key?'

'Some people read palms, some read tea leaves, some people read between the lines. I read hearts,' smiled Mother Collops. 'Tell me all about your journey here.'

So they told her everything, and when they reached the part about the echo cavern Mother Collops was shocked. 'It was lucky you didn't stay. It's the home of a honey dragon and it's got a dreadful temper. Much worse than yours and mine, Storm.'

'But I thought honey dragons had the sunniest disposition of all the members of the lizard family,' said Aurora.

'Oh, that's the two-headed version,' said Mother Collops. 'This one is so angry about having only one head that it eats small girls and any passing royalty for breakfast. It's had two princesses and a minor duchess in the last year alone.'

Then Mother Collops opened up the map and showed the sisters where to find the secret entrance to Piper's Peak. She entrusted Storm with the gold key, but her face was grave as she had told them of the journey ahead. 'You have to go over the mountains, which are treacherous. Then you are in DeWilde country. Trust nobody. Keep watch for spies. They will be on the lookout for you, particularly if the doctor knows that you have the pipe, Storm. It makes your journey doubly perilous.'

'Why is he so desperate to have the pipe anyway? What use is it to him?' asked Aurora.

'All the use in the world, chick. He had it once, and he gave it away before he truly under-stood its power,' said Mother Collops. 'It may not look it, Storm, but that little instrument is very powerful indeed.' Storm's hand went unconsciously to where the pipe hung around her neck. It glowed.

'You both know the story of the Pied Piper, of course?' Mother Collops asked. 'How, long ago, he rid the town of a plague of rats by bewitching them with the music from his pipe. The rats hurled themselves into the river and were drowned. But the elders of the town refused to pay him the agreed fee. So he took his revenge. He played his pipe again and all the children of the town followed him into the mountains. One of those children was your great-great-great-great-great-great-grandfather. Only he couldn't hear the piper's air because he was deaf and therefore immune to its tune. He ran after the others because one of the little girls who followed the piper was his sweetheart. But he had a terrible limp, and he couldn't keep up. When the children reached Piper's Peak, he was far behind. He was just in time to see the last child disappear into the mountain before the rock swung closed and the mountain was sealed. By the entrance he found the piper's pipe. It has been passed down in the family ever since.'

Storm fingered the flute. 'So how did Dr DeWilde get it?'

Mother Collops looked guilty. 'I gave it to him,' she admitted. 'It was a terrible misjudgement. But he was just a boy, an unhappy slip of a thing, and I didn't know his true nature. I loved him for his vulnerability and I thought it might help him. But I think that like everything with him, it was only a ruse to manipulate me. He likes to find a person's weakness and exploit it.'

'So what does the pipe *do*?' Storm demanded.

'It beguiles people. Makes them dance to its tune.'

Storm blew, and a haunting air floated across the room. 'Are you beguiled, Aurora?'

'No, not in the least bewitched.'

'Oh, it doesn't work on family,' said Mother Collops. 'We're all descended from the little deaf boy who first found the pipe. Like him, we're all immune to the negative effects of its witchery. Some others are unaffected too, I don't know why. Maybe you have to want to be seduced by it for it to totally work. But, one thing's for sure – it is absolutely *not* a plaything.'

'But if it doesn't have any effect on anyone in the family, how do we know it really is magic?' Aurora protested. 'How do we know it's not just a silly old legend?'

Mother Collops looked uncomfortable. 'I don't think I'd have got a husband without it. I wasn't a picture, and my temper was legendary.' She shivered. 'But once was quite enough. It is easy to be corrupted, particularly by something that offers our heart's desire. That's why it mustn't fall into Dr DeWilde's hands. He's powerful enough already. I fear that on the other side of the mountains his rule is unchallenged, and in

Piper's Peak he has created his own kingdom based on slavery and immense wealth. His aim, I am sure, is to enslave us all. And with that pipe he could be invincible!'

16
THE Icy
Ice-Field
of Certain
Death

It was mid-afternoon when the girls left Hell Heights. Mother Collops begged them to stay for the night, but the children knew they wouldn't be able to sleep knowing that Any was a prisoner under some dark, distant mountain. So after Mother Collops had given them some clothes more suitable for climbing mountains, thrust a large bag of jelly babies and a packet of sprouted alfalfa sandwiches into each of their pockets, armed them with rucksacks, heavy with ropes, sleeping bags and ice axes, and made them promise to stop by on the return journey for a grand tiddlywinks contest, they set off once more into the unknown.

It was a gloriously crisp clear day. The distant mountains were etched sharply against the horizon, their snow caps sparkling like jaunty little diamanté hats. In their centre rose a slash of dark rock, its jagged summit rising like a deadly serrated knife cutting the air. This was Piper's Peak – their destination. On the snaking road they passed through several desolate villages that had suffered the same grim fate as Netta's.

As night closed in, an enveloping dampness made them shiver with cold and fatigue so that when Storm spied an abandoned pig-sty even the fastidious Aurora agreed they should stay the night there without too much protest.

The stars winked in the sky as Storm shut the sty gate and she saw something glinting in the moonlight on the road up ahead. From a distance it looked as if a star had fallen from sky to earth, but on closer investigation Storm saw that the star was edged with tiny midnight-blue threads. She gave a little hiccup of excitement: it was one of the silver stars from Any's blanket. A few metres further on she spied another star in the hedgerow. She claimed it and discovered another before she heard Aurora anxiously calling her name.

Back in the sty, where Aurora had been doing a little knitting to help her forget the hardships of the journey, Storm held out the stars to her sister in the upturned palm of her hand. Aurora whispered a single word: 'Any.'

'Yes,' breathed Storm. 'She must have been tearing them off her blanket and leaving a trail behind her to let us know we're on the right track.

'Such a clever little thing,' sighed Aurora.

'She is,' agreed Storm like an especially fond mother. She looked into the depths of a star. 'I feel as if I can see her little face reflected in it.'

Aurora leaned over. 'I can see the way her chin dimples when she smiles.'

'And how her eyes dance when she's happy . . .'

'And are as dark as millponds when she's scared.'

'I can see the way she hides her face in her

hands and thinks that no one can see her.'

'How she curls her fists into tight balls when she's asleep . . .'

'And stretches out her arms to be lifted up and hugged when she wakes up . . .'

The litany of love and memory went on until the girls drifted into sleep. They slept soundly, both dreaming of their little sister, while outside all was darkness but for the occasional gleam of ice-blue and silver-grey eyes stalking each other through the night.

By the following afternoon the lush pastures of the lower mountain had given way to more difficult terrain. The sisters picked their way slowly across slopes of loose gravel and mud dotted with huge boulders. Their hands and knees were badly grazed, and they were weighed down by the heavy rucksacks filled with the equipment that Mother Collops had insisted could make the difference between life and death in the mountains.

They toiled on, occasionally breaking into laughter when they spied one of Any's little stars. It was like a treasure hunt and it kept them going despite their exhaustion. Great banks of boiling cloud swept across the face of the mountains above them, and every now and again it would part to reveal the glowering summit of Piper's Peak. They reached a gully that rose steeply upwards to a forbidding wall of rock at least two hundred metres high. They scrambled up to its base, removed their rucksacks and crouched at the bottom, looking up at the vertical barrier in front of them. The surface was as smooth as glass. It would have defeated even the most experienced mountaineer. Storm's sturdy heart sank into her sturdy boots. The map must be wrong. There was no way up. They would have to retrace their steps and try to find another way. She pushed her rucksack angrily and it rolled down the gully, hit a boulder and bounced off to one side, scattering the contents as it went.

Aurora stood up wearily. She felt slightly guilty. If she was to tell the truth – which, being Aurora, she always made it a habit to do – she was rather relieved that she would not have to climb the daunting wall of rock. She did not think that mountaineering was her sort of thing at all. She looked over at Storm, whose head was buried in her hands, then hoisted her rucksack onto her shoulders and started slowly to traverse the gully in pursuit of her sister's strewn things. Slipping and sliding, she picked her way down and across, collecting up Storm's belongings, until she reached the far edge of the gully where the rucksack had rolled to a halt. She bent down to pick it up. A cascade of small stones on the rock face made her look up and, as she did so, her eye was attracted by something glinting in the shadows in the far corner of the gully, where it met the edge of the vertical drop. She peered more closely, wondering whether what she thought she was seeing was merely a trick of the light. It was not. It was one of Any's stars.

'Storm! Storm!' she called, her voice high with excitement. 'Over here. There's a way up.'

Storm traversed the gully to take a look. Someone had cut rough steps all the way up the side of the rock face. From the front of the rock they were impossible to detect. On either side of the hewn footholds were two fixed ropes. With mounting excitement, Storm pulled hard on the rope. It was quite secure. She scrambled onto the first ledge of the rough staircase, hung hard on the ropes to haul herself up, and found the next foothold with no difficulty. This was going to be easy.

'Come on, Aurora,' called Storm. 'You won't find it hard.'

'With two rucksacks I'll probably find it well-nigh impossible,' Aurora said tartly.

Guiltily Storm leaped from the staircase as nimbly as a goat and slid down the scree to where Aurora stood with her rucksack.

'Thanks,' she said, hoisting it onto her shoulders. Aurora knew it was for more than rescuing the rucksack.

Storm climbed the rock quickly, renewed hope giving her a burst of energy. She hauled herself over the top, stood up and surveyed the scene. It was a dazzling blur of blue glaciers, magnificent and terrible in its icy beauty. To the left was a wide path that ended at a large rock outcrop which appeared to drop away to nothing. To the right was a narrow path leading to a spur of rock. Beyond it Storm could see a high, narrow ridge that eventually tapered away into the sea of ice and snow below. That must surely be their way forward. Storm narrowed her eyes, trying to stare into the shimmering brightness to locate a pathway through. Yes, that must be it. She was so certain, she didn't think of checking on the map. She heard Aurora breathlessly struggling up the final steps and gave her a helping hand. Still panting, Aurora looked at the view in silence.

'It quite takes your breath away, doesn't it,' said Storm.

'It would if I had any left to be taken,' said Aurora lightly. 'Actually, sweetie, it's a bit daunting, the idea of us against all that.'

'We'll just have to think of it as an adventure.'

Aurora sighed. 'You should know by now that I'm not the adventurous type. My idea of excitement is a large roaring fire, homemade bread cooking in the oven, and a pair of socks with a satisfyingly large hole to darn.'

Storm smiled at Aurora sending herself up as she got the rope out of her rucksack. She looped and tied one end around her sister's waist, then, after letting a length trail loose between them, tied another loop around herself. She hoped that if one of them slipped on the cold, slippery ground ahead, the other would be strong enough to haul her to safety.

'Which way?' asked Aurora. Both paths looked equally treacherous to her, although she could see the imprint of what looked liked the tracks of a hare leading off to the left.

Storm pointed down the icy spine to the right.

'Are you quite sure? Have you checked on the map?'

'Look, I'm absolutely certain,' said Storm testily.

Aurora gazed at the narrow ridge again.

'How invigorating,' she said with a little laugh. She took a deep breath. 'Let's get going.'

The ridge was as treacherous as Storm had feared. Initially the path across the top was wide, but it quickly narrowed until it seemed no more than a fragile thread suspended in a great gulping sea of blue nothingness. Storm looked around anxiously. Night was falling and the wind was getting up. One big gust and both of them would topple over the edge, smashing like rag dolls on the rocks below.

At the next rocky outcrop Aurora slipped and started a heart-stopping slide towards thin air, and it was only because Storm was already braced for such an eventuality that they were not both swept off the ridge into oblivion. Aurora scrabbled wildly on the end of the taut rope, then managed to haul herself back up to Storm's side, where she perched on the ridge taking in big, scared gulps of air.

It began to snow again in great squally blasts.

Storm threw back her head, and railed at the sky, 'Why me? What have you got against me?' Her words echoed around the void.

'Now you've woken the whole world do you feel better?' enquired Aurora irritably.

'Much,' said Storm gruffly.

To stay where they were was certain death. There was no way but onwards, although Storm's arms felt like lead and Aurora's legs felt like jelly. Long into the night they edged their way across the ridge, two tiny, lonely specks battling their own fear and the immensity of nature, and so intent on their survival that they did not notice they were being watched.

Storm awoke in the snow-hole that they had managed to dig at the spot where the ridge descended into the ice-field. She pushed herself free of the fresh snow, troubled by a thought so terrible that she knew she would never have the courage to confide it to Aurora.

She had been dreaming about the story of the Pied Piper leading the dancing children over the mountain, and the shard of dream had been sharp enough to wake her. Something about the story nagged at her. Suddenly she realized what it was: how could the Piper have led hundreds of children, some of them only tiny, over the treacherous ridge that she and Aurora had traversed during the previous night? It was impossible. Most of them would have slipped to their deaths. Her heart began to beat very fast. She and Aurora must have come

270

the wrong way! There must be another and easier way to get to Piper's Peak, a way that Dr DeWilde was also using to transport the children. She thought back to the towering rock face that they had climbed. Somebody had fixed the rope and cut the steps in the seemingly impenetrable rock to make it passable with care. Surely that same person would have also made certain that the rest of the journey was possible. She pictured the summit of the rock face and the outcrop that had seemed to end abruptly in a sheer drop. What if it hadn't? What if there had been another hidden way down that avoided having to traverse the ridge and the ice-field? She hadn't bothered to check it out. She had just assumed that the path across the ridge must be the right one because it was the obvious one, stretching away in the direction they needed to go.

Storm looked at Aurora sleeping gently in her sleeping bag. It was too late now. The idea of telling her that they had come the wrong way and that they would either have to retrace their steps across the ridge or take their chance on the ice-field was not pleasant. She reckoned that Aurora would only be slightly less angry than if she told her that knitting had been permanently outlawed. Particularly as Aurora had questioned whether she had checked the map. Her sister had trusted her and she had let her down. Aurora stirred, opened her eyes and smiled at Storm. Storm looked down at her and guiltily decided that what Aurora didn't know probably wouldn't hurt her.

'Come on, sleepy-head, let's get moving,' she said with a forced little smile.

The way across the ice-field was as nerve-racking as their crossing of the ridge. The wind blew a constant spray of snow into their faces, the glare from the glacier was intense, and the ground was not solid, as Storm had assumed it was from a distance, but a honeycomb of ice-bridges across crevasses that were overlaid with a deep coating of snow. Before every single step forward she had to prod the snow with an ice axe until she was sure it met firm ice underneath. One ill-considered step could send them plunging into one of the gaping crevasses below. It was like trying to walk across a lacy paper doily.

Aurora stared deep into the bottomless blue depths of one of the crevasses and shivered. There was something about the sharp teeth-like ice formations that reminded her of a shark's mouth, ever-open and ready to receive its prey.

'How deep do you think it is?' she asked uneasily.

Storm shrugged. 'As tall as a cathedral, maybe taller. Fall down there, and you'd have no chance. You would be entombed for ever. You would become part of the mountain itself . . .' She trailed off, realizing that she was frightening her sister. 'But you're not going to fall down, Aurora,' she added hastily. 'I'm going ahead to make quite certain that the ice is solid and safe. All you have to do is follow me, making sure you step exactly into my footprints. Even if you slip you'll be fine – I can pull you up with the rope like before.' Storm hoped she sounded more confident than she felt.

Aurora still looked uncertain. 'But are you quite sure this is the right way?' she asked.

'Of course I'm sure,' said Storm shortly, and began pressing down with her axe on the ground ahead.

Progress was painfully slow and the physical effort was soon taking its toll on Aurora. She lagged further and further behind her sister, forcing Storm to let out more and more rope until it trailed like a long, limp snake between the two girls.

Eventually, after a lengthy period of standing

still, shivering and watching her sister's painfully slow progress, Storm lost patience. She turned and ploughed on ahead, not noticing that the rope had caught on a particularly sharp rock sticking out of the ice and had been severed neatly in two.

The snow turned to a dancing blizzard.

After several minutes Aurora reached the spot where the rope had parted. She looked up in alarm, expecting to see Storm just a little way off. But ahead of her was just a wall of snow. She could see nothing. She shouted her sister's name over and over, but her words were blown away on the wind.

The snow became so clotted that Aurora could see no further ahead than her own hand and she felt completely disorientated. She looked around blindly. She could see the indentation of Storm's foot in front of her but the snow was falling so thickly that the impression was filling up fast. Aurora took a step forward and then another, trying to move quickly through the enveloping blanket of white. Her breath came in panicky little gasps. She saw another faint imprint ahead. She stepped into it and cast around for the next, but the expanse of snow in front of her was completely smooth. She took a tentative step forward, hoping desperately that the ice beneath her was thick enough to bear her weight. It held firm. She shuffled forward again. The ground felt blessedly solid. She took a third panicky step.

As soon as she did so, Aurora realized she had made a terrible mistake. Her foot passed through the drifting snow like a hot knife through butter, and instead of finding solid ice it found thin air. She didn't even have time to call out as she fell through the mouth of the crevasse into the gaping dark hole below.

Up ahead, Storm looked around. She was frightened. The dense whiteness was so disorientating that she had lost all sense of direction. They were completely adrift in a sea of ice; for all she knew she could be leading them round and round in circles. She wished suddenly that she hadn't pressed on so speedily. Huddling down, she waited for Aurora to catch her up, peering back through the murk, expecting to see her sister's anxious face appear any minute.

'Aurora!' she roared into the wind. 'Aurora . . .' The wind spat Aurora's name back at her. Storm felt the pipe around her neck glow like a hot ember in a dying fire. Panic rising, she set off to retrace her steps, but she had only taken three or four when she realized with a sick feeling that she could see an end to the rope and that there was no Aurora attached to it. She stared down at the rope in horror and disbelief. Beyond it, the snow had obliterated her tracks completely. There was no telling which way she had come.

'Aurora!' she screamed, and, quite oblivious to her own safety, broke into a stumbling run. After a few steps she sank to her knees, aghast at her own stupidity. One false step and she would have fallen to her death. She hugged herself and forced back hot tears. Had Aurora already fallen? Was she already dead, deep in the underbelly of the mountains? Or was she still somewhere out on the ice-field, lost and frightened and needing Storm's help?

Storm hauled herself to her feet. She felt her way back with her ice axe in the direction from which she thought they had come, all the while muttering to herself, 'For ever and for always,' 'For ever and for always,' until it became a comforting mantra as she moved trance-like through the blinding snow. Time crumbled away. Storm was soon so exhausted that every step required a supreme effort. 'For ever and for always,' she muttered to herself. She felt terribly sleepy. Perhaps she would lie down in the snow and have a rest. She shook herself. 'For ever and . . . for . . . always.' She knew that she mustn't lie down, that if she slept, then she would never awake again. But she couldn't help herself. The wind had dropped and she was alone in a silent world of snow. 'For ever . . . and . . . for . . .' She would just lie down for a moment and then she would get up again. She prodded the snow in front of her with her ice axe, then she knelt, curling her body up into a little ball. The pipe was burning her skin but she didn't care. She was far too sleepy. 'For ever . . .'

The snow continued to fall, covering her with a warm, treacherous blanket. After a very short while it began to drift around her body, so that Storm became part of the landscape. A silver-grey hare ran across the snow and huddled its warm body against her cold one.

'Left shelf. Seven plain tea towels. Seven coloured tea towels. Seven hand towels, blue. Seven hand towels, various colours. Right shelf. Six large bath towels, white. Six large swimming towels, multi-coloured. Next shelf up. Left-hand side. Eight cream Irish linen double sheets, embroidered with a leaf motif, two darned. Sixteen cream linen lacy pillowcases, embroidered with a leaf motif, one with an iron scorch-mark in top left-hand corner. One patchwork quilt . . .'

Storm blinked dozily. She was sure she could hear Aurora's voice. She smiled sleepily and shut her eyes again, drifting back into warm sleep.

'Right-hand side. Eight single white Irish linen

sheets, four of them darned, one very badly in bottom left-hand corner. Sixteen white Irish linen pillowcases . . .'

Storm awoke again. She was confused. She seemed to be entombed in warm, wet cotton wool. Foggily, she remembered what had happened. She struggled to sit up, fighting against her aching body, which was screaming for a return to the oblivion of sleep. She pushed her upper body through the layer of snow that encased her. It had stopped snowing. The sun was warm on her face. She cast desperately around for Aurora. The white landscape was utterly empty. She must have been dreaming her sister's voice. Carefully Storm stood up, every bone protesting and her knees clicking like knitting needles. Somehow she had survived, but she had lost Aurora.

Storm was beyond tears. Beyond despair. She felt as if she was carved out of stone. She stared at Piper's Peak. A squall of snow raced across the cruel face of the mountain. Her face set hard, she prodded the snow in front of her and took a step in the direction of the mountain.

She took several more steps.

'Four brushed-cotton cot sheets, white. Two small goose-feather eiderdowns with blue piping. Four soft white towels. Twenty-two nappies, six badly worn . . .'

Storm couldn't believe her ears. It *was* Aurora's voice. She wondered whether she might be hallucinating. She took a tentative step in the direction of the voice and shouted, 'Aurora! Aurora!'

'Six vests, white—' The voice broke off. 'Storm? Storm! Is that you?'

Storm looked around frantically. The voice was coming from somewhere in front and below her. Trying to contain her excitement, she tested the ground and moved forward.

'Storm?' The voice was coming from under the snow. Kneeling, Storm prodded the ground directly in front of her. It crumbled away to reveal a yawning hole. She peered down. Several metres below on a small ledge she saw Aurora's ashen face staring back at her. Beyond the ledge loomed a dark blue, apparently bottomless drop. A series of ledges, smaller than the one upon which Aurora was perched, rimmed the crevasse mouth. They would be impossible to climb unaided, but with a rope and some help from her, Storm reckoned that Aurora would be able to scramble back out.

'Hold on, Aurora,' she called. 'I'm going to get

you out.' She double-tied the length of severed rope to the spare in her pack and secured one end to her ice axe, which she then jabbed as hard as she could into the snowy ground. Then, casting a loop around her waist, she slowly lowered the rope towards her sister.

'Aurora? Have you still got your ice axe?'

'Yes.'

'Good. You're going to have to use it to help lever yourself out. I won't be able to pull you up on my own.' Storm dug her feet into the ice and braced herself. 'Ready?'

'Yes,' said Aurora in a small voice.

Storm felt her sister's weight on the rope. It was like fifty sacks of potatoes. Storm's forehead beaded with sweat as she tried to stop her feet from slipping. She felt her ice axe move ominously in the ice. Summoning all her energy, she heaved on the rope. Aurora's head appeared over the top of the hole. The ice axe moved again. Storm pulled with all her strength. Just as Aurora scrambled over the edge, the ice axe flew out of its lodging. The sisters collapsed in a heap on the snow, gasping.

After a few moments Aurora felt for Storm's gloved hand and clasped it in her own.

'Tell me,' Storm said as her breathing returned

to normal, 'exactly why were you itemizing the entire contents of the linen cupboard at Eden End?'

Aurora blushed. 'I thought I was going to die. I was trying to take my mind off it by thinking of something nice.'

'Something nice . . .' said Storm wonderingly. 'The linen cupboard? Something *nice*?' She broke into gales of laughter. 'I love you, Aurora Eden. You are so unpredictably predictable.'

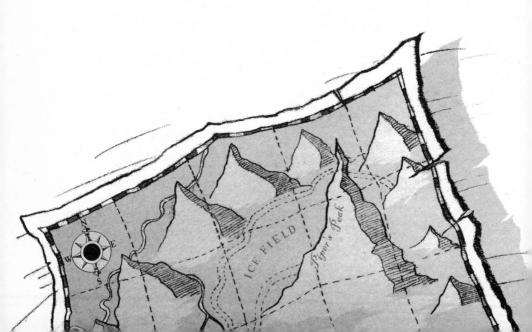

17
Down a Deep, Dark Hole

*I*t was noon the next day by the time they reached the base of Piper's Peak. They had found several silver stars left by Any, so Storm knew that they were back on the right track.

A gale had kicked up off the ice-field and the girls were sheltering behind a lichen-covered boulder amongst the stones and rubble at the foot of the mountain. Storm was studying the map. Aurora had collapsed on a large flat stone and was nervously eyeing the mountain that rose out of boiling clouds. She resolved that if she survived this terrible adventure she would spend the rest of her life indoors, only venturing outside for weddings, picnics and visits to the dentist. She cocked her head. Somewhere behind the wind she thought she heard the guttural snarl of wolves. She got out her knitting needles: knitting would take her mind off things.

Storm paced, muttering to herself, taking first forty steps in one direction and then forty steps in another, until she completed three sides of a triangle and came to rest in front of Aurora, still mumbling under her breath and looking around as if she had lost something important.

'Where is it, stupid? Where is it! It must be here somewhere, stupid.' Storm craned her neck, looking at the flapping map from different angles. Then she counted out the steps again, arriving back at the exact same point in front of Aurora.

'I don't understand. It must be here,' she said angrily.

'What must be here?' asked Aurora pleasantly.

'The entrance to the abandoned mineshaft,' Storm replied impatiently. 'Look, it says here on the map: *X marks the spot.*'

'Are you reading the map upside down?' ventured Aurora.

'What do you think I am? Stupid?'

'Of course not, sweetie,' said Aurora soothingly. 'But it's not here, is it? If it was we would be able to see it.'

'Well, if you're so good at reading maps, you find it,' said Storm huffily.

Aurora looked at the map. The boulder with its distinctive lichen markings was clearly shown. She took the forty steps in one direction. Then the forty in another. Finally, with Storm close behind her, she paced forty more and came to a rest in front of the wide flat stone where she had been sitting. Engraved where she had been perched was a faint but distinct X.

There was a tiny bubble of silence. Aurora expected Storm to explode, but her sister merely took the map and said in a tight arctic voice, 'Ah, so *Aurora* marked the spot.' Then she sighed. 'Come on, Aurora, give us a hand.'

It took several minutes of back-breaking exertion before the girls succeeded in moving the heavy stone to reveal a round wooden lid with a rusty handle. Storm lifted the lid and the girls stared into a vertical tunnel of darkness. Storm threw a pebble down the hole and counted. She had reached nineteen and a quarter before they heard a distant splash.

'Well,' said Aurora with a nervous little laugh, 'either this mineshaft is very deep or that stone fell very slowly.'

Storm grinned. She felt into the shaft and located a rickety, rusty metal ladder fixed to the side. Then she busied herself with the rope.

'You stay here and hold the rope,' she decided. 'I want to check the ladder. It doesn't look very safe but I think it's the only route to the tunnel that leads into Piper's Peak. I just hope it's above the waterline and hasn't been flooded.' She tied one end of the long coil around her waist and the other around Aurora's.

Aurora was only half-listening. She had been peering fearfully around into the gathering gloom. She had the uneasy feeling that they were being watched. 'You're going to leave me all on my own?' she gulped.

'Only for a few minutes,' replied Storm impatiently. 'Please try to pull yourself together,

Aurora. Nothing is going to happen to you. I'm doing the dangerous bit. All you've got to do is hold on to the rope and brace yourself in case I slip.'

'But what if the rope snaps again?' Aurora protested.

Her sister looked momentarily contrite. 'It won't. Look – there are no rough edges for it to snag on here. And besides' – she tried a smile – 'we've had more than our share of bad luck already, don't you think?'

Her sister didn't look convinced. She peered around again, still unable to shake the sensation of being watched, but there was no sign of movement amongst the rocks or out on the ice-field. 'I'm scared,' she whispered. Storm ignored her and began to descend into the shaft.

Aurora gave a shriek so shrill it nearly made Storm lose her footing.

'What's the matter now?' she asked, pulling herself frantically from the hole.

'I thought I saw something,' said Aurora tearfully.

Storm stared around. 'I can't see anything, can you?' she enquired with a nasty little sarcastic edge to her voice. Aurora shook her head miserably.

'Well then . . . If you're quite sure, I'll try again,' said Storm, descending into the dark. She got a few rungs down when Aurora gave another piercing cry. Storm scrambled breathlessly back.

'What is it?' she hissed irritably.

'There's something there,' sobbed Aurora, pointing up into the gloom of the mountainside. Storm sighed. She was getting really fed up with Aurora's never-ending anxiety.

'There's nothing there, it's your imagination playing tricks. You're such a baby, Aurora. Now, I'm going down again; all you have to do is hold the rope. Can you do that?' she asked, adding nastily, 'Or will the scaredy little baby run away?'

'But I *did* see something,' said Aurora in a tiny voice. 'Please don't leave me here alone. I'll come with you. I don't want to be left on my own.'

'Oh grow up, Aurora. Do you really want to climb down this dark, wet hole if it leads to a dead end? And besides, it'll be quicker if I go alone. You're always so slow.' And with that, Storm's head disappeared into the darkness.

The coil of rope slowly unwound. Aurora shivered. She peered into the gloom and her heart skipped a beat. Staring back at her was a pair of eyes like tiny dirty headlamps. She closed her own momentarily and rubbed them. When she opened them, the single pair of eyes had been joined by several more. She screamed a scream that was like a thousand shivers. The eyes moved closer.

Down in the mineshaft, Storm thought she heard a distant cry. She listened hard. Nothing. It must have been the wind. She continued towards the bottom, testing each rung of the ladder before putting her full weight on it. After more than a hundred metres she thought she could see water, dark and deceitful, waiting to swallow her up if she slipped. She sighed – it was just as she'd suspected. The entrance to the tunnel was below the water level. They would have to climb Piper's Peak and find another way in.

She began to climb back up, her exhausted legs protesting. Halfway to the surface she made a stupid error. She stepped onto a rusty rung and grabbed another a few metres above without testing it first. As she put her other hand on the rung to haul herself upwards it broke away. Storm fell. She grabbed at the ladder desperately and an entire section ripped away from the wall and dropped into the water below. Storm lurched sickeningly through thin air on the rope, then stopped with a jerk. Silently she blessed Aurora for absorbing the impact of her full weight on the rope.

When her stomach returned to its proper place, Storm tried to claw her way through air to the wall. But although her fingers grazed the shaft's sides, there was nothing to get a grip on. Only bare wall stood where the ladder had once been. She stretched upwards as far as she could. The section of ladder above the piece that had broken off was tantalizingly close – no more than a couple of metres above her. But however hard she tried to reach it, it remained beyond her grasp.

Her situation was desperate, but not hopeless. Aurora had broken her fall and before long she would surely realize that for some reason Storm was unable to take her weight off the rope. Then her sister would haul her upwards. If Aurora could just manage to lift her a couple of metres higher, she could reach the ladder. She called up, 'Aurora. Aurora.'

There was silence. A terrible thought crossed Storm's mind. Perhaps somehow, in breaking her fall, Aurora had knocked herself unconscious, maybe with the rope caught beneath her. Maybe Aurora was even dead. Then Storm would be suspended for eternity in mid-air until she herself died or, even more chillingly, until her weight dragged Aurora's body over the edge of the shaft and sent it tumbling down on top of her.

Storm tried again to reach the next rung of the ladder before tumbling back exhausted. Tears of frustration began to course down her cheeks.

Up at ground level Aurora stood frozen with shock and effort. She had felt the jerk of the rope as Storm fell and had held on for dear life, the rope biting viciously into hands. Her arms were shaking uncontrollably with the effort.

She couldn't understand it. Storm couldn't have fallen very far — there had only been a metre or so left of the rope to uncoil. She couldn't be seriously hurt. So why hadn't she moved her weight back onto the ladder?

Aurora shut her eyes briefly to black out the pain in her arms and the terrifying circle of yellow eyes that now surrounded her. She heaved on the rope, but Storm's body was heavy and her own arms too numb. There was a small stunted bush nearby. She wondered if she might be able to reach it and secure the rope around it. She took a tiny shuffle towards the bush. As she did so the yellow eyes morphed into grey bodies and saliva-flecked jaws, stretched with twisted smiles.

Trembling, Aurora took another minuscule step

towards the bush. The wolves moved
closer. Then they threw back their heads and
bayed.

From out of the darkness stepped Dr DeWilde,
followed by Kit, the beautiful odd-eyed boy. The
boy's shoulders were slumped and there were violet
circles under his curious mismatched eyes. He
would not, or could not, meet Aurora's pleading
gaze.

Dr DeWilde's cruel eyes surveyed Aurora's
sweaty forehead, her shaking arms and the rope
wrapped around her clenched fingers.

'Let me help you take the strain, my dear,' he
said smoothly, and with a diabolical smile. Aurora
saw the diamond flash of a knife in the air, and a

blade sliced through the rope like butter. She watched aghast as the rope flew through the air and vanished down the mineshaft like the tail of a disappearing cat. She looked down stupidly at her hands, which still clasped the frayed end of the cut rope. At that moment, the wind paused for breath and from far away there was a cry followed by a splash. She looked speechlessly into Dr DeWilde's cold eyes, and her lips formed a single word. 'Murderer.'

Dr DeWilde shot her a callous look. 'Come, come, my dear. Don't be so emotional. You've still got one sister. That would be quite enough for most people. I suppose you would like to see little Any? What a dear she is. I do so love children — especially when they cry. This way.'

He took the shocked Aurora by the arm and guided her towards Piper's Peak with the wolves following slavishly in his wake. The boy, his shoulders hunched, turned to follow, but Dr DeWilde stopped him.

'No, pup, you stay. Follow my instructions to the letter, or it will be the worse for you.'

Storm's body hit the water, cut the inky surface and dropped like a stone. Panic rose as she sank. She was going to drown. She opened her eyes underwater. She could faintly make out the brick walls of the mineshaft through the murk. She felt her feet touch the bottom of the shaft. She pushed hard against the floor with bended knees and propelled herself upwards. Her lungs felt as if they were going to explode. She thought she was never going to reach the surface in time. Her head was full of stars and white flashes; snapshots of Aurora, Any, her dead mother and Eden End pulsed inside her brain like the click, click, click of a camera shutter. Her chest felt as if it was being squeezed by twenty-five full-grown boa constrictors. Then her head bobbed above the water and Storm took a great gulp of air before sinking helplessly again. She thrashed about, and one of her hands closed over a rung of the ladder on the wall. She pulled herself upwards and clung to it, taking enormous, shuddering gulps of air into her bruised lungs.

The rope was dangling above her. Warily she gave it a little tug. It was slack and several coils came tumbling towards her. She climbed upwards, testing each untrustworthy rung carefully, until she came to the place where the ladder had broken away to leave several metres of unscaleable wall. She peered upwards and saw, with a gasp, that the end of the rope was snagged around a rung, high above.

She couldn't understand it. Aurora couldn't have just let go – the rope had been tied securely around her waist. It could only have fallen if she had. Storm tugged hard until the rope unsnagged. As it fell she caught the end in her hand. She stared at it with mounting shock. She felt sick and shaky. The rope had been deliberately cut! She clung to the ladder to stop herself plunging once more into the water below. She was certain that her sister would never have cut the rope. But then an image of Aurora's white, panicky face flashed across her mind. Alone and frightened in the dark, Storm suddenly felt less certain. She replayed their last fraught exchange in her head and regretted her unkindness. Perhaps she shouldn't have left Aurora at the top of the mineshaft when she was in such a nervous state. But would she have been scared enough to cut herself free? Aurora must have known that cutting the rope would almost certainly have been her sister's death warrant. She would never have done it.

From a distance she suddenly heard a soft voice calling 'Hello.'

'Hello,' she yelled back excitedly. 'Down here! I need help.'

'I'll help you,' returned the voice from the top of the mineshaft. She knew that she had heard that voice somewhere before but in her panic she couldn't place it.

'Have you got a rope?' called Storm.

'No,' returned the voice.

'Is my sister there?' Storm asked urgently.

'There's no one here but me,' returned the voice. 'But I think I may have met your sister on my way up here. She was going round the mountainside. She had a knife in her hand. I called out to her, but she didn't stop. She seemed to be in rather a hurry, as if she wanted to get away from somewhere as quickly as possible.'

Storm's insides turned to water and she felt sick. So it was true! Aurora had cut the rope! Exhaustion, hopelessness and fear swept through Storm, and disbelief turned to boiling anger that lodged in her stomach – a red-hot burning coal

of bitter resentment. Aurora must have been so
scared that she had cut the rope without thinking
of the consequences. *She* would never have done
that to Aurora. It was one thing for a rope to snap
accidentally, like on the ice-field. It was something
else to deliberately cut it – to purposefully abandon
a sister in trouble. Storm would never have just
tried to save her own skin. But Aurora had. She
must have thought she was going to be pulled into
the mineshaft and had cut the rope to save herself.
Storm felt utterly betrayed. Tears of corroding
self-pity poured off her cheeks. 'Together and for
ever,' she muttered to herself with a bitter little
laugh. 'Hah!' Then, craning her neck upwards, she
yelled, 'Do you think you could find a rope to
lower down?'

'I can try,' said the puzzlingly familiar voice.

'Please,' said Storm.

'I'll do my best to help you, but it may take
time.'

'I'm not going anywhere,' Storm said dryly. 'I'll
be here.'

At the head of the mineshaft, Kit turned and
headed in the direction taken by Dr DeWilde.
As he walked across the inhospitable terrain, his
ice-blue eye glittered with excitement but his

emerald-coloured one was wet with tears.

Left alone in the cold, dank hole once more, Storm's feelings of betrayal overtook her. How could Aurora have deserted her? How could she have been so selfish? Well – Storm scowled – I'm not finished yet! If Aurora doesn't need me, I certainly don't need her!

The red-hot coal glowed viciously inside of her. She was better off without her sister anyway! Aurora didn't have a chance of surviving out there without her, but *she* could do anything without her silly, stupid, cowardly sister. The nugget of rage in the pit of her stomach flared and burned itself out, leaving her charred and empty. And so very, very alone. She had never felt so bereft. Not even when her mother had died.

'Aurora,' she sobbed in the gloom. 'Why did you do it? Why did you run away? Why did you abandon me?'

She clung precariously to the ladder, weeping for her loss. Eventually her sobs turned to dry hiccups. She looked at the severed end of the rope in her hand. A thought grew in her mind. Maybe she wouldn't have to wait for help to come. Perhaps she could throw the rope high enough to get it over one of the rungs of the ladder and pull herself up. It was a long shot, but better than just hanging there. She untied the rope from around her waist and pulled the other end up from under the water. She tossed the rope upwards. It didn't get near the bottom rungs of the ladder. Muttering angrily to herself, she threw the rope again and this time it sailed over the nearest rung. Carefully she fed the rope upwards, threading it through her hands. The other end slowly descended towards her.

Storm was thrilled. She had never hoped it would be so easy. She grabbed the swinging end, trying not to look at the cut marks that showed Aurora's betrayal, and tied it to form a long loop. She looked up. It was a long way to shin up to the first rung, but she was confident she could do it. Just so long as the rung held. She tugged hard on the rope before she began her climb, just to be sure. It felt fine. She swung out and heaved herself upwards. Still the rung held. She heaved again and used her feet to scramble closer. One more monkey-like shimmy and she would be there. The rung creaked suddenly. Storm made a desperate lunge just as it gave way, plunging her once again into the dark water below.

Storm bobbed up, spluttering, and clung to the

ladder. The rope was now submerged at the bottom of the shaft. She tried to squash the growing feeling of despair in her heart. She would just have to be patient until help came.

She waited

And waited.

She didn't know how long it was she stayed there, hanging just above the waterline, the cold and wet chilling her to the bone. It seemed like hours, but she knew from past experience, particularly during long, boring arithmetic lessons with Aurora, that although time is supposed to pass at exactly the same rate, it doesn't. Sometimes it passes very slowly − mostly during maths and spelling tests − and sometimes it whizzes by. So she tried to remain patient, even though she was shivering uncontrollably. Several times she called up the mineshaft, but only silence answered. She began to feel doubly abandoned and certain that she was doomed to die in this cold, twilight world. Eventually, she knew, she would lose consciousness and slide into the water for the very last time.

Finally she lost all hope that the owner of the disembodied voice would ever return to help her. She would just have to try to help herself.

If she couldn't go up, Storm decided, she would

try going down. She knew from her double dunking that the bottom of the shaft was no more than a few metres beneath her. Perhaps she could dive down and find the entrance to the tunnel. Even if it was flooded here, she was pretty sure it couldn't be flooded all the way up into Piper's Peak. Perhaps she could swim through it until it climbed above the waterline! She had nothing to lose. If she stayed where she was, she would certainly die. If she could find the entrance to the tunnel, she might survive. Storm took a deep breath, put her head under the water, and began her descent.

18
THE PIPER UNDER THE MOUNTAIN

Storm hauled herself above the water's edge and lay gasping for air, the water still lapping over her ankles. Exhaustion spread like a bruise through every limb of her body. Ahead she could just make out the sides of the tunnel. She was afraid

302

of the smothering darkness, but she had no choice but to go on. She certainly wasn't going back. She had easily found the entrance to the tunnel lurking below the surface of the water. But swimming through had been nightmarish, her body pushed to its limits and her mind full of terror as the waterlogged passageway seemed to stretch endlessly onwards. She had begun to fear that she had been wrong about it sloping upwards, and that she would drown and lie in a watery tomb for ever. But just when she had thought she could go no further, she sensed that the tunnel was rising and had managed to propel herself forward to dry land.

As her breathing evened, Storm became aware of a curious booming sound from far away. It sounded like thunder coming right from the very heart of the mountain. She struggled wearily to her feet and set off up the tunnel, feeling her way carefully along the knobbly walls, and leaving a diminishing trail of puddles in her wake.

In the thick darkness she edged her way along, occasionally stumbling on the uneven floor, but always keeping a picture of Any in her head to give her the courage to keep going. Whenever she thought of Aurora, the uncomfortable burning coal settled miserably in her stomach again, so she simply banished her sister from her mind.

After a while Storm saw a glow in the far distance, at first just a pinprick. She paused and listened. She could hear nothing except the distant booming and a strange tinkling sound like a mobile in child's nursery. At last the light grew stronger and the tunnel opened out into a vast cavern, its ceiling covered in hundreds and thousands of tiny stars. Entranced, and quite forgetting any thought of her safety, Storm wandered into the middle of the cavern staring upwards. She had never seen anything so beautiful. It was then she realized that it was alive. She was not seeing stars, but hundreds of thousands of tiny glow-worms whose bodies were emitting a beautiful, ghostly light.

Dragging her eyes away from the astonishing sight, Storm looked for a way out of the cavern. Tucked away in one of the darker recesses was a small wooden door with a tiny golden keyhole. Storm put her eye to the keyhole. She could see nothing, but the booming noise was louder than ever. She felt for the key Mother Collops had given her. For a dreadful moment she thought she had lost it but, after a panicky search, she located it at the bottom of her left pocket. It was under two empty toffee wrappers, the phial of magic potion from the Ginger House, the metal file, a twist of gunpowder, a large quantity of fluff and the sodden box of matches given to her by Any so long ago in the forest. Scraping the sticky remains of a peppermint toffee from the key, she put it in the lock and turned it. Carefully she opened the door and slipped through.

She was right in the heart of Piper's Peak, and a terrible sight met her eyes. In a massive cavern, taller than several large cathedrals and lit with the eerie luminous light of more glow-worms, were thousands of toiling men, women and children. All were as pale as ghosts, and thin as paper, and all scrabbled in the dirt as if they were searching feverishly for something precious they had lost. Standing guard were several packs of huge wolves.

Occasionally a worker would delve into the dirt and triumphantly hold something bright and glittering up to the light. Immediately a wolf would bound over, open its jaw wide, and extend its long pink tongue, and the man, woman or child would drop the object onto the wolf's tongue. At first Storm thought that the workers were giving the wolves brightly coloured sweets, but then she realized that they were not extracting candy from the earth, but precious gemstones – rubies, amethysts, sapphires, diamonds and emeralds.

Storm watched as a little girl, only just older than Any, found a ruby in the dirt. She clearly thought it was a fruit gum because she put it in her own mouth. Immediately a wolf bounded up to the child, growling menacingly. With a look of fear, a female worker bent over the child and coaxed her to give the crimson gemstone up to the wolf's massive jaws. They closed over the jewel with a snap that only narrowly missed the child's fingers. The wolf took the ruby to a table where other workers were counting the gems and tipping them into small pouches.

Storm watched, appalled, peeping out from behind a huge boulder, as the people went about their work, their bodies cowed, their eyes clouded with fear. Those who were not looking for the precious stones were bearing huge loads of earth and trying to avoid the attention of the wolves. A young woman, her ringlets stuck damply to her pale, sweaty face, struggled with a huge sack on her back, stumbling as she tried to stay upright. Another woman, with faded cornflower eyes, was desperately pulling a heavy load of stones and rubble on a sled. Storm saw that the woman would once have been pretty, but now she was pale and sickly. It was as if all the colour had been washed out of her. Like those of the other workers, her mouth sagged and her eyes were dull from working in the semi-darkness for many years.

The booming noise that Storm had heard was produced by massive excavation machines, driven by huge wheels suspended high above the floor of the cavern. Each wheel was powered by at least a hundred people, crammed forlornly onto steps that had been carved inside. As the people marched on the spot, the steps moved beneath them, making the vast wheels turn and powering great drills that tore lumps of rock from the cavern walls. The marchers looked exhausted, but they dared not slow down – any that stumbled risked falling to a horrible end on the rocks below.

Storm watched, horrified, as an elderly silver-haired man with a small goatee beard tumbled from his place high on the steps. She saw his mouth open in a scream, and then he hit the floor below with a terrible thwack. None of the other workers missed a beat; none of them even looked in the direction of the old man; they simply powered onwards, their eyes cold and dead.

Storm wanted to cry out, implore the workers to stop and help the fallen man, but she had already seen enough to know that to do so would be to invite the unwelcome attention of the wolves. Two had already ambled up to the prone man, sniffed him and were beginning to drag him away by the scruff of his neck.

A long howl from the pack leader cut through the booming din. The workers stopped. Leather-skinned bottles were passed down the lines. Those in the giant wheels began to clamber exhaustedly down a series of rickety ladders. No sooner were they all down than a fresh team of forced labourers scrambled up to replace them. Then the lead wolf howled again and the backbreaking work resumed.

Storm cautiously threaded her way through the boulders towards a long table where gems were being sorted into pouches. A dark-haired woman, her fingers permanently atremble, was counting emeralds. Her hands were shaking so badly that she knocked several pouches over and their contents skittered across the floor. A wolf gave a little snarl of irritation and two children hurried to pick up the gemstones. With a jolt Storm recognized them as the plump little twins from the orphanage, Arwen and Aisling. Only they were no longer plump. Their skin had turned grey and they were so thin that they looked more like wizened old ladies than nine-year-olds. She called out to them as loudly as she dared. 'Arwen! Aisling!' The children looked around suspiciously. Storm put a finger to her lips. The taller twin edged towards Storm's hiding place, looking anxiously around.

'My sister?' whispered Storm desperately. 'Have you seen Any?'

Arwen nodded imperceptibly. 'She's in Dr DeWilde's parlour. At least, that's what I've heard.' She pointed towards a tapestry hanging at the far end of the vast hall, depicting a jolly Pied Piper leading a throng of laughing children towards an open crack in a mountain. 'Wait until the end of the day and fall in with the column,' she whispered. 'It passes right by the tapestry.' Then she melted back into the crowd.

The pack leader howled again and Storm scurried back to her hiding place. She watched the labourers from the wheels climb wearily down and crawl away to fall in exhausted, sweaty heaps. But the wolves refused to let them rest, harrying them to replace the sorters, who in turn were sent to the far side of the cavern to join hundreds more people piling earth into large sacks. Others carried the sacks away, bent double under their heavy loads.

A new crowd of workers were forced up the ladders to the wheels by the wolves. Many looked so thin and pitiful that they hardly seemed capable of walking, let alone powering the giant machines. Storm realized then why Dr DeWilde needed an endless stream of plump new workers – he had to have a constant supply of replacements for those whose bodies were broken by this horrendous work.

The final stragglers – a teenage boy, a paunchy man and an elderly woman – scrambled into places high on the steps of the wheel. The old woman was so bent over that Storm could tell straight away that she would have difficulty marching on the steep steps. Then her stomach pitched and tossed like a ship in a wild sea, and a wave of icy cold swept over her. The old lady had looked up just as the wheel had begun to turn. It was Mother Collops!

Before Storm could move or cry out, the wheel was turning swiftly and her great-grandmother, staring blindly into the distance through milky cataracts, was hopping frantically up the steps in a desperate effort to keep up. The old lady was stronger than she looked, Storm knew, but she could never keep up the pace, especially without her stick. Storm cast about frantically, wondering how she could stop the dreadful machine, but there was no way she could reach her great-grandmother before the wolves spotted her.

The wheel completed a circuit. And another. Then, as it made a third turn, Mother Collops stumbled. Storm bit her tongue to stop herself crying out as her great-grandmother lurched from side to side. But somehow Mother Collops steadied herself. And the wheel turned again. Storm let out her breath in a whoosh of relief. And the old lady slipped again. She flailed briefly at the workers closest to her, but her fingers clutched nothingness and, with a terrible cry, she tumbled through space, arms and legs flailing.

Mother Collops hit the ground with a dull thud and then lay still like an ancient, broken doll.

A scream forced its way through Storm's lips and her legs took her from her hiding space towards the broken body of her great-grandmother. She was oblivious to the shouts from all around and to the growl of wolves.

The old lady was alive – but only just. Her eyes fluttered open and shut as Storm reached her. She took the old lady's hand and stroked it. Mother Collops looked up at her through filmy eyes. 'Our little Storm, our wild one,' she whispered. 'They took me almost as soon as you left. But I knew you'd come. I never doubted you'd save us.' She closed her eyes and was still.

'Don't die!' screamed Storm. 'Please, please, don't die!' She was suddenly aware that the entire cavern had fallen silent and everyone was watching her. She was surrounded by a circle of wolves, all tensed and waiting for a signal from their chief. Still she did not let go of her great-grandmother's hand. She felt the pipe around her neck glow so hot that it blistered her skin. She started to rip it off, but as she did so her mother's dying words floated through her mind: 'Use it wisely and only if you have desperate need.'

Things were certainly desperate. Storm lifted the pipe to her lips and blew. Its eerie, shivery sound, the most beautiful and the most terrible song that the world has ever heard, filled the cavern and echoed off the walls, but Storm didn't hear it. She leaned over her great-grandmother, murmuring a desperate incantation. 'Please, don't die. I need you so much. Please be well. I need you to be well.' With each word the tune from the pipe didn't fade but grew louder. It grew as deep as the most sonorous bell and as high as the sound of breaking crystal, its tones sweet as honey and as sad as a funeral lament. As soft as a whisper and as loud as a mighty wind, it filled the vast cavern and the minds of everyone present, including the wolves. It made all those who heard it want to laugh and weep, exclaim with delight and shiver with horror. The sound hung like a shimmer in the air until at last the final quivering notes faded away and, at that moment, Mother Collops sat bolt upright and said cheerfully, 'You know what I could do with, duckie, a nice cup of tea and a sprouted alfalfa sandwich followed by some jelly babies.'

Storm gasped. The workers looked astonished and took a step backwards, murmuring to each other. The wolves grumbled and growled. Realizing the danger, but feeling a sudden, wondering thrill, Storm put the pipe to her mouth and blew again. Once more the beautiful, terrible sound filled the cavern, and those who heard it wanted to dance and lie down to sleep at the same time.

'Let us pass,' said Storm, and taking Mother Collops by the arm, she walked through the ring of wolves towards the tapestry at the far end of the cavern. As they passed, the pack leader silently put his head between his front paws and the other wolves did the same. Music continued to echo around the cavern.

At the tapestry Storm turned. Hundreds of faces were staring back at her. Swallowing hard, she called out, 'Sit down, everyone, and have a nice rest. There'll be no more work for today.'

A ripple of astonishment passed through the cavern and it echoed to the sound of cheers and laughter – something not heard in the heart of the mountain for hundreds of years.

Storm pushed past the tapestry and found a small door beyond. She leaned against it, trembling uncontrollably. Her legs were quaking so violently she sank to her knees. She had wished for her great-grandmother to be saved and the pipe had cured her! It wasn't just a silly trinket; the pipe really did have tremendous power. It had made even the wolves tremble! Storm finally understood her mother's warning, and why she must never let the pipe fall into Dr DeWilde's hands. She turned to Mother Collops, aghast. 'Why didn't you tell me what it could do? Why didn't you tell me just how powerful it could be?'

314

Mother Collops sighed. 'Oh, chick, because you have to work it out for yourself. That's the way it works.'

'But it is truly terrible,' whispered Storm, her voice still shaking. 'If it makes everything your heart desires come true, then you could use it rule the entire world.'

'I know,' said Mother Collops sadly, but then she brightened. 'But now you know its power, you'll be able to use it to rescue Any and Aurora quite easily.'

'Aurora? She's here!' Storm demanded sharply. 'Dr DeWilde has her too?'

She wanted to find out more, but before she could question her great-grandmother they heard running feet and angry shouts. It was time to get going.

Storm felt in her pocket for the key, slid it into the lock and turned it. The pair opened the door just wide enough to scuttle through, then Storm locked it again from the inside.

They were in a small library; the walls were lined with leather-bound books. Storm peered at the titles. There were hundreds of different volumes, but apart from a few reference books and a dictionary they only told one story. The entire library was devoted to versions of the tale of the Pied Piper.

At the opposite end of the room was an oak door, slightly ajar. Tiptoeing across to it, Storm peered through the gap into a simply furnished antechamber. Inside were two human guards, hunched over a table, playing cards. Beyond them was another door, this one magnificently worked with scenes of rats being devoured by wolves and, in its centre, a huge ornate carving of the Pied Piper dancing a merry jig.

Storm was wondering whether they could creep past the guards unnoticed when she felt Mother Collops' hand touch her arm. The old lady made a gesture for her to use the pipe. Storm shook her head. The pipe and its power terrified her now. Somehow she knew that it must be used sparingly and only when there was no alternative. She feared not just what the pipe could do to others but also what it could do to her. When she had blown it in the cavern and her heart's desire had come true, she had experienced a feeling she had never known before: she felt as if she was master of the universe. She had felt huge and completely invincible. It was a feeling to which it would be all too easy to become addicted, and Storm didn't entirely trust herself to be strong enough not to fall into that trap.

Now she knew its power and had experienced its seductive thrill, what was to stop her reaching for it in times of anger and greed as well as times of peril? Nothing. The thought made her feel panicky. She could use the pipe to get everything she wanted, any time she wanted it! But to do so would make her no better than Dr DeWilde, who wanted to bend the world to his will. The thought made her shiver.

Mother Collops was staring at her expectantly. Storm felt in her pocket and her fingers touched the potion bottle that Aurora had given her in the Ginger House. She removed her still-damp cardigan and sprinkled it carefully with the remaining drops from the phial, taking great care not to breathe in any of the fumes. Even so she felt deliciously light-headed. Cautiously, Storm pushed the door open a little further and, as quietly as she could, threw her cardigan towards the guards. It landed softly, a few metres from their backs. The two guards were so engrossed in their game that they didn't even look up.

Indicating to Mother Collops that she must hold her nose, and pinching her own, Storm peeped through the crack in the door. After a few moments one of the guards lifted his head and sniffed.

'What's that delightful smell?'

'I can't smell anything,' said his companion, yawning loudly. 'Come on, let's finish the game. I'm feeling tired.'

'It's lovely,' said the first guard sleepily. 'Sort of tangy vanilla overlaid with the scent of oranges and lemon rind.' He spied the cardigan lying on the floor and blinked. 'Here, mate, what's that?'

The second guard looked up. 'What's what?' he asked.

'Don't know, mate. Looks like a kid's cardigan.'

The second guard glared at the garment. 'What's it doing there?' he asked sharply.

'I don't know, do I? Someone must have dropped it, mustn't they?' said the first guard. He stretched languidly. 'Anyway, I don't care. I feel too sleepy to worry about it.'

'You ought to pick it up, though,' said his mate, yawning again. He sniffed the air. 'You know . . . I *can* smell something. It's quite delicious. Sort of tangy vanilla overlaid with the scent of oranges and lemon rind.'

'I told you,' said the first guard. Then he smiled as a cunning idea occurred to him. 'You pick the cardigan up,' he said.

'No, *you* pick it up. I'm too tired.'

'So am I,' said the first guard.

'Tell you what, let's pick it up together.'

'All right,' said the first guard. He paused. 'Nah, I can't be bothered.'

'Neither can I. I'm just going to have a little nap.' The second guard's eyelids flickered and drooped.

'So am I. Sweet dreams, mate,' said the first guard, and his chin dropped to his chest. Within moments the room was reverberating to the sound of their snoring.

Behind the door, Storm was also feeling pleasantly sleepy. She wondered if she could be bothered to walk all the way across the antechamber. Maybe she would just have a little nap herself . . . She felt her eyelids getting heavy when an image of Any floated into her brain. She shook herself violently and gave Mother Collops a prod. The old lady had fallen fast asleep where she stood.

Taking deep breaths and holding their noses, the pair tiptoed across the antechamber and past the sleeping guards to the ornate door at the end. Storm slowly opened it and stepped through, the pipe raised towards her mouth. As she passed the great carving it seemed as if the Pied Piper on the door was laughing at her. Then Storm's eyes fell on the beauty of the room beyond and she gasped in delight. Just before she felt a sharp pain to the back of her head.

19
AN IMPOSSIBLE CONTEST, A TRICKIER CHOICE

Storm emerged back into consciousness to find herself with a sore head and her hands tied behind her back. She was in a beautiful room, light and airy with a vaulted ceiling encrusted with precious gems that twinkled and danced in a brilliant rainbow of colour.

'Welcome to my parlour,' said Dr DeWilde lazily. 'I've been expecting you. I've been following your progress with intense interest since you left Hell Heights. In fact, I only just missed you there.' He gave a wolfish grin. 'I'm sorry to say that your great-grandmother seemed less than delighted to see me, so I decided to bring her here for a grand family reunion. Oh, I have been quite riveted by your adventures, Storm. A truly epic journey. Such courage, such pluck. I must say I've been quite impressed, although I did think you were a goner on the ice-field. My heart was in my mouth, I can tell you. As to the mineshaft and the secret tunnel! It is years since I've encountered such bravery, and it was so exceptionally helpful of you to survive – it saved me the bother of having to retrieve your body.' His smile was twisted and deformed.

Storm struggled to her feet and stared back at him stony faced. She was in shock. To have come all this way, to have survived so much, only to be beaten now – and so easily! She couldn't believe that all her efforts had been for nothing. All along, when she had thought that she and Aurora were defying the odds, he had been toying with them just as a cat plays with mice. Storm gritted her teeth. Well, she thought, he might have won, but she wasn't going to give him the satisfaction of knowing how much she cared.

'Now then, to business,' Dr DeWilde continued in a cold voice. 'I think that you have something I want, and I have something you have lost.' He grinned again. 'It's mighty clever of you, my dear, to have mislaid your entire family in such a very short space of time. Many struggle for years with far less impressive results.' He gave a little whistle. Two wolves appeared, pushing Any, Aurora and Mother Collops forward with their muzzles.

Inside, Storm felt destroyed, but she was determined not to show it. She ran to Any and covered her chubby face in kisses. She felt as if she could gobble her little sister up, such was the intensity of her feelings.

Any hugged her back, then looked deep into her eyes. 'What kept you?' she asked with her characteristic mixture of cheekiness and solemnity. Mother Collops patted Storm on both cheeks and shook her head sadly.

'He had guards behind the door, ducks. I knew it was a mistake not to use the pipe. But don't fret, chick, we're not finished, he hasn't won yet.'

Aurora hung back, a little adrift from the rest. She itched to throw her arms around Storm, but there was something about the way Storm ignored her that made her hesitate. Storm caught Aurora's expectant look and felt a confusing mess of emotion. She wanted to rush to her sister, but the image of the severed rope kept dancing in front of her eyes. Aurora had let her down badly.

Miserably, Storm turned her back, so she didn't see the look of hurt and puzzlement on Aurora's face. Any did, however, and she tugged at Storm's sleeve. 'Storm, you haven't kissed Aurora,' she said, and with one arm still around Storm she reached out to her other sister. 'Storm, Aurora has been so brave—'

The burning coal of resentment flared in the pit of Storm's stomach. 'Has she?' she cut in, in a clenched voice.

Pain and bewilderment were etched across Aurora's face as if a most terrible thought had occurred to her. 'Storm,' she whispered urgently, 'surely you don't think that I—'

'I don't want to hear your excuses,' Storm snapped, in a voice that even to her sounded as thin and spiteful as broken glass.

'But Storm . . .' protested Any tearfully.

'Just forget it for now,' said Storm. This much-longed-for meeting was not working out how she had imagined it at all. She saw Dr DeWilde staring

325

at them intently and sensed that he was enjoying a private joke, the punch line of which only he knew.

'Storm, listen to me!' cried Aurora desperately, but Dr DeWilde cut in.

'I don't want to spoil this delightful and deeply touching family reunion,' he said. 'But I'm afraid I must.' He turned to Storm. 'I asked you this once before, young lady. Rest assured this will be the final time. Hand over the pipe.'

Storm looked at him defiantly. 'If I do, will you let us all go?'

Dr DeWilde hooted with derisive laughter.

'I hardly think that you are in a position to bargain with me.' He indicated to a wolf to bite through Storm's bindings and held out his hand for the pipe.

Storm lifted it carefully from around her neck, the chain looped around her hand. The pipe seemed to dance in midair, catching the light, and Dr DeWilde reached out hungrily for it. He closed his hand around its length, and just as quickly dropped it again, shaking his fingers as if they'd been burned. Swearing angrily, he picked the pipe up and quickly blew into it. The sound that came out was thin and reedy and the skin around his mouth began to blister.

Dr DeWilde dropped the pipe and fell to the ground himself, clearly in tremendous pain. In the centre of his palm was a livid red representation of the pipe. It had branded him.

The pipe lay on the floor where it had fallen. Puzzled, Storm bent down and gingerly touched it. It felt perfectly cool. But before she could pick it up, a wolf stepped forward, teeth bared. Storm quickly drew back her hand.

Dr DeWilde was snarling with rage and pain on the floor. Mother Collops tapped her way over to Dr DeWilde and nudged his shoulder with her stick. 'Now then, duck,' she said. 'You know that isn't the way it works. You know you can't just take the pipe, Wolfie. It has to be given freely, and given with total and unconditional love. Otherwise it's quite useless. Just a piece of metal, nothing more. It's the love that makes it powerful. It's the love that makes it work.'

Storm's heart did a back flip. Given freely and with total love? Zella had given it to her. That meant that her mother must have loved her after all. Totally, with an unconditional love. Storm's eyes filled with tears, but inside she was smiling.

Down on the ground, Dr DeWilde gave another howl of rage and pain, then curled up

327

into a ball, whimpering.

'Silly boy,' said Mother Collops sternly. 'You always knew that was the way it worked. You knew when you gave the pipe to Zella—'

'To Zella!' Storm was shocked. 'He gave the pipe to our mother? That must mean that he . . . that he . . .' Storm's voice trailed off.

'Yes. He loved her,' said Mother Collops sadly. 'Right from when he was a boy and she was just a baby. It's what turned him so bad – her running off with your father like she did. Mind you, he always was a moody one, right from the time I brought him from the town orphanage to be my kitchen boy. Moody and unhappy. As if he didn't fit his own skin. I should never have given him the pipe or told him of its power in the first place, but he was such an unhappy little scrap of a thing, he seemed so powerless and frail, that I didn't see the harm in it and I thought it might help him.'

'So what happened?' asked Aurora wonderingly. 'With Zella and Wolf – I mean Dr DeWilde?'

Mother Collops sighed. 'Zella came into my care after my daughter died. Her father was a terrible gambler, you know. In the end he staked the only thing he had left – his own baby daughter. He lost, and he brought Zella to me and begged me to hide her away in the tall tower of Hell Heights where his creditors would never find her. He had to salvage some pride though, so he started a rumour that I was an ogress who had claimed Zella from him as a promised child and that I was keeping her imprisoned in a tower. People in the village had always been wary of me, but that was when they really started to turn against me. I think even Zella believed the story. I never had the heart to tell her the real truth about her dad.'

Mother Collops smiled at Aurora. 'Your mother was an exquisite child who grew into a beautiful young woman: white skin, red mouth, raven hair. And with a throaty laugh like diamonds in a drain. And her smell!' She closed her eyes as if remembering.

'Like caramel pineapple crossed with night-scented stocks!' chorused Storm and Aurora together.

'Yes,' agreed Mother Collops delightedly. 'With undertones of cherry tart and hot buttered toast, I always thought.' She blew her nose loudly. 'Of course, she was lazier than a three-toed sloth. But I suppose that comes of growing up in a tower with very few opportunities for exercise. Wolfie used to follow her around, fetching and carrying. He adored her. But I knew she'd never look twice at him.' Mother Collops gave the figure on the floor a pitying look. 'When your father arrived on the scene, Wolfie was wild with jealousy. And when they ran off together, love turned to rage and spite. That's when he started going into the forests and the mountains. He did make one more effort to win Zella though. He stole my invitation to Aurora's christening and went disguised in my place. He failed, of course. And there was a terrible scene.' Mother Collops sighed again. 'After that he spent more and more time in the forests and mountains, and every time he came back he was a little more tipsy on his own power, a little more twisted. I guessed what he might be up to – I knew the legends surrounding Piper's Peak as well as anyone. But it wasn't until I found the map and key under the mattress in his room that my worst fears were realized. It's in his blood, you see. He belongs in the barren mountains and the dark forest, not our sunlit world. It is in his nature to seek power and exterminate things.'

'Who was his father?' asked Storm in a small voice.

'Nobody knows for certain, but on the night he was found abandoned on the orphanage steps, wolves were seen running through the streets, led by a large grey beast who held a baby wrapped in a nettle blanket in his mouth. When the orphanage matron took the bundle in, at first she thought that it was a wolf cub. It was only when she unwrapped the nettle blanket and lifted up the little scrap of a thing that she realized it was a baby boy.' Mother Collops leaned heavily on her stick. 'I think the orphanage was the closest place to a home he ever found. I know he always blamed me for taking him away. But, despite everything that's happened, I still pity him.'

'I don't want your pity,' snarled Dr DeWilde. He rose to his feet. 'But I *do* want that pipe – and I know how to get it.' He cradled his injured hand to his chest, but his look was triumphant. 'There is another way. Your pretty little story reminded me.'

Mother Collops looked stricken. 'Me and my big mouth,' she mumbled, a hand clasped across her face.

'Too late,' the doctor crowed. 'Now tell them what I mean.' It was an order, not a request.

Mother Collops' shoulders drooped. 'There are only two ways that the pipe can be passed from one person to another,' she said hesitantly. 'Either it must be freely given in total, unconditional love or it can be' – her voice trailed to a whisper – 'won.'

331

'Won?' said Storm sharply.

'Yes, won in a wager,' said Dr DeWilde with an evil smile and a flash of sharp, white teeth. 'Either in a fight or a game. Which is what we'll be playing. A game. Winner takes all: the pipe and your sisters.'

'And Mother Collops,' added Storm sharply.

'Oh,' said Dr DeWilde lazily, 'I'll throw the old hag in too – *if* you win.' He chuckled. 'Which you won't.' He gave Storm a nasty look. 'Choose your game.'

'Poker,' said Storm confidently.

Dr DeWilde eyed her with stony amusement. 'You're prepared to lose your sisters at cards?'

'I'll take my chance,' said Storm, trying to sound completely assured.

'Oh, there is nothing quite so depressing as boundless optimism,' murmured Dr DeWilde. 'Remember – these are high stakes.'

'The highest,' said Storm, meeting his gaze and holding it.

'Well,' said Dr DeWilde, 'since you want to play poker, I think we'll choose something else.' His expression turned sly. 'Since I hold all the advantages here, I'm going to choose the game after all. And the game I'm going to choose is . . .

spelling. We'll have a spelling contest.'

Storm's insides turned to water.

'I won't do spelling. I can't do spelling. I refuse,' Storm stormed.

Dr DeWilde raised an eyebrow.

'You'll regret it.' He gave a little whistle and a wolf moved closer to Any and, with a snarl, bared its teeth. Storm stared at the doctor, aghast. She knew that he had her trapped. She felt as desperate as an animal backed against a wall. She saw the others' shocked, frightened faces. It was up to her to save them. She took a deep breath. 'All right,' she said sulkily. 'We'll do spelling.'

Dr DeWilde clicked his fingers and Alderman Snufflebottom stepped into the room with a dictionary. 'Since I'm a fair and honest man,' he drawled, 'we'll have the alderman and the hag check the dictionary to make sure that there is no cheating.'

Storm felt sick: she knew that she was going to let everyone down. How had it come to this?

The doctor ignored her stricken face. 'Let's begin,' he said, in a voice tight with excitement. 'First to five wins – and if we're both even at that point, it's' – he paused for effect – 'sudden death!' Aurora gave a little mewl of despair and Any covered her face with her hands. 'And I have just the word to start with . . . Spell Chihuahua.'

Storm smiled. That was easy. She had always wanted a pet dog and had spent hours studying dog breeds.

'C–H–I–H–U–A–H–U–A,' she spelled triumphantly. The doctor's face fell.

'My turn,' said Storm. And she tried to think of the longest word she'd ever heard. 'Discombobulated,' she challenged.

But Dr DeWilde reeled the letters off as if it was a word he used every day. Then, 'Spell broccoli,' he spat.

Storm hesitated. 'B–R–O–C . . . O . . . no, that's wrong,' she said, correcting herself. 'B–R–O–C–C–O–L–I.' Aurora and Any breathed huge sighs of relief as Storm racked her brains for a more difficult word. 'Lycanthropy,' she said finally, not really sure what it meant.

The doctor shot her an odd, twisted look, then spelled it perfectly.

He considered her coolly. 'Phosphorescence.'

'I can spell that,' said Mother Collops excitedly.

'Yes, but you don't have to,' said Storm tensely, 'I do.' And she reeled off the letters like an express train with her eyes tight shut. Aurora, Any and

Mother Collops clapped loudly. Fury flashed across Dr DeWilde's face as Storm cast around for another word.

'Coccyx,' she said triumphantly.

Mother Collops looked puzzled. 'What's that?'

'Tailbone,' said Any.

'How do you know that?' Aurora asked admiringly.

'Oh, I've been reading that dictionary while we've been locked up here,' said Any airily. 'Although it's taking much longer than *Astrophysics for Beginners* and *Trepanning for the Moderately Gifted* took me. I'm only up to D. At this rate I'll be ancient – maybe even three – by the time I get to zymurgy.'

'Zymurgy?' asked Mother Collops.

'It's the chemical process for brewing,' said Any. 'And it's the very last word in the dictionary.'

'What's the first?' asked Mother Collops.

'A, of course,' laughed Any. 'Are you completely dumb?'

'No, I'm partially blind,' chuckled Mother Collops.

'Oh, do shut up,' said Dr DeWilde menacingly. 'Or I'll rip both your tongues out and have them for my tea. You're deliberately trying to put me off.' He shut his eyes and thought hard.

'C-O-C-C-I . . . No, that's wrong. It's a Y. C-O-C-C-Y-X!'

Only Alderman Snufflebottom clapped politely.

Dr DeWilde considered Storm through narrowed eyes. 'Spell blancmange,' he challenged.

Storm's heart raced. She ought to know this one. She dimly recalled that Aurora had told her it quite recently. If she could only remember when, she might recall how to spell it. But she couldn't think straight.

'B-L-A-N-C . . .' She paused and looked around. Aurora had her eyes screwed tightly up and Any had her head in her hands. 'H-M-A-N-G-E.'

There was a bubble of silence and then Dr DeWilde shouted in delight. 'Wrong! You've got it wrong! There's no H in blancmange!'

Storm couldn't bear to look at the others. If Dr DeWilde spelled his next word correctly, he would win.

bleu mang

'Don't worry, Storm. He's going to get his next word wrong,' said Any confidently.

Storm's mind was whirling. She couldn't think of a single word, let alone a hard one. But then she had an idea. 'Diarrhoea,' she said.

Dr DeWilde looked nervous. He thought hard.

'D-I-A-R-R-H-O . . .' He didn't look too sure of himself. 'E . . . no that's wrong.' He pressed his knuckles against his head. 'No it's not. It's right. D-I-A-R-R-H-O-E-A,' he spat with a triumphant little snarl.

Alderman Snufflebottom cleared his throat. 'I declare Dr DeWilde the winner. Three cheers for Dr DeWilde. Hip, hip . . .' Nobody joined in.

Any ran and hugged Storm's legs.

'You did your best, Storm,' said Mother Collops soothingly.

'Yes,' said Storm bitterly. 'But my best wasn't good enough, was it?'

Aurora moved towards her.

'I suppose you're going to tell me that I should have paid more attention for all those years in spelling lessons. That a failure to prepare is preparing to fail.' Storm scowled.

blanchmanche
blahma

'No, Storm, of course not, sweetie,' said Aurora, looking deeply hurt. 'You were amazing. I know that you don't find spelling easy.'

'About as easy as you find holding ropes,' whispered Storm viciously.

'Storm, you must let me explain!' cried Aurora. But it was too late. Dr DeWilde was upon them.

'Give me the pipe, Storm Eden.'

Watched closely by the wolf, Storm bent to retrieve the pipe and dropped the tiny instrument into the doctor's outstretched palm. This time it didn't scald him. He nodded at the wolves. 'Take Mother Collops back to the workers' pens and take Any and Aurora into the garden. I am going to have a talk with this young lady.'

Two wolves harried Aurora and Any through an arched doorway that led into an exquisite rose garden right in the heart of the mountain. Beyond the roses, a pair of intricate wrought-iron gates gave way to the rugged mountainside.

'Storm,' whispered Mother Collops urgently under her breath, 'whatever he offers you, don't trust him. Even if you had won the game, he would not have kept his promise to set us free. Believe me, he can lie the blue right out of the sky.'

'I'm not a fool,' said Storm irritably.

'I know you're not,' said Mother Collops, looking anxiously around. 'But I'm not sure you realize how much you and your family have humiliated him. First Zella, when she wouldn't return his love, then you when you outwitted him and escaped from the Ginger House. He will never, ever forgive you, and he will prey on any weaknesses you display. Beware!' A wolf nudged Mother Collops' bottom and snarled, indicating that she should leave.

Dr DeWilde beckoned Storm to sit. For a moment there was a charged silence between them and then he spoke.

'I like you, Storm Eden. I like your spirit. I like it a lot. So, after careful consideration, I am going to let you go. On the understanding, of course, that you do nothing further to bother me. Although now I have the pipe, I am, you understand, quite invincible. Opposition would be futile. If you make any attempt to thwart me, in any way, I will crush you.'

Storm lifted her head and looked at him, dazed. 'You're going to let me go?' she whispered, amazed.

'Yes,' said Dr DeWilde in a soft velvety voice, 'and what's more, I'm going to throw in one of your sisters too.'

Storm's face lit up, and then just as quickly her smile collapsed. 'Only one sister?'

'Come, come, my dear. I'm not stupid. I need the other one and your great-grandmother as my insurance policy. Just to make sure you don't try stirring up trouble.'

Storm felt a cold knife of knowledge cut through her heart as she began to understand the choice that Dr DeWilde was asking her to make. Her tongue felt as if it had tied itself into a reef knot inside her mouth. A small smile played around the corners of Dr DeWilde's lips and his eyes appraised her as if she was a particularly interesting specimen that he was examining under a microscope. At last Storm found her voice.

'You want me to choose between my own sisters?'

'Their futures are entirely in your hands.'

'You're asking me to decide which of them will go free and which of them will be doomed to stay here in Piper's Peak for ever?'

'Precisely,' said Dr DeWilde with another devilish smile. 'I am impressed. You have grasped the situation remarkably quickly.'

Storm's eyes smouldered with hate and rage. 'Have you no pity?'

Dr DeWilde laughed, a desolate sound.

'None at all, I'm afraid. My emotional range is limited: greed, boredom, revenge . . . that's about it.' With an exaggerated gesture he patted the left-hand side of his chest as if looking for something he had lost. 'No, I'm sorry. I just can't seem to feel any pity. All I feel is mild indifference.'

'What you're asking me to do is barbaric. I won't do it. I refuse to choose. You can't make me.'

'Oh, I think I can,' said Dr DeWilde evenly. 'If you *won't* choose, you condemn your entire family, not just yourself. Any is so small, the little poppet. It would be a crime to have to put her in the wheel. The thought makes me feel quite tearful. So I think you had better choose. I have you all in my power; in the circumstances I am quite astonished by my own benevolence. Make up your mind quickly, before I change mine and have you all thrown to the wolves.'

Storm walked over to the window. Outside Aurora and Any sat side by side, their heads bent close together.

Sensing they were being watched, the girls looked up. Any gave an expectant little smile. Aurora's worried eyes briefly met Storm's. Storm's

341

heart lurched. She felt nauseous. Her eyes were blind with tears.

'Have you made your choice?'

'I can't.'

'You must. I ask you for the final time, have you decided?'

Numbly, Storm nodded.

'Then listen carefully. This is what you will do. Any deviation and you will regret it for the rest of your extremely short life. You will go into the garden and you will kiss on the cheek the sister that you have decided to sacrifice.'

Storm's eyes flashed with anger. 'This is an outrage,' she stuttered.

'Yes, it is, isn't it,' smiled Dr DeWilde pleasantly. 'I just want everyone involved to be clear who is the betrayed and who is the betrayer. I always think the kiss on the cheek sends an unmistakable signal.'

'Kill me. Kill me instead,' pleaded Storm.

'Oh, my dear, that would be too easy,' said Dr DeWilde. He leaned forward and hissed in her ear, 'I want you to suffer. I want you to live with what you've done every day and every minute for the rest of your life.'

The doctor led Storm into the garden, where

the wrought-iron gates onto the mountainside beyond were slowly swinging open. Tears misted Storm's eyes so she could hardly see. She stumbled and would have fallen if Dr DeWilde had not held her arm in a vicious grip. Aurora and Any rose to meet them. A few metres from the sisters, Dr DeWilde pushed Storm forward, murmuring, 'You know what you have to do.' Storm stumbled and Aurora put out her hands to support her.

'Don't! Don't touch me,' cried Storm, recoiling from Aurora as if her sister's fingers were red-hot pokers. Aurora took a step backwards, puzzled and frightened. Storm looked into the chaos of her sister's face. For a moment it was as if time stood still, as what had been, what might have been and what would be became distilled in the essence of a single moment. Without speaking the two sisters looked deep into each other's eyes and read what was written there. Aurora suddenly stiffened as she understood exactly what Storm's desperate, beseeching silence was telling her. Then she smiled gently at Storm, with a look that Storm couldn't quite work out – not pity, but compassion – on her beautiful face.

'It's all right, Storm,' she said, gently placing her hand on her sister's shoulder. 'I understand.

343

You had no choice.' Storm's eyes blurred with fresh tears. She stood on tiptoe and planted a whisper of a kiss on Aurora's cheek. Aurora didn't flinch. She simply closed her eyes, tears glistening like tiny, fragile stars on her thick lashes.

'Love you, Storm. Love you, Any,' she murmured. 'Go now, lovelies, while you still can,' and she turned her back on Storm and Any and walked towards Dr DeWilde, who took her hand proprietorially in his. Storm took Any's hand tightly in her own and began pulling her towards the gates. Baffled and scared by her sisters' tears, Any tried to pull away.

'What's going on, Storm? Why are we leaving Aurora behind?' She planted her sturdy little feet in the ground and refused to budge. 'I'm not going anywhere, Storm, until you tell me what's happening.'

Storm could see the open gates beginning to close. Beyond them she could see the mountain. She could smell freedom. She had to get herself and Any through those gates before it was too late. She scooped Any up in her arms. Any responded by nipping Storm on the cheek. Storm dropped her with a yelp.

Any looked at her with stony eyes. 'The kiss.

It was some kind of a signal, wasn't it?'

'Yes.'

'Well, I'm not coming. I am not leaving Aurora. How could you even think I would, Storm?' asked Any in an outraged voice. 'Have you forgotten? For ever and together.'

'I had no choice,' screamed Storm. 'He made me.' Out of the corner of her eye Storm could see the gates swinging shut. Another few seconds and they would close, trapping them all inside Piper's Peak for ever. She began to run towards the gates, her legs feeling like sludge, her brain turned to mush.

'Of course you had a choice,' Any screamed after her. 'You could have chosen to stay with us, to face whatever was thrown at us, even if it was the very worst. Better that than betraying your own sister!'

Storm felt Any's critical words like tiny pinpricks all over her skin. It was so unfair. After everything she had been through, after everything she had suffered to try and save Any. She felt furious that Any was choosing Aurora over her. Aurora, whom she still loved, but who had deliberately left her to die. Who had betrayed her. Still running for the gates, Storm yelled back, 'She betrayed me, she cut the rope to save her own skin, and look what good it did her.' She slipped through the wrought-iron gates just before they clanged shut. Then she crouched on her knees, trying to catch her breath and calm the roaring in her head.

Storm heard footsteps behind her and then a little voice from the other side of the closed gates said very coldly, 'She didn't betray you, Storm. She didn't cut the rope. Dr DeWilde did. Aurora was desperate about it. She tried to tell you what happened. But you wouldn't listen.'

Storm spun round, her face a spasm of shock and utter despair. Any gave her a look of terrible pity, and then, clutching her blanket, she toddled back towards Aurora and Dr DeWilde. Storm stared into his face. His cruel smile was the very last thing she saw as, with a great creaking of thunder, the mountain closed itself up before her eyes. Crying, she threw herself against the hard rock again and again until her body was bruised and battered. The rock did not yield.

Storm had never felt such despair. She had set out to save one sister and in the process she had lost them both. And even if she could find some way back into the mountain, she knew they would never forgive her now. Hot tears ravaged her face as she realized that she had played right into Dr DeWilde's hands: he had the pipe, Aurora and Any, and she had nothing. Nothing at all. She was an outcast to her own sisters. Storm's legs and heart turned to lead as the creeping exhaustion of the defeated enveloped her.

20
LiTTLe ReD FiREWork MaKER

The gates at the end of the drive to Eden End were wide open. Storm stood at the entrance as if turned to stone. A very battered Ted Bear hung limply from one of her hands. She had been standing in the same position for at least twenty minutes. She longed to rush towards the familiar old house, but she felt paralysed, as if she had forfeited the right to call Eden End home. Despite the wide-open gates it felt as if the way forward was barred to her. She stared at the ramshackle house with its lopsided chimneys and winking windows that rose up out of the ravelling morning mist. It was all silence, as if the house was waiting to be awoken from a long, deep sleep. A silver-grey hare streaked across the park, leaving a visible path towards the house in the dew-drenched lawn.

Storm hardly knew how she had made her way this far. She could remember almost nothing of the journey from Piper's Peak. She had scrambled and clambered her way blindly across the mountains, taking no care for her safety whatsoever, just wanting to get as far away as she could from the scene of her betrayal of Aurora. She had wanted to die more than to live. As she had passed the disused mineshaft she had stopped and rummaged in her abandoned rucksack for Ted Bear, but she had taken nothing else to help her on her journey. It was a miracle that she had survived it, yet Storm felt that that in itself was a punishment. She was consumed with regret. Every waking moment was scorched with the image of Any's pitying face and

Aurora's sad one, and her fitful sleep was troubled
by terrible dreams that echoed with Dr DeWilde's
sneering laugh and the howl of hungry wolves.

And yet somehow, here she was – so close to
home, but unable to enter the grounds. Storm
was about to turn away when Desdemona came
hurrying down the driveway, clucking self-
importantly, followed by Tabitha and her latest
litter. Storm sighed deeply and moved leaden-footed
up the path to greet them. Clucking and mewling,
this odd menagerie urged her towards the house,
like sheep dogs attempting to round up a lost
sheep.

At the front door they stopped, apparently
waiting to see what she would do. Desdemona
sat down firmly on one of Storm's feet and Tabitha
on the other, as if to prevent her from turning
and running. The cat reminded Storm of Netta's.
She felt sick at the thought. She had betrayed
everybody's faith in her: her mother's, Netta's and
most of all Any and Aurora's. She felt completely
worthless.

She stared at the front door. The children had
not been away from Eden End for long, but in
that brief time the old creeper that covered the
walls of the house had slithered its way across the

entrance, and the rambling roses had rambled through the knocker and meandered across the door, their thorns making a vicious necklace around the handle. The downstairs windows of the old house were completely covered with creeper too, and huge stinging nettles had sprung up all around the edge of the building and in the cracks in the steps leading to the front door, as if providing a natural barrier to unwanted visitors or intruders. For a split second, Storm imagined Aurora pursing her lips at this invasion of the wild; her sister would quickly set about taming and tidying unruly nature, cutting back the creeper and pinning the roses to the trellis. The thought of Aurora made her feel faint again.

She walked up to the door, oblivious of the nettles attacking her bare legs, and laid her hand upon the handle, not flinching as the thorns tore at her flesh and tiny pinpricks of blood erupted across her palm. She opened the door and walked into the hall. Even from here she could see the violence that Dr DeWilde had inflicted on the poor old house in his search for the pipe. Furniture was upturned and trampled, and drawers had been emptied out, so that paper lay like banks of huge snowflakes across the floor. Ghost-like, she wandered into the kitchen. It too had been turned upside-down, pots and pans higgledy-piggledy all over the floor, the kitchen table and chairs hacked about in a frenzy of rage and destruction. She picked up a single crumpled sheet of paper. It was Aurora's recipe for madeleines. It could not have hurt Storm more if it had been a dagger.

She wandered through the silent house, followed at a respectful distance by the posse of watchful animals. She carried Any and Aurora's absence with her in her bones. Every room was full of whispered sadness; every mirror mocked her with her reflected solo image; the bedrooms, kitchen, library and drawing room all screamed their reproaches. She found traces of her sisters everywhere, and jagged memory crowded upon jagged memory. In the kitchen she thought of Any laughing as Storm made Aurora toss marsh-mallows up in the air so that she and Any could catch them in their mouths like sea lions. Aurora had pretended to disapprove, but really she had enjoyed the game as much as the others. In the library Storm stumbled across the old dressing-up box and the billiard table, now broken and collapsed, that one afternoon she had persuaded Aurora and Any to pretend was a boat. The three of them had spent a happy few hours atop it, with Storm dressed as the ship's captain, imagining that they were intrepid explorers sailing around the world pursued by cut-throat pirates and a giant squid with nine tentacles.

Upstairs she remembered how Any would clap her hands when Storm slid down the banisters and how Aurora would shout how dangerous it was and that Storm was irresponsible, although there had been a curl at both corners of her mouth even as she protested. She also recalled Aurora's shocked face when she had walked into the house one afternoon to find Storm and Any tobogganing down the stairs on an old tea tray with a broken handle. Aurora had been furious, but after much coaxing she had been persuaded to try it herself on the lower stairs and had sped down pink-cheeked and laughing, although afterwards she had said breathlessly that one go was quite enough to last her a whole lifetime. At last Storm wended her way up the 147½ steps of the nursery turret to the girls' empty bedrooms. There in the corner of Any's room stood her little cot, still intact. Storm leaned over and carefully placed poor, worn Ted Bear in the cot, and pulled up one of the sheets and nuzzled it. She could smell her sister's warm, sweet honeysuckle smell. As she dropped the sheet a tiny silver star fell out. Storm gave a dry sob and rushed out of the room and down the stairs.

She ran along the polished gallery floor towards the room that had been her parents', and skidded to a halt as she encountered a small mountain of trampled, tangled sheets and towels all over the gallery floor. They were ripped and dirty. Storm pulled open the door to Aurora's beloved linen cupboard. It had been wrenched apart: torn sheets were wrapped around splintered wood in wanton destruction. Dr DeWilde had brought his full fury to bear upon the cupboard and its contents. It was too much. Her knees buckled, she fell to the floor of the linen cupboard and, clutching a heavily darned Irish cotton pillowcase, she sobbed until she had no tears left. She lay slumped on the floor, staring sightlessly and hiccupping quietly. She had never known before that it was possible to feel quite this lonely and quite this miserable. She couldn't think of any reason why she should ever stand up again. It wasn't worth the bother: she was completely without hope. Gradually her hiccups subsided and she fell into a listless doze.

She was roused by the creak of the great oak

front door and a soft voice calling, 'Hello? Is there anybody there?'

Storm drew back into the linen cupboard. 'Storm! Are you here?'

She blinked. Who knew that she was here at Eden End? Who could be calling her name? Cautiously she crawled along the gallery floor and peered through the struts of the balustrade. She caught a glimpse of the face of the most beautiful boy she had ever seen. He was a few years older than her, and he looked like an angel. A very thin angel. Despite the bitter weather he was wearing only a grey jerkin over soft brown trousers and, beneath it, Storm could see his alabaster skin and his ribs rising and falling with every breath. He caught sight of her tear-wrecked face and smiled, full of concern. It was a smile so dazzling it was as if it had been polished to a shine. Blinded, Storm smiled uncertainly back; then she realized that this was a stranger in her house and stood up indignantly.

'Who are you and what are you doing in my house?' she demanded.

'I'm a friend, offering you a helping hand,' he said. His voice had a seductive country burr touched with a beguiling hint of melancholy. Storm knew that she had heard it somewhere before.

'I don't need a friend or a helping hand,' she said, and she marched down the stairs, walked pointedly to the door and held it open for him.

The boy laughed again. He moved closer to her. 'I've a message for you.'

Storm stared at him. Her heart was racing. He smiled again, and as she basked in its warm glow she saw with a start that his eyes were different colours: one as green as emerald; the other an icy blue. She blinked. She was sure she'd seen those eyes somewhere before, but his smile was so dazzling that she was finding it hard to think straight.

Storm shook her head to clear it. 'How do you know who I am?' she asked coolly.

The boy leaned very close to her. 'You're lost, like me.'

'How do you know?'

'I can read it behind your eyes,' he said.

Storm laughed, a tiny tinkle of derision. 'A lie, told quite beautifully. You'll have to do better than that.' She drew herself up to her full height, pulled the door wider and indicated he should leave.

'Wait,' called the boy urgently, a note of panic rising in his soft voice. 'I do have a message.' Storm stared at him. He suddenly seemed desperately young and vulnerable. There was a shadow of fear in his mismatched eyes.

'Well, spit it out, then,' she said.

The boy opened his hand and brought it up towards her face. Storm stared at the handkerchief in his grip. The ornately embroidered 'A' in the corner was unmistakable. The handkerchief belonged to Aurora.

'How did you get that?'

'Your sister gave it to me. She needs your help.'

Storm's breathing quickened. 'Why does she need my help?' she whispered.

The boy's breath was hot in her ear. 'She is to be married tomorrow night. To Dr DeWilde. Only you can prevent it.' The boy's icy-blue eye burned bright.

'Married? To him! But she can't!' cried Storm.

'He's forcing her. She has no choice. If she refuses, the consequences for her will be terrible. And for Any, too.'

Storm's brain slowly started to click and whir. 'Where is this marriage taking place?'

'In Piper's Town. The ceremony is to be quite sumptuous. They have already put up the bunting and there is to be a huge firework display.

Catherine wheels, foaming fountains of fire, gigantic rockets to light up the sky. Dr DeWilde has ordered a public holiday. And the next day, he is to be made honorary mayor and given the keys to the town, although he rules the roost in any case.' A flush rose across the boy's ravishing cheek. 'It will be quite a festival, two days of celebration.'

Storm shivered, not with cold but with excitement. 'Do you know if Any will be there too?' she asked urgently.

The boy nodded. 'She is to be a bridesmaid,' he said, smiling his gleaming smile.

Storm felt its radiance as much as she saw it. She clutched at the boy's sleeve. 'Did Aurora ask for my help?'

'Of course,' said the boy comfortingly, laying his warm hand on top of Storm's own. 'She knows that only you – her sister – can save her.'

Storm felt as if a tiny flame had been re-kindled inside her, as if she was springing back into life after a long hibernation. Aurora *needed* her, and if Aurora needed her it meant that Aurora must have forgiven her! She felt dizzy with excitement.

Her brain whirred even faster. 'You say there are to be fireworks?'

'Well . . . there's supposed to be. But I heard

that the firework maker has fallen sick. When I left town they were putting up posters everywhere advertising for a firework maker capable of organizing a grand display – the biggest ever seen. Bee Bumble and Alderman Snufflebottom at the Ginger House are in charge of finding someone else who can do the job.'

A gleam crept into Storm's eyes and she looked thoughtful. 'What time is this wedding?' she asked.

'As darkness falls. Six o'clock,' said the boy. He looked her deep in the eye. 'I'll help you rescue her,' he promised. 'I'll meet you at the southern corner of the square, at five-thirty. I know one of the Piper's police: he is my uncle, he'll let us through. We'll be able to get right up to the platform where the ceremony is taking place.'

'And how exactly are we supposed to free Aurora and Any?' asked Storm impatiently.

The boy looked earnestly at her, his blue eye glittering. 'I'll leave you to come up with a plan. Aurora said that you are clever and brave, that she trusts you to know what to do. She has every confidence in you.' Storm felt the tiniest swell of pride.

At that moment the landing clock with its carved wooden figures and calendar began to strike the hour. The clock face only had one and a half hands, and the elaborately decorated carved figures had long ago lost their heads but they still moved jerkily in their prescribed hourly dance below the face of the clock. Storm looked upwards, and as she did so the clock struck the final chime of the hour and one of the little figures pointed to the calendar. Storm stared at the date and felt a shock along her spine, as if somebody had run their fingertips lightly down her back. Tomorrow would be Aurora's sixteenth birthday.

She remembered the christening curse that Aurora had told her about. How she was doomed to prick her finger on her sixteenth birthday and fall into a sleep from which she would never awaken. Aurora was in double danger! She must go to her. She must save her.

A little cry rose in Storm's throat. Tears and hopelessness all forgotten, a new determination fired her. She would put the past behind her and do everything she could to save her sister. If Aurora had had the extraordinary generosity to forgive her, then the least she could do was to prove to Aurora how much she loved her, and how bitterly she regretted leaving her in Dr DeWilde's clutches. And if she died in the attempt, so be it. At least

Aurora and Any would know that she had tried to make it up to them and undo the terrible damage she had done. 'All right,' she said. 'I'll meet you tomorrow at the south end of the market square.'

The boy nodded, something sad in his smile, and, with a bow, slipped quickly away through the door. Storm watched him go, his shoulders slumped as if in defeat as he started to dissolve into the mist. Then her heart skipped a beat. She remembered now when she'd seen him before – he was the boy she'd met in Piper's Town on the day she'd first seen Dr DeWilde! And with the return of that memory several things clicked into place. She was suddenly sure that it had been his glittering emerald eye that she'd seen in the darkness of the liquorice pipe in the Ginger House – and his warning that had stopped her from eating the food. And he must have been the boy who had broken the enchantment binding Aurora to Bee Bumble. Kit, Aurora had said his name was – in a voice that had quivered as though she was speaking the most beautiful name in all the languages of the world.

Well, Storm thought grudgingly, he is beautiful. But dangerous too. For she was now almost certain that it had been Kit who had tried to steal the pipe from Eden End, and that he was the one who had convinced her of Aurora's betrayal at the well. Storm frowned. She wondered how her mind could have been so sleepy. But then, there was something about Kit's smile that made it easy to forget things.

Storm leaned against the door-frame, thinking hard. What was he up to? Was he helping her this time? Or was he telling more lies? There was something as odd about Kit's behaviour as there was about his beautiful mismatched eyes: it was as if the good and the bad in his nature were in constant struggle with each other. Could he be trusted? Believing that he really had come as a messenger from Aurora was a risky strategy, but she had no choice but to do so. She couldn't risk it not being true.

Whirling, Storm ran into the library, delved into the dressing-up box and pulled out a long red hooded cloak. She put it on and took a good look at herself in the mirror. With the cowl shadowing her face she barely recognized herself, and she was sure it was a good enough disguise to get her through Piper's Town unnoticed. Satisfied, she hurried to her room to get some ingredients and several timing switches from her old wooden firework box. Then, with barely a backward glance, she flew down the driveway and headed for town.

Back at the house Desdemona shooed the kittens outside and Tabitha nosed the front door shut before leaping out of an open first-floor window to join them. For a moment it seemed as if the whole building shuddered and sighed before settling back into a deep sleep.

Storm slipped like a wraith through the shadows of Piper's Town. Chilly fingers of fog crept up the narrow cobbled streets from the oily river below and curled around her head like the wispy branches of trees in a wood. It was bitterly cold. The fog wrapped its clammy arms around her as she moved silently down Shroud Alley, across Butchery Lane, past Angel Court, where the squat derelict houses leaned against each other like drunken dwarves, and into Cripplefields. A wolf howled nearby. Storm shivered, gathering the hooded red cloak around her more tightly, and set off quickly through a dense forest of streets into DeVille's Gap, passing through Bedlam Yard into Bleeding Heart Mews and cutting down Drowned Man's Alley. She hesitated for a moment, sensing that some-body was following her. She listened hard, but could hear nothing except the icy, melancholic howl of a wolf, somewhere to the east.

She walked down Black Crow Passage into Cutpurse Alley, eyes peeled for anything that might leap out of the shadows and catch her unawares. As she moved, she thought she caught the sound of something moving too. She stopped suddenly. Whoever was following her stopped too, but not quickly enough. In the hush, Storm heard the shift of a foot on the cobbles. She hurried onwards in the velvet darkness of Crooked Lane, and it was with some relief that she caught the spicy whiff of cinnamon and toffee mixed with ginger and cran-berries that indicated that she was close to the Ginger House. She sniffed the air. The smell was much less pungent than when she'd last been there, as if a vestige just lingered in the air. She turned the corner and the orphanage with its spun-sugar towers stood in front of her. After everything that had happened at the Ginger House, the thought of entering the orphanage again was repugnant to her. But it had to be done. Storm took a deep breath, opened the gate in the picket fence, walked up the Ginger House steps and knocked on the door.

After a few moments, the door opened a crack and a dishevelled-looking Bee Bumble peered out.

'Who are you, and what do you want?' she snapped suspiciously.

'I've come about the advertisement,' said Storm, keeping the hood covering her face and holding out a tattered piece of paper that she had torn down from a wall. It read:

Required Urgently

Experienced Firework-Maker capable of making Grand Wedding Go with a Bang

Must be able to create show-stopping and unrivalled pyromania display. Excellent timing a pre-requisite. No time-wasters please. No convicted arsonists. Previous applicants need not apply. All materials supplied.

Apply: THE GINGER HOUSE, PIPER'S TOWN

'It says experienced,' said Bee Bumble sourly. 'You don't look nearly big enough to have the level of expertise required.'

'My name is Jill and I am a very experienced firework maker,' said Storm, and from out of her pocket she produced several firecrackers and flung them onto the cobbles; with a crack and a bang, several glittering silver and blue dragons chased each other down the street. She pulled out two sparklers, handed one to Bee Bumble, lit them both and the air was filled with huge fizzing golden, green and crimson sparks that formed themselves into intricate patterns, including the national flags of several minor countries.

'I can make them into everlasting sparklers, if required,' said Storm with a little bow.

'Well, Jill, you look far too small and underfed to be able to do anything properly, but you seem to know your stuff,' said Bee Bumble grudgingly. 'You had better come in.' Storm followed her into the hall of the Ginger House. There was no sign of any children.

'Didn't this place use to be an orphanage?' Storm asked with exaggerated casualness.

There was a little pause.

'It did,' said Bee Bumble tightly. 'But some

claimed that there were security problems and it was closed down. Quite unnecessarily, in my view.'

'What happened to the children?' asked Storm.

'Oh, they were all sent on elsewhere,' said Mrs Bumble evasively, and she pushed open the dining-room door. The tables had all disappeared. Only a dusting of icing sugar clung to the toffee walls. Suddenly Bee Bumble's manner changed. Her sour face was replaced by a sweet one; her hard voice became soft and wheedling.

'Oh, my little Snuffy Bottom, we have an applicant for the job of firework maker for Dr DeWilde's wedding.'

Alderman Snufflebottom was lying sleepily on an old chaise longue. He gave a cursory glance at Storm, who kept her face well-hidden under the red hood. 'She's just a child. She won't have the experience.'

'I know she looks small, my little Snuffy Bottom,' gushed Bee, and she popped a cheese straw into the alderman's mouth, 'but I've seen what she can do. And it's not as if we've been inundated with applicants, is it? The last one had an allergy to gunpowder and sneezed all over it, making it too damp to light. The one before that was terrified of loud bangs and the first applicant was an out-of-work fireman. Entirely unsuitable. Come on, my little Snuffy Bottom, let's give her a try. If Dr DeWilde is pleased, perhaps I'll get my sugar supplies restored and then I'll be able to make Snuffy Bottom's favourite chocolate-chip cheesecake.'

Alderman Snufflebottom yawned sleepily as she fed him another cheese straw. Storm wondered if Bee Bumble was using her special potion on him.

'Oh all right, my sugar honey bumble,' said Alderman Snufflebottom. 'I can't resist you. Have it your own way, my little sugar dumpling. Show her the supplies and let her get to work.'

Bee Bumble turned to Storm and poked her with a bony finger. 'You've got the job, Jill. Now make sure you do it properly, or it will be the worse for you. Dr DeWilde's got a terrible temper and if anything goes wrong at his precious wedding, he will be a very angry man. He will be so angry he will roast you alive.' Her eyes had a faraway look and she licked her lips. Storm shuddered under the cloak.

'Come this way to the kitchen,' Bee commanded. 'I won't be needing it tonight. Cooking is not so satisfying without a good supply of sugar. Savouries have their place in a cook's repertoire, but it's gateaux and mousses and charlotte russes that make people saucer-eyed. It's granulated happiness they want, and it's granulated happiness that Bee Bumble does best. You'll find everything you need to make the fireworks in the kitchen: gunpowder, fuses, timers. It's all there.'

21
An Unfortunate PinPrick

I t was close to dusk. Storm moved through the owl-light towards the market square. She could hear the crowds cheering and chanting, 'Long live Dr DeWilde!' Something about the intensity of their chants chilled her. She knew that they were people who could not be reasoned with. They had been mesmerized by the magic pipe.

When she reached the square, Storm found it packed with hundreds of revellers and thousands of flickering candles. Scarlet and gold bunting waved in the wind, and phalanxes of fireworks stood ready to be ignited. Storm had worked unceasingly all the previous night and during the day that followed, creating a firework display that she hoped would take the town's breath away. She had spent hours setting up timing devices that would ensure that the fireworks exploded with split-second precision.

In the centre of the square a large wooden platform had been constructed. The dais was covered in ivory silk and scattered with white rose petals. The smell of candle-wax mingled with their heavy scent. A canopy over the dais was secured by poles garlanded with red and white roses. A long red carpet, flanked by rows of Catherine wheels, ran from the edge of the dais and down through the middle of the square.

Storm looked at the town clock. It was almost five-thirty and she had finally decided to keep her appointment with Kit. All day she had been at war with herself. Her own plan, crazy though it was, might be enough to save Aurora and Any.

371

Why put herself at risk, when there was a chance that she could pull off the rescue alone? If the boy's message was a trap, then her rescue attempt would be over before it had begun. And yet, she desperately wanted to believe the boy had really been sent by Aurora to ask Storm to save her. It was her reason for living. And so meeting him was a risk she had to take. Besides, if the boy proved stalwart, then another pair of hands would be very helpful indeed. She was worried that the timing mechanisms on some of the fireworks might fail, and that the element of surprise that her plan required would be lost.

Storm slipped through the crowd, heading for the south side of the square. Wolves were patrolling everywhere. They had encircled the crier's tower to ensure that nobody could enter by the small wooden door at its base, and they were swarming round the wedding dais.

Edging to the back of the crowd, Storm caught sight of the boy, lurking in the shadows near a group of street cleaners who were working frantically to make the cobbled square shine. She looked carefully around. Kit seemed to be alone.

Squaring her shoulders, Storm walked purposefully towards him, but with her body tensed, ready to turn and fly. She could see the boy's face quite clearly now: a white mask with those odd-coloured eyes burning brightly. He raised a hand slightly, in what she took as a gesture of acknowledgement, but then she saw that his look was fixed, almost desperate. She hesitated and at that moment Kit yelled, 'It's a trap, Storm. Run!' Immediately, the street cleaners downed their tools and began hurtling towards her and the boy. They were not cleaners at all, but Dr DeWilde's spies in disguise!

For a moment, shock prevented Storm's legs from working and she was almost taken. But just as the hands of the lead man reached for her, Kit leaped forward and sent him flying with an agile kick. Then he spun and bowled into the others, giving Storm a chance to speed away into the crowd. She heard shouts of protest as the attackers began pushing through the people behind her. But she quickly gained ground, slipping between the revellers and racing off into the crooked winding lanes beyond the square. Down Desolation Lane she went, into Hangman Gate, down Damnation Alley and then through DeVille's Gap into Rat Trap Wynd.

Breathless, she slumped behind a small wall, hardly daring to breathe as her pursuers thundered by, their shouts and cries disappearing into the distance. What a fool she had been to trust the boy! Why did he always offer hope with one hand, only to snatch it away with the other? And how stupid she had been to believe that Aurora had really forgiven her and asked for her help. Of course Aurora wouldn't want anything more to do with her. Storm buried her head in her hands.

As the distant clock struck the quarter hour, she rose wearily and retraced her steps. Kit was waiting for her in Damnation Alley, his beautiful face bruised, one eye a pool of misery. Fixing her gaze on a distant point, she marched right past him as if he simply didn't exist. The boy, his face a mask of pure despair, ran after her, his move-ment reflected in the eyes of a silver-grey hare that looked on from the shadows.

'Storm,' he called urgently. 'Forgive me. I didn't want to betray you. Dr DeWilde made me. I wanted to warn you, but I couldn't. He has spies everywhere.' Storm, her eyes fixed ahead, just kept on walking.

'Please, please,' Kit begged, running after her. 'I want to help you and Aurora. I . . . I love your sister.'

Storm stopped and looked at him with contempt. 'Help?' she spat. '*You* want to help *me*! All you've ever done is deceive me. You almost got me captured and killed! And you tried to make me believe that Aurora deserted me on Piper's Peak. You're contemptible!' she hissed. 'You can't be trusted. You're a betrayer.'

'Yes,' whispered the boy miserably. 'I am a betrayer. And I know what it feels like – just as you do.'

Storm glared at him. Fury welled in her stomach and spread into every nerve-ending.

'I'm nothing like you,' she whispered. 'I had no choice. I thought I was doing the right thing. But you! You have a choice, but you are just a coward who betrays out of fear of what will happen if you disobey Dr DeWilde.'

'You're right,' said the boy sadly. 'I don't have any courage. I don't have the strength to resist him. But neither do you. *You* let him make you choose between your sisters – and because you let him, you lost both of them.'

Storm stared at him, white-faced. He was right. She was no better than he was! And she hated him even more for voicing this terrible truth. She hated him more than she had ever hated anyone in her life. She wanted to hurt him; she wanted him to shrivel up inside and feel as bad as she did. She took a step closer to him, raised her trembling hand and slapped him hard across the cheek.

'My sister would never love someone like you,' she said, her voice cold and harsh. 'When I tell her what you are really like, she will despise you as much as I despise you. She will hate you for for ever and a day.'

With that, Storm turned and fled, so she did not see the agony on the boy's face. It was not the crimson mark left by her hand that hurt Kit so unbearably, but her words and the certain knowledge that now Aurora could never ever love him and that he would be doomed to be Dr DeWilde's creature for ever. The pain was too intense for him to bear; it radiated in tight bands across his chest so he could hardly breathe.

Kit sank to his knees, and as he did so there was a crack like breaking glass, and the boy's heart broke in two and the sliver of ice at its centre melted. He began to sob, and his tears washed the blue splinter of ice right out of his eye and down his cheek. In a twinkling, the blue faded from the iris and the green crept back in again, so that he had two perfectly matched, perfectly beautiful emerald eyes. But still he could not stop sobbing. Not even when the silver-grey hare hopped silently towards him and rubbed against his knee.

An Unfortunate Pinprick

After a few moments, Kit became aware that he was being held by a gentle woman with serious silver-grey eyes. 'It's all right, Kit,' she was saying gently, over and over. 'Just cry. A heart is not a proper heart until it has been broken, and the same applies to spells. The enchantment is broken and you are free at last.'

The boy looked up at her and his eyes – as dark green as the deepest sea – danced and sparkled as one.

Fury drove Storm on as she ran back towards the Ginger House. The boy's words stung her and had goaded her into action. Well, she would show him. And she would show her sisters. She would save Aurora and Any, even if they hadn't asked to be saved, and she would do it all on her own. If she was successful, perhaps Aurora and Any would forgive her for her betrayal at Piper's Peak. Perhaps they would all be together again, and Storm would no longer have to lug her loneliness and guilt around with her like a heavy suitcase. A look of determination on her face, Storm ran faster. It was time to put her plan into action.

Bee and the alderman had already left for the wedding ceremony when she reached the orphanage and she was able to slip into the vast kitchen unseen. She shifted the empty sugar barrel, picked up the lamp and the rope, slipped through the trapdoor and made her way along the dank, musty tunnel. As she passed under the market square Storm could hear the roar of the crowd overhead.

She opened the trapdoor in the floor of the crier's tower, and ran up the stairs, emerging onto the platform with its stone surround and supports that rose to a thatched roof. She stayed crouched down low so her head could not be glimpsed over the stone parapet and scanned the roof supports for a place to secure her rope. Above the crowd's noise, she could just hear the chime of the clock in the meat market. It was exactly six.

A band struck up and the crowd gave a huge roar. Storm guessed this marked the arrival of the bride and groom. She calculated that everyone's attention would be on them and so risked popping her head cautiously above the parapet. She watched as Dr DeWilde handed Aurora out of a magnificent carriage drawn by gold- and scarlet-plumed horses. Aurora looked as beautiful as the first flush of a pale dawn but she was quite as white as her dress. The only colour came from her hair, which was studded with hairpins and topped with rubies so that it looked as if her head was splashed with drops of precious blood. The wickedly sharp points of the pins gleamed white gold in the candlelight. With Dr DeWilde holding her arm firmly, Aurora walked down the red carpet as if in a dream from which she hoped to very soon awaken. Behind her, staggering under the weight of Aurora's heavy train, tottered Any. She was dressed all in crimson and her face was one vast scowl. She looked like a very disgruntled dwarf. Storm smiled. That's my Any, she thought.

The bride and groom made their way up the steps of the canopied dais towards Alderman Snufflebottom, who was looking very pleased with himself, and Bee Bumble, who was dressed un-becomingly in sugar-pink with a matching hat deco-rated with crystallized fruits. Then the archbishop stepped forward, the crowd fell silent and the wedding service began. Storm waited nervously. If her plan was to have the smallest chance of success then her timing had to be perfect.

The archbishop droned on. On the dais Aurora swayed as if about to pass out. Her skin gleamed like alabaster in the glow of the candles. The pins in her hair sparkled viciously every time she moved her head. The archbishop was talking about the importance of marriage, clearly oblivious to the fact that Aurora was being married against her will.

The moment had come. Storm climbed onto the parapet and quickly tied the rope around the roof supports. There was a howl and her stomach fluttered and swooped. She had been spotted! She saw a pack of wolves bound towards the tower. There was no time to be lost. She gave the rope an anxious tug, and looked nervously towards the rockets. Please, please, let the timers work, she prayed. Please don't let them fail. The archbishop was still droning on monotonously.

'Get on with it, man,' she heard Dr DeWilde snarl. Then, down below, came the sound of the tower door being forced. On the dais everyone was oblivious to the drama unfolding behind them.

The archbishop turned to Dr DeWilde and said, 'Do you take this woman to be your wife?'

'I do,' he replied loudly. The crowd cheered as if someone had raised a cue board and, right on schedule, there was a huge *whoosh*, a violent bang and suddenly the sky blazed with scarlet and silver explosions. Storm smiled with satisfaction and scrambled onto the edge of the parapet, holding tight to the rope. The crowd below oohed and aahed, totally bedazzled by the magnificence of the spectacle, obviously believing that it had been planned for this moment. Paws thundered on the tower stairs.

Down on the dais confusion reigned. The archbishop looked questioningly at Dr DeWilde, whose face was as black as thunder. Another roar went up from the crowd as the rows of Catherine wheels that lined the red carpet ignited and a whiz of silver sparks showered everywhere.

'Carry on, carry on,' snarled Dr DeWilde at the archbishop. The archbishop looked doubtfully at Aurora. Brilliant silver and crimson flowers opened in the sky.

'Aurora Rose Grace Eden, do you take this man to be your husband?' Aurora looked wildly around; her mouth opened and closed and nothing came out.

'Of course she does,' said Dr DeWilde impatiently to the archbishop. 'Get on with it, you stupid man. Just pronounce us man and wife.'

Teetering on the parapet ledge, Storm clutched the rope and swung outwards as hard as she could. To the crowd's delight, another raft of rockets rose in the air with a rat-a-tat-tat like the sound of a hundred drums beating. From the corner of her eye, Storm saw a blur of fur at the top of the stairs and a flash of bared teeth. There was snap of jaws, but they were too late. She was already flying outward towards the dais.

And then time seemed to slow down. Storm heard the archbishop repeat, 'Do you take this man?' and saw her sister raise her hand to her head. Then the light from the Catherine wheels was reflecting off the golden glint of a hairpin, and Aurora was plunging the sharp end of the pin towards her finger.

'No, Aurora, no!' Storm screamed as she soared through the air. But she was too late. As Aurora turned her head towards Storm, the pin hit her finger and a spurt of crimson blood spattered the rose petals on the podium. Aurora's mouth formed the words 'Storm' and 'forgive', then with a smile she sank to the ground, just as Storm crashed into the canopy above the dais, which collapsed into Dr DeWilde, toppling him and the wolves standing sentry in a rather pleasing domino effect.

Aurora lay apparently lifeless on the ground. Any, who had dropped Aurora's train, and had been happily bashing the archbishop over the head with his copy of the marriage service, leaned over her, and gently slapped her face, trying to wake her.

Entangled and pinioned by a mess of skewed

poles, ripped silk and rose petals, Dr DeWilde
was roaring in fury, 'Stop that girl! Stop that girl!'
But most of the crowd's attention was still taken
up with the brightly coloured stars that were
falling from the sky, and nobody could hear him
over the whiz and bang of the fireworks.

Storm looked around desperately. She had assumed that she, Aurora and Any would be able to make a run for it down the crimson carpet, but Aurora's action had made that impossible. She had chosen to fulfil the terrible prophecy of her christening rather than spend her life as Dr DeWilde's unwilling bride.

The wolves had made it down from the tower and were snapping and snarling their way through the crowd, but it was so densely packed that Storm thought she might still have a chance. She ran over to Any and Aurora. Any's eyes were wet and shining.

'You came, Storm! I knew you would. I told Aurora that you would save us. Whatever had happened between us, I always knew that you would remember: '*The three of us alone. The three of us together. For ever and for always.*'

'Any,' replied Storm urgently, 'lovely though it is to see you, I think we better concentrate on getting out of here alive.'

'It's hopeless,' said Any with grim practicality. 'We can't carry Aurora between us.' She squeezed Storm's arm. 'You go,' she said, flinging the archbishop's book at the advancing Alderman Snufflebottom and hitting him so squarely on the chin that he tumbled right off the dais.

An Unfortunate Pinprick

'Never!' said Storm, seizing one of the canopy's fallen poles and taking out Bee Bumble, who was attempting to creep up on her from behind. Then she threw a handful of firecrackers to keep the advancing wolves at bay.

'You must,' Any yelled, biting the tail of a wolf so hard that it yelped and ran off, clearly realizing that its teeth were no match for a toddler's.

Storm swung her pole again, sweeping a dozen wolves off the dais and into a snarling heap. 'I won't leave you again!' she insisted.

'It's no good, Storm,' said Any, seizing a pole herself and jabbing it into the chest of the rising Bee Bumble. The matron's hat wobbled alarmingly and two small crystallized pineapples tumbled off its brim to knock a wolf unconscious. 'There's too many of them. Get out of here while you can. Live to fight another day!' She swept Bee's feet from under her with another well-placed strike.

'I won't leave you and Aurora,' cried Storm, turning and delivering a thwack on the nose to an approaching wolf and a smack on the bottom to Alderman Snufflebottom just as he struggled back onto the dais.

More rockets rose into the sky and cascades of brilliant sparks fell to earth. Out of the corner of her eye Storm could see Dr DeWilde struggling to get to his feet. Things were about to get much nastier.

A pack of wolves moved up the red carpet to join him. Others leaped onto the dais behind them. Capture was inevitable. Storm looked wildly around. There was no way out. She picked up a pole, ready to fight, to the death if necessary. Any did the same and, hopeless though it seemed, the two girls stood back to almost back, resolutely facing the lines of wolves.

The first ranks moved in and the girls unleashed a welter of blows. But although it won them a temporary reprieve, their cause was hopeless. More wolves poured onto the platform until the girls were completely surrounded. Eventually, Any dropped her pole in exhaustion and Alderman Snufflebottom knocked her to the ground beside the lifeless Aurora. Storm was still snarling like a caged tiger, raining blows hither and thither, but she too had little strength left. She was beaten. In her heart she knew it was over. She had failed again.

Suddenly there came a terrible, war-like cry and a thunder of hooves, and Pepper the pony, ridden by Kit, galloped up the red carpet, dispersing all before him. At the dais, Pepper didn't halt for a second but, with a neigh as his battle cry, made a giant leap right into the ruckus, scattering wolves in all directions. The pony reared, his eyes wild, his hooves knocking out any of the beasts that dared come too close. Snorting and neighing as he rose on his hind legs, his muzzle flecked with foam, his eyes big and furious, he looked like some monstrous avenging beast from hell.

Tossing firecrackers in every direction, and swinging a flaming torch to disperse the wolves, Kit leaped from the horse, hit a recovering Alderman Snufflebottom over the head, and struck a wolf in the belly with an expertly directed kick. The boy was a whirling dervish, yelling at Storm and Any to mount Pepper, and trying to drag Aurora towards the horse while beating off his attackers.

Storm raced to help him, and together the two of them heaved Aurora's unconscious body over Pepper's neck. Then Kit swung Any up and Storm leaped on behind.

'What about you?' gasped Storm to the boy as she scrambled onto the horse's back. Kit was fighting furiously with no regard whatsoever for his own safety.

'I can look after myself. Save yourselves,' he yelled, and then he leaned forward and whispered in Storm's ear, 'Nettles. You need nettles! Nettles and a forest fire are the only things I've ever seen that scared him.' He slapped Pepper on the rear and cried, 'Go, boy, go!' Pepper neighed, dispensed with two wolves who were trying to drag Storm off with a nifty kick of his back legs, and galloped away.

Storm looked back through the parting crowd to see Kit fall to his knees, surrounded by wolves. Bee Bumble was viciously raining blows down onto his beautiful, bruised face. But still he fought with the ferocious bravery of a lion. Until Dr DeWilde strode into the fray. He'd finally freed himself from the wreckage of the canopy and the pipe was at his lips. A lilting, shivering tune floated across the square.

The crowd fell silent. Bee Bumble's arms fell to her sides and Kit slumped to the ground. The wolves raised their muzzles expectantly. Dr DeWilde began speaking in low, guttural tones, whipping the crowd into a frenzy. Their eyes gleamed excitedly in the candlelight, fired by his words. 'That girl – that Storm Eden. She is a witch!' he declared. 'It was her that brought the rats to Piper's Town and she is still trying to destroy it. We must not allow that to happen!' He paused and played another note on the pipe, before continuing. 'She has bewitched and stolen her own sister, my beautiful, beloved fiancée. She has turned this treacherous cub against me.' He indicated Kit, who lay unconscious on the ground. 'She must be caught and made to pay before she destroys us all. We must hunt her down and burn her at the stake!'

The crowd, many still craning their heads to hear the last dying notes from the pipe, roared their agreement. 'Hunt the witch! Burn the witch!' The Piper's police thrust the larger candles into their eager hands and they poured out of the square in a delirium of hysteria, eyes red in the firelight. Dr DeWilde watched them go with a twisted look of satisfaction on his face.

22
HUNT
tHe WiTch!
BuRn
tHe WiTch!

Out in the winding lanes Pepper
thundered towards the derelict
church. He galloped between the graves
and across the flagstones of the ruined
nave, and halted beside the long-
disused altar, pawing the

390

ground with his hoof and waiting for the children to dismount. Storm lifted Any and the unconscious Aurora down, laid her sister gently beside a broken lectern, then turned to hug the pony's neck. 'Thank you,' she whispered. Pepper nuzzled her ear, then tossed his head and raced away.

The candle-bearers at the head of the mob caught a glimpse of the pony and set off in frantic pursuit. Storm and Any crouched behind the altar as the people surged past, the torchlight showing their faces all twisted up with hate, but their eyes devoid of any expression.

The words they chanted were equally clear: 'Hunt the witch! Burn the witch!'

For a second it felt to Storm as if the whole world had fallen away. It was as if she was entombed in an icy cold place of shock and silence. It seemed that as fast as she rescued her family from one horrible predicament, fate contrived to cast them into a worse one. Another throng surged past, clutching flaming torches and yelling excitedly, 'Hunt the witch! Burn the witch!' Storm felt Any's little hand squeeze hers; her sister's eyes were wide with fright.

But then the yells began to fade. Pepper the pony had successfully led the mob away and Storm finally had a moment to think. She looked down at Aurora. Her sister was still fast asleep and appeared perfectly content to be lying on the cold flagstones. Storm tried shaking her, but Aurora didn't even stir. Storm chewed her lip. Would Aurora ever wake up? Or had the curse come true?

Gesturing for Any to stay quiet, Storm stood up to look for a better place to hide. As she did so, some nettles that were growing out of cracks in the altar-base stung her ankles and made her hop from foot to foot.

Nettles! What had Kit said? Dr DeWilde was scared of nettles. Storm stood completely still, oblivious to the pain radiating through her feet. Could it be? It hardly seemed possible that he would be bothered by anything so insignificant. But then Storm remembered what Mother Collops had said about the night that Dr DeWilde had been left at the orphanage and how the young matron had thought she had been left a wolf cub, not a human baby, until she had lifted him up out of the nettle blanket. An extraordinary thought occurred to her and she gave a tiny little whoop of excitement.

'Come on, Any,' she said, pulling her sister towards the churchyard. Crouching beside a grave under an ancient yew, she began pulling up nettles in great clumps from the frozen ground. 'We need to pick as many as we can.'

Any looked puzzled. 'Did you hit your head on something, Storm? This doesn't really seem like a good time for gardening.'

'It's our only hope of showing the people of Piper's Town Dr DeWilde's true nature,' her sister answered impatiently. 'So start pulling!'

Any didn't look convinced, but she plunged her arms into the nettles anyway and began tearing them up by the roots. Soon the sisters' fingers were red and raw from the nettles' scorpion sting, but they ignored the pain. A silver-grey hare crept from behind a stone angel and sat watching them intently.

At last Storm judged that they had enough and they returned to the church. As they approached the altar, Storm asked Any, 'Do you know if Aurora has still got her sewing kit?'

'I wouldn't go anywhere without it, not even on my wedding day,' came a familiar voice, and Aurora's smiling face appeared from behind the altar. Storm and Any gasped and the girls fell upon each other in delight.

Finally Storm broke away. 'So you didn't fall into an irreversible coma, then?'

'It appears not,' said Aurora briskly. She raised an eyebrow. 'I never believed in that old prophecy, anyway.' She looked at both the girls' faces. 'Surely *you* didn't, you silly geese?'

Storm and Any glanced at each other. 'So when you deliberately pricked yourself with the hairpin, you didn't – not for even one tiny second – think that you were about to fall into a sleep from which nobody would be able to awaken you?'

'Of course not,' laughed Aurora. 'I wouldn't have done it, if I had. I just wanted to make sure that I fainted so that the marriage service couldn't continue, although of course if I'd known you were going to turn up . . .' She leaned closer to Storm. 'I've never admitted this before, Storm, but although I am inordinately fond of sewing I have a terrible fear of needles. Just the thought of one pricking my finger makes me feel faint. So I suppose it is a kind of curse in a way.'

'But how could you be so certain that pricking your finger on your sixteenth birthday wasn't going to send you into a permanent sleep?' Any protested.

'Well,' said Aurora serenely, 'I always suspected that maybe the whole prophecy was an exagger-ation hit upon by Mama to keep me at her beck and call. But it was only when we met Mother Collops and she wasn't quite the old hag Mama had led me to believe that I really began to wonder. Added to that the story she told us about Dr DeWilde stealing her invitation and turning up at my christening unannounced, and I knew the whole thing was rubbish.'

The freezing call of a wolf cut the air.

'Aurora, where are those knitting needles?' Storm asked urgently. Aurora patted her pocket.

Storm smiled. 'Good. We're going to make a shirt.'

Her sisters looked confused.

'I am, of course, delighted by this sudden interest in things domestic,' said Aurora. 'But what exactly are we going to make a shirt from?'

'Nettles,' said Storm triumphantly, and she told them what Kit had whispered in her ear.

'We'd better get started, then,' said Aurora. She looked up: tears were coursing down Storm's cheeks.

'What is it, sweetie?' she asked gently.

'I don't know how you can ever forgive me for what I did to you!' sobbed Storm. 'First I jumped to the conclusion that you had deliberately cut the rope at the well, and then I left you in Dr DeWilde's clutches. I didn't keep our vow about always being together,' she wailed. 'Nothing can ever be the same between us.'

Aurora pulled Storm to her.

'Storm, there's nothing to forgive. I've never stopped loving you, and I know that you've never stopped loving me. It was just anger and shame that blinded you. As to nothing ever being the same, well, different can sometimes be just as nice as what you already know and like. Like tinned peaches are nothing like fresh peaches, but they are both perfectly delicious in their different ways.'

Aurora was relieved to see a smile spread across Storm's features.

At that moment another mob dashed through the churchyard, their cries of 'Kill the witch! Burn the witch!' filling the night air.

Aurora looked at Storm in horror. 'Oh, sweetie,' she said softly, 'I just hope you're not wrong about the nettles.'

'Don't worry,' said Storm airily. 'I've got a plan, but I have to get really close to Dr DeWilde for it to work.'

The girls set to work as fast as they could and, with Aurora's superior sewing and knitting skills, it was not long before the shirt was almost complete, but for one of the sleeves.

It was then that they were discovered. The

wolves had finally caught their scent and had led
the mob back to the church. The throng moved
through the gravestones, their faces red and sweaty
in the torchlight, something feverish and wild in
their eyes. 'Hunt the witch! Burn the witch! Kill
the witch!' they chanted incessantly.

'Here we go,' said Storm with a gulp, and she
took the shirt and needles from Aurora and stuffed
them into her pockets. The crowd grew bigger
and the noise more tumultuous as people swarmed
through the churchyard and filed up the nave, led
by the wolves. 'Hunt the Witch! Burn the Witch!'
The chant of the crowd echoed off the crumbling
walls.

Holding tight to each other's hands,
Storm, Aurora and Any rose to their
feet from behind the altar. The
crowd fell completely silent,
and then the wolves lifted
their heads and howled
as one. Trembling,

Storm moved around the front of the altar and the crowd, which had spread out across the narrow church, began to advance towards her in a line. Their chant began as a low murmur and gradually bubbled to a crescendo. 'Hunt the witch! Burn the witch! Hunt the witch! Burn the witch!' Then they parted, and Dr DeWilde appeared at the back of the church. 'Well, Storm Eden,' he drawled. 'It seems you've broken our little agreement.' His scarred face took on a hurt look, as though he'd suffered a great wrong. Then he grinned wolfishly. 'No matter. You may have spoiled one celebration today, but there's still time for another.'

The sky had turned a dark purple and the wind had grown spiteful, trying to sting the cheeks of the people who were again gathering in the square. The crowd was inflamed with excitement, and small children had been hoisted onto their fathers' shoulders, so that they would get a better view of the witch as she was burned. A low murmur of excitement passed around the crowd as bundles of kindling were added to the base of a hastily erected pyre.

A cheer went up as Dr DeWilde appeared on the dais. He acknowledged the throng with a little bow, and then nodded towards Aurora and Any, who were huddled within a circle of slavering wolves. The train of Aurora's wedding dress, now rather crumpled and dirty, was pooled at her feet like a puddle of spilled milk.

A roar went up from the people at the farther reaches of the square and it carried like a wave towards the centre. A cart rumbled across the cobbles with Storm shivering inside. She was deathly pale. Her lips were forming the words 'together and for ever' over and over and her fingers were busy trying to finish the as yet uncompleted arm of the nettle shirt. The crowd jostled and jeered as the cart passed by. 'Witch! Witch!' they hissed. Storm ignored them and continued to sew desperately, wishing she had Aurora's speed and expertise. Then the cart came to a halt and she was grabbed roughly by either arm and pulled towards the pyre. Lifted atop the high pile of wood and kindling, Storm was thrust against a stake and bound at the feet and the waist. Somehow she managed to keep hold of the nettle shirt, and her needles clicked in a furious frenzy as she completed the last few stitches.

'Witch! Witch! Burn the witch!' taunted the crowd, their faces deformed with hostility. 'Kill the witch!'

As Dr DeWilde stalked toward the pyre he looked long and hard into Storm's eyes. She read the pure hatred that was written there. It was as if the two of them were the only people left in the world, locked in a silent battle as the crowd roared around them. The doctor willed Storm to break the gaze and look away, but she didn't flinch.

The crowd screamed again. Dr DeWilde raised a hand to quieten them. Hush fell. The world seemed to stop turning. With a vicious little smile, Bee Bumble handed him a brushwood torch and a lighted taper. Dr DeWilde smiled and lit the torch. It burst into flames and the crowd roared their approval.

'Burn the witch!' they screamed again. Dr DeWilde gave another little bow, as if he was a mere servant doing the crowd's bidding. The crowd held its breath as he walked with a swagger towards the pyre. A full moon slipped suddenly from behind a dark cloud and cold, harsh light spilled over the square, a witness to the scene of a crime.

Dr DeWilde raised the flaming brushwood torch above his head; then, with an exaggerated gesture, he dropped it into the kindling around the pyre. There a crackle and snap as flame licked dry wood. A tongue of fire curled into the air. An aromatic wisp of smoke wafted into the crowd. They gave a huge whoop of delight and, as they did so, Storm – horribly aware of a sudden warmth close to her toes – tossed the nettle shirt over the shoulders of her enemy.

For a second Dr DeWilde was still, then he reared up like a wild animal.

Whether it was a trick of the light or a reality, nobody could be entirely sure – and for years later some people would claim one thing and others another – but silhouetted against the flame of the burning pyre was the image of a wolf. The crowd took a collective breath. There was a tiny silence, but for the pop and spit of burning wood. Then Any's clear, confident voice carried across the square.

'That's not a man. It's a wolf.'

'That's not a man. It's a wolf,' said another child carried aloft on his father's shoulders. Other children took up the cry, 'Not a man, a wolf!' The adults looked at each other and then they began whispering. 'The children are right. They speak the truth. That isn't a man, it's a wolf.'

The whisper carried across the square and quickly it became a shout and the shout became a chant. 'Not a man, a wolf!'

The moon, her job well done, slipped back behind a cloud, and in the blink of an eye Dr DeWilde stood in manly shape before the crowd. But the damage was done. He took out the pipe and held it to his lips. It was no good. The noise of the crowd, a mixture of derision and anger, was so great that its tune was swallowed up. A look of fury flickered across his face. It quickly turned to uncertainty and then to fear as he realized the extent of the feeling against him and understood that now the townsfolk had seen the wolf within, they would no longer accept his iron rule. He threw back his head and howled, a sound of such desolation that a shiver ran around the crowd and every person present felt as if they had been touched by a sudden deep sadness. Wolves began to gather at the edge of the square, silent and watching. Dr DeWilde leaped from the dais and the crowd parted and started pelting him with stones as he loped and limped across the square towards the wolves. Then he fled the square, blood pouring from his head – a man running wild in the midst of the pack.

Aurora and Any raced to untie their sister and Storm immediately leaped down in pursuit of the doctor.

'Where are you going?' yelled Any, grabbing her leg.

'Let me go, Any,' she cried. 'I have to catch him!'

'But why?' gasped Aurora. 'He won't be back. I reckon that is the last Piper's Town will see of him for a very long while.'

Storm shook her head. 'He's still got the pipe. And as long as he has it, the slaves at Piper's Peak can never be free. Nobody's safe. I've got to get it back and destroy it.'

'But he'll be deep in the forest by now,' her sister protested.

'No, he won't,' said Storm confidently. 'He's hurt. He'll have gone to the Ginger House to lick his wounds. It's the closest thing to a home he has in Piper's Town.'

'Then we'll all go after him together,' said Aurora, her chin jutting determinedly.

'No,' said Storm. 'This is between him and me. Just the two of us.' And she raced away across the square.

The Ginger House reared up in front of Storm, its spun-sugar spires rising into the clear sky. The moon bathed the gardens in a milky light, illuminating a hundred wolves in formation, like soldiers silently standing guard. More of the beasts lined the pathway up to the front door.

Storm took a deep breath. The wolves stared at her, unblinking. They watched every step she took towards the Ginger House with an intensity that made it hard to put one foot in front of the next. She sensed that if she showed the slightest sign of fear or weakness, they would pounce. Yet, even more curiously, she sensed a respect from them, as if they recognized something wild deep inside her that made her as recklessly brave and completely untameable as they were. She knew she must keep calm at all costs.

She carefully opened the gate in the picket fence and started up the path towards the front door. The wolves' eyes glowed red and yellow like the embers of a dying fire but Storm forced herself to look squarely at each animal as she passed. Each time she did so, the wolf would lie down with its chin between its paws in a gesture that suggested submission.

After what seemed like a lifetime, Storm reached the front door. She lifted the knocker and let it fall. The sound echoed around the building. Then from the highest tower she heard a mournful cry that sounded half human and half wolf. She felt a million muscles in a hundred wolf bodies tense, ready to spring, but she didn't flinch and she did not look back.

Her legs quivering, Storm pushed at the door. It opened and she stepped through, conscious of the eyes of the beasts watching her every move, but not of the gaze of the silver-grey hare that looked on from beneath a gooseberry bush.

The smell of ginger and cinnamon and toffee in the Ginger House was gone. Instead there was an odour of something truffly, of musky fur, ripe sweat and fear. In the half darkness Storm started slowly up the stairs. At the landing, she stopped, listened, and then pressed on to the tower bedroom that she had once shared with Aurora and Any. At the threshold, she paused, before pushing open the door.

Dr DeWilde was no longer the commanding figure he had been. He was crouched in a corner, dirty, hair matted, with a trickle of blood across his scarred cheek. His clothes were ragged and rent where the angry crowd had torn at them.

He eyed Storm with a yellow glare. Storm eyed him back.

'I've come for the pipe,' she said boldly.

His mouth twisted in something like a grimace.

'I knew you would.'

Storm held out her hand.

He made a sound between a snarl and a growl. 'You'll have to win it off me.'

'I know,' said Storm quietly.

He laughed derisively. 'A child against a fully grown man? A girl against a wolf!' He sniggered.

Cold fury rose in Storm's stomach. Her nostrils flared. She felt as if she had physically doubled in size.

'Try me,' she said, smiling.

Suddenly there was a flurry of fur, a flash of red-yellow eyes, and a swipe of claw. Blood spurted across Storm's cheek. She opened her mouth to scream and the noise that came out was not the high-pitched cry of a frightened child but a roar – the roar of a furious wild animal ready to attack. She was incandescent with rage. She saw the flicker of fear in Dr DeWilde's eyes at the same time as she saw his fangs coming towards her; she ducked nimbly away so that he lost his balance. He was on his feet immediately, growling at her and pushing her towards the wall. He had her cornered now. He crouched and sprang and she leaped to meet him, in a crunch of chin and muzzle, skin and pelt, bone and bone. They both rolled away, but the doctor was up first, breaking for the door and bounding towards the spiral stairs. Storm flew to the banisters, balanced on the edge for a fraction of a second and then threw herself over, landing on top of him, so they rolled down together a whirling mass of girl and animal, man and child, entwined grey hind legs and pale limbs, white and yellow teeth. He tore away from her again, and bruised and battered though she was, she charged after him like a wild thing, determined that her prey should not escape.

He hurtled down more steps towards the kitchen, a long, lean streak of grey, and slammed the door in her face. She pushed hard against it. He was holding it shut. She kicked the door. It didn't budge. She stood back for a second and caught her breath. She put her hand on the handle and tried again. The door opened easily.

By now, Storm had had enough experience of walking too casually through doors to know it was a trap. So, cautiously, she pushed it open with her foot. She could see the vast oven, its door wide, bright flames licking at the logs within. Otherwise the room appeared to be empty. The trapdoor that led down to the secret passage was wide open. Storm felt surprised and disappointed: she had expected

Dr DeWilde to fight to the death, not run for his life. But then his head popped up from the open hole.

Forgetting her caution, Storm rushed through the door, only to be grabbed from behind. She smelled Bee Bumble's crystallized-violet breath mixed with a scent of tangy vanilla, orange and lemon rind. She heard the matron's triumphant 'Got you!' heard the door bang and the key turn in the lock and felt the strength ebb out of her body.

Storm held her breath so that she wouldn't breathe in any more of Bee's potion-perfume, then elbowed her hard in the ribs. The matron doubled up in pain, hissing, 'You'll pay for that, my girl. I'll roast you to a crisp. I'll bake you into a pie.'

But before she could reply, the doctor had sprung from the trapdoor and leaped on top of her. Storm whipped out from underneath him and rolled to the far side of the large wooden preparation table. The doctor instantly blocked her escape from one side and Bee Bumble quickly moved to the other, close to the great oven and its gaping fiery mouth.

'I am coming to get you,' she threatened, a sly look on her face.

'So am I,' leered Dr DeWilde unpleasantly.

'I'm going to mince you and turn you into sausages and feed you to your sisters,' Bee added viciously.

Storm was trapped, but she had surprise and lithe suppleness on her side. As the grown-ups stepped in and reached for her, she rolled under the table again and came up the other side. She lurched towards the closed door.

Seeing his quarry escape, Dr DeWilde gave another howl of fury and gave chase. In his haste, he collided with the matron and their limbs became entangled. He tried to push her away, but her bulk prevented him. 'Get out of my way, you stupid woman,' he screeched, and gave her an almighty shove. A look of fury and surprise crossed Bee Bumble's features as she lost her balance and, with a terrible, blood-curdling cry, fell into the roaring flames of the oven and disappeared entirely.

Storm ran to the oven, but the white heat of the inferno drove her back. The fire crackled and hissed and popped loudly. She turned to face Dr DeWilde, her eyes wide and her face chalky with shock. He laughed at the look of pity and horror on her face.

'The old hag was always entirely dispensable,' he panted. 'Oh dear, dear. Is kind-hearted little

Storm upset? Well, don't waste your pity. The old witch would have made you into toast and eaten you if I'd given her a chance – and if you don't concede, that's what I will do too!' He bared his fangs again. 'Will you finally accept that I have won?'

Storm's mouth opened and closed like a fish. She was numb with shock at what he'd done to Bee, and even more so because of his total lack of concern. Nobody – not even witchy Bee Bumble – deserved to die so horribly. She was still trying to find her voice when a red-hot log, which had been dislodged when the matron fell, rolled from the oven and crashed to the floor. Sticky with spilled sugar, the floor caught light instantly. Flames licked immediately up to the tablecloth and it too burst into flames.

Fire spread up the walls and raced across the floor at an alarming rate. The doctor made a dash for the trapdoor, but a wall of flame repelled him. Roaring in anger, he came at Storm again, taking a vicious swipe at her shoulder and knocking her away from the door.

The pain and the heat from the fire brought Storm to her senses. As Dr DeWilde yanked the door open, she dodged around him, and fled towards the front door, coughing as her nose and mouth filled with the stench of burning sugar. The doctor was right behind her as she fumbled for the latch.

Then a bag of flour exploded in the kitchen and a ball of flame shot down the hallway towards them. With a cry of wolfish terror, Dr DeWilde leaped away from safety, and raced for the stairs.

For a moment Storm hesitated by the half-opened door. Another step and she would be safe. But the doctor would be trapped. And even after all he'd done, she couldn't just leave him to burn alive. And he still had the pipe. Spinning round, she sprinted after him.

The pop and crackle of the fire had turned to a roar now and the air was thick with the scent of caramel. Molten toffee poured off the walls. Above them Storm could see the spun-sugar towers shift and start to buckle. Every time a spot of burning sugar fell onto the floor another flame sprang up. She heard and felt an ominous rumble and realized at once what it was. The vast oven was about to explode!

Dr DeWilde pelted into one of the bedrooms overlooking the front lawn and she raced after him. 'We've got to get out!' she yelled. 'The oven's going to blow up and the whole building will explode with it. We must leave now.'

The doctor backed away from her, red-eyed and wild. He bared his teeth ferociously. There was another rumble, as if the bowels of the building were in terrible pain. A shower of sparks fell past the window where he stood trembling. Storm took another step towards him and put out a hand. 'We must leave or die,' she gasped.

He snarled and backed further away, but with a look of intense fear as he saw flames lick up the walls of the bedroom.

'Take my hand,' she urged him, one final time. But her enemy shrank further against the wall, growling and spitting. Then, from the depths of the building, came a sound like rising thunder and she knew she could wait no longer. Storm turned and bolted down the fiery staircase and out through the front door into the cool night air. The wolves had long gone, terrified by the fire and the building that blazed against the night sky, sending a red glow across the horizon.

Storm stood on the lawn, gasping for breath, beneath the window where Dr DeWilde stood. Suddenly she heard the shattering of the window pane above. Looking up, she saw Dr DeWilde, his mouth open in a howl of despair and completely surrounded by flames. Something fell to the ground at her feet. It was the pipe. She bent to pick it up, then looked back at Dr DeWilde. Their eyes met, and for a second she thought she saw him nod his head in submission and raise his hand as if in salute, a tiny gesture of *au revoir*. Then there was an almighty explosion, and gouts of flame burst from all the windows of the Ginger House.

Storm felt herself being dragged backwards by someone as the spun-sugar towers started to teeter and collapse and the building began to fold in on itself in a great inferno of sparks and explosions. Then she heard a voice say softly, 'You've done it, Storm Eden. You've done what had to be done. Your mother would have been so proud of you.'

Storm looked up into a pair of gentle silvergrey eyes and realized that the voice belonged to Netta. She sank back into her arms. Then she heard the sound of running feet and the concerned voices of her sisters. She looked up to see Aurora's worried face and Any's beaming smile.

'Are you hurt?' asked Aurora anxiously.

'No, I'm fine,' Storm said stoutly, struggling to her feet.

Any hugged her tightly. 'You're a heroine, Storm.'

Storm blushed and said shyly: 'No, I'm not.'

'Oh yes, you are,' chorused Aurora and Any together, and Storm felt a warm pink toffee feeling seep into her tummy.

She allowed herself to enjoy the sensation for a second. Then, aware of the pipe tingling in her hand, she said, 'I haven't finished quite yet. Come on.' And she set off determinedly through town, leaving the others looking wonderingly in her wake.

Sometime later, the girls stood shivering by the sea just to the south of Piper's Town. It was drizzling with rain and the sky was dark and sulky although it was near dawn. From further up the beach, Kit and Netta could see Storm turning something over and over in her hand. She looked as if she was turning something over and over in her mind, too.

Suddenly, without hesitation, she strode down onto a narrow finger of rock that stretched out into the dark sea. Aurora and Any followed.

'Are you quite sure that this is what you want to do?' Aurora asked.

'I've never been more certain of anything in my life,' said Storm. They all looked down at the pipe in her hand.

For a moment Storm felt as if it was calling to her, urging her to put it back in her pocket. She shivered and closed her ears to its beguiling call. Then she raised her arm and flung the pipe as hard and far as she could into the sea.

As it hit the water, the rain stopped and the sun skulked out from behind a cloud. The pipe bobbed and danced across the waves, its surface glinting, then the surf closed over it and the sisters saw it no more.

They stood for a second in silence, then Storm gave a little whoop that sounded half like a cry of triumph and half like a sob, turned on her heel and walked away.

'Where are you going *now*?' called Aurora.

Storm turned round and her face was one huge smile. 'Home, of course, sillies.'

Any and Aurora gave a great cheer of delight.

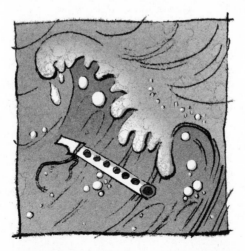

23
An end and A Beginning

Netta took the sisters back to Eden End in her wagon. The girls were delighted to see Pepper again, and relieved that no harm had come to him.

Kit rode with them for a short time, but jumped off near Piper's Port. He planned to go to sea and travel the world. Storm suspected he'd soon return, though, because whenever his and Aurora's gaze met, their eyes flew away from each other's like shy birds.

Their route from the port took them through crowds of escaped slaves heading back to their homes from the mines beneath Piper's Peak. And then, just a few kilometres from Eden End, they spotted Mother Collops, hobbling along with her stick. They helped her aboard the wagon and threw themselves into her arms.

Over a snack of jelly babies and Netta's finest soda bread and flapjacks, their great-grandmother told how the wolves had suddenly fled from the mountain and how the slaves had made a dash for freedom. In turn the girls relayed how Storm had finally defeated the doctor in Piper's Town.

Mother Collops clucked and gasped at all the appropriate moments and then her face turned thoughtful. 'Do you think that Dr DeWilde escaped from the Ginger House?' she asked.

'I don't see how he could have done,' Kit called back, from his seat beside Netta. 'I don't think anyone could have escaped alive from that inferno. Bee Bumble certainly didn't.'

'That's true,' said Aurora. 'The firemen told me

that all they found left of her was her heart. It was made of lead, which proves that she was a witch.'

'But they never found a body or anything belonging to Dr DeWilde,' Any said, in a small voice. 'So maybe he *did* escape. What do you think, Storm?'

Storm shrugged. In her bones she knew that he was out there somewhere, but she didn't want to talk about it. She just wanted to get back to Eden End as soon as possible.

Pepper must have heard her thoughts, because he quickened his pace and soon the wagon was flying through the lanes towards home.

A few days later the sisters, Netta and Mother Collops were enjoying a picnic in the warm sunshine in the garden at Eden End.

'I'm so very gruntled,' sighed Any, stretching out her bare toes.

'Gruntled? I don't think there's such a word,' smiled Aurora.

'Well, there should be,' said Any firmly. 'If you can be disgruntled, you must be able to be gruntled. And I am *extremely* gruntled.'

'So am I,' laughed Aurora. 'I'm very, very happy. We all are.' She swept Any into her arms and, giving Storm's hand a quick squeeze, carried her baby sister across the lawn to Eden End.

Storm watched them go, a nugget of envy lodged in her heart. She suddenly realized what she was missing: that warm chocolate fudge sundae, pink sticky toffee feeling in her tummy that she associated with happiness. Its absence gnawed at her. It was making her crabby and resentful. She wondered if there was something wrong with her. The others were elated by their safe return to Eden End. Why wasn't she?

A sudden terrible, shameful thought swept over Storm, making her flush with embarrassment, even though she was quite alone. Perhaps she had actually preferred being out in the world pitting her wits against the wolves and Dr DeWilde to being safe and sound. The adventure had made her feel important. It had made her feel certain of her place and role within the family. She thought of the terror of being lost in the woods and being alone in the town and wondered wearily why it was that being lost had seemed so much more like being found. She turned her back on Eden End and walked down to the lake to be alone in her misery.

For a while Storm sat dejectedly, her legs

dangling in the water. Then she felt a hand clasp her own, and Netta was beside her.

They sat in silence for several minutes and then Storm said haltingly, 'I thought that it would feel different. I looked forward to this moment so much. I imagined what it would be like when we were all together, safe and . . .' She paused and gave a bitter little laugh 'And happy.'

'And you're not happy?' asked Netta gently.

'Of course I'm happy,' said Storm indignantly. She looked up into Netta's wide silver-grey eyes and sighed heavily. 'No . . . No, I'm not. It just doesn't feel like the happy ever after that I thought it would be. Everything's changed and nothing's changed. Mama's still dead, Papa hasn't come back, and Aurora's gone back into housework overdrive. You should have seen her face when she saw all the dust when we got back − it was as if she had discovered gold at the end of rainbow. She'll be delirious with happiness for weeks getting rid of it all and putting the house to rights.'

'Maybe she's got the right idea. Maybe you do have to get rid of some things so you can go on,' Netta suggested.

'I don't think I can ever forget how I betrayed her,' Storm mumbled.

'You shouldn't be so hard on yourself, Storm. You were in desperate circumstances. Aurora's forgiven you, why can't you forgive yourself?'

Storm sighed. 'Because that wasn't how I saw myself. I used to imagine what I'd be like in peril and how I'd always speak up for what was right and true and always be heroic. Aurora and Any called me a heroine, but when the crunch came, I was a coward. I left them alone in Piper's Peak.'

'But, Storm, you *are* brave and tenacious. If it wasn't for you, neither your sisters nor Mother Collops would be here now. You saved them all. In a way you even saved Kit. You broke his enchantment when you broke his heart by telling him that Aurora would never love him. And you took on Dr DeWilde and you won. You got back to Eden End.'

'So why don't I feel triumphant, then?' scowled Storm. 'Why do I just feel . . . empty?'

Netta hugged her tightly. 'You can't turn back the clock. You can't bring your mother back to life, or make a different decision at Piper's Peak. This isn't a fairytale. It's real life. But you can find a way to deal with the past, find your own way of getting rid of the bits you don't need, just as

Aurora gets rid of her dust.'

'I don't think a purple feather duster would be much help to me,' said Storm, with a shaky attempt at a joke.

'No,' smiled Netta. 'But perhaps writing it down and casting it away would be.'

'You mean like you do, with the paper boats?'

'If you think it might help.'

Storm thought for a second and smiled.

'It might. But in my case I don't think I'd need one boat, I'd have to make an entire fleet.'

'Well,' smiled Netta, her silver-grey eyes sparkling, 'in that case you better get started.' And she removed several large folded sheets of paper from her pocket and a stubby pencil. She pressed them into Storm's hands and walked away.

Storm crouched on the grass, sucked the end of her pencil and started writing. After a few hesitant lines she scribbled furiously. As she wrote she was dimly aware of the warm sun on her back and the sound of Netta and Aurora laughing, as Aurora sat sewing replacement silver stars onto Any's midnight-blue blanket. Looking over to the field, she saw Pepper rolling in the buttercups, delirious with the sheer pleasure of the long meadow-grass on his back. Looking up the garden,

she saw Mother Collops practising her tiddlywinks
skills and occasionally pausing to pop a jelly baby
into her gummy mouth. Then Any ran across
Storm's field of vision, chasing a large yellow ball:
a laughing, happy toddler without a care in the
world. Storm's eyes misted with tears, but they
were not tears of self-pity.

An hour later, with the sun low in the sky, she
was still writing fast, pouring out all her pain and
shame onto the paper. By the time she had finished,
the sun was sinking quickly and the others had
already slipped inside the house to make broccoli
soup, more madeleines and hot chocolate. Storm
stood up, her knees protesting from being in one
position for too long. She carefully folded the sheets
into the shape of small boats and, feeling into her
pocket, found a pin and a piece of string and linked
them all together. She dug further into her pocket
and pulled out a little twist of gunpowder and
placed a smidgeon in each of the boats.

Feeling to the very bottom of her pocket she
found a sorry box of matches – the very same
ones that Any had given her a lifetime ago in the
forest. There was just one match left inside.
Carefully she placed the little flotilla of boats on
the lake, then she struck the match and dropped

it into the first boat as it drifted away from the shore. As the boat caught light, and the flames took hold, the fire spread until, one after another, each vessel was lit up with an explosive little pop.

Storm watched the luminescent fleet bob across the surface of the lake. Then, as the final boat flamed, flickered and burned itself into ash, she turned her back on the lake and walked quickly towards the house. For the first time since their return to Eden End she felt a sudden fierce need to be with the others.

She was about to enter the house when she saw a familiar figure trudging up the drive, a large carpet bag over his shoulder and a raft of maps under his arm. She rubbed her eyes in disbelief, but when she looked again he was still there.

'Aurora! Any!' she yelled.

'What is it?' asked Aurora anxiously, rushing outside. She looked to where Storm was pointing. 'Papa!' she cried. 'It's Papa!' She ran towards him, followed by the others.

'Hello, girls,' he said cheerily. 'Been having fun?'

'You could say that,' said Storm dryly. 'Where have you been all this time?'

Captain Eden looked rather sheepish. 'Oh, just off on one of my expeditions. I thought that this time I really *had* found the four-tongued, three-footed, two-headed honey dragon, but it turned out to be a false lead. Terribly disappointing.' He saw his daughters staring at him open mouthed, and had the grace to look embarrassed. 'It's not as if I just disappeared,' he mumbled defensively. 'I *did* leave you a note. And I'm sorry if I was away a trifle longer than I had intended, but I knew that you'd cope fine without me. I had no doubt you would all be safe at Eden End.' He smiled winningly at Aurora. 'I do hope you've got something nice and hot bubbling on the stove. I'm so famished, I could eat a wolf.'

Aurora and Any glanced at Storm. Her colour was rising dangerously; she looked as if she was about to explode. She did, but it was with gales of laughter. Captain Eden gave her a funny look, and picked Any up. 'So you must be Anything,' he said with a smile.

Any looked at him crossly. She opened her mouth as if to bite him, changed her mind and said, 'Really, Papa! Have you got any idea what my sisters and I——?'

Surprised, Captain Eden set her on her feet. 'Anything talks? Now that's really quite something.' Then, without a pause, he added, 'Right, I've got my next expedition to plan. It's going to require all my attention, so you may be left to your own devices for a bit.' And he hefted the carpet bag onto his back and marched into the house.

The girls stared after him, then Any said very slowly, 'Are you quite sure that that man is our father?'

'I'm afraid so,' Storm answered sympathetically.

'Well,' said Any, in her most mournful voice, 'he is a severe disappointment.'

'I know,' smiled Storm. 'We'll just have to hope that he improves with age.'

She looked at Aurora, and was surprised to see her big sister's normally serene face wet with tears.

'What is it, Aurora? What's the matter?'

'Oh, I'm just being silly,' she sniffed. 'It's just that seeing Father and him being so particularly Fatherish, reminded me of Mama and the fact that she's not here – that she really is dead.' She choked back the tears and her nose began to run. She fumbled desperately in her pocket for a handkerchief and couldn't find one.

'Here,' said Storm, proffering her sleeve. 'I've a got a clean . . . well, a fairly cleanish sleeve. It's all yours if you want it.' Aurora fell into Storm's arms and hugged her sniffily. Then Storm bent and lifted Any so that her face was level with theirs. The three children watched their father's disappearing back.

'We're never going to change him,' said Aurora wistfully.

'No,' agreed Storm sadly. 'I don't think we are.'

Aurora sighed. 'Oh well, I suppose we'll just have to have lots of hot baths.'

Storm and Any looked at her, nonplussed. 'Hot baths?'

'Of course,' said Aurora brightly. 'Everyone knows that a good scrub in a hot bath is the best cure there is for when you're feeling blue.'

Storm and Any grinned at each other. 'No it

isn't,' said Storm. 'It's having sisters.' And she wrapped her arms around the others, who encircled her with their arms too. 'The three of us alone, the three of us together. For ever and for always.'

The end?

Into the Woods

was brought to you by . . .

Lyn Gardner works as a theatre critic for the *Guardian*. She goes to the theatre five or six nights a week, which should leave no time for writing books at all. In fact she is quite surprised to have written a novel, as she never believed the cliché that everyone has a book in them. Prior to joining the *Guardian* she was a tea lady, a waitress, sold (or failed to sell) advertising space for a magazine called *Sludge*, wrote for *The Independent* and helped found the London listings magazine, *City Limits*. She and her two daughters have one venerable goldfish (there were two, but one came to a tragic end) and a horse – who is the most demanding, temperamental and expensive member of the family.

Mini Grey was given her name after being born in a Mini in a car park in Newport, Wales. She studied for an MA in Sequential Illustration at Brighton under the tutelage of John Vernon Lord. When she is not writing and illustrating, Mini works part-time as a primary school teacher in Oxford, where she now lives.

Aurora's Madeleines

115g (4oz) butter
115g (4oz) caster sugar
115g (4oz) self-raising flour
2 medium eggs, lightly beaten
3 tablespoons of bitter marmalade
3 tablespoons apricot jam
75g (2¾ oz) cold dark chocolate, grated finely
75g (2¾ oz) cold milk chocolate, grated finely
Glace cherries, halved.
Butter for greasing.

Preheat the oven to 220°C (425°F or Gas Mark 7). Grease 12 dariole moulds very well. Cream together the butter and sugar until light and fluffy. A little at a time, beat in the eggs. Fold in the sieved flour. Spoon a little of the mixture into each dariole mould until it is ⅔ full. Bake for 10-12 minutes. Remove from oven and allow to cool for a few minutes. Then very carefully run a knife around the edge of each cake and turn out onto a wire tray. Allow to cool thoroughly.
Heat the marmalade in a saucepan until runny. In another saucepan heat the apricot jam. Using a pastry brush, paint half the cakes in marmalade and the other half in apricot jam. Allow to cool for a few minutes. Roll the marmalade-painted cakes in the dark chocolate until coated and the apricot-jam-painted cakes in milk chocolate. Put half a glace cherry on top of each madeleine. Arrange on a plate.
Eat in front of a roaring fire.

'There were over a hundred very sweet words on this page, but Any swallowed them all.'

'There would have been words on this page but they were tidied up by Aurora.'